MURDER IN MOONLIGHT

SILVER AND GREY
BOOK 1

MARY LANCASTER

ARE YOU SIGNED UP FOR DRAGONBLADE'S BLOG?

You'll get the latest news and information on exclusive giveaways, exclusive excerpts, coming releases, sales, free books, cover reveals and more.

Check out our complete list of authors, too!

No spam, no junk. That's a promise!

Sign Up Here

www.dragonbladepublishing.com

Dearest Reader;

Thank you for your support of a small press. At Dragonblade Publishing, we strive to bring you the highest quality Historical Romance from some of the best authors in the business. Without your support, there is no 'us', so we sincerely hope you adore these stories and find some new favorite authors along the way.

Happy Reading!

CEO, Dragonblade Publishing

Additional Dragonblade Books by Author Mary Lancaster

Pleasure Garden Series
Unmasking the Hero (Book 1)
Unmasking Deception (Book 2)
Unmasking Sin (Book 3)
Unmasking the Duke (Book 4)
Unmasking the Thief (Book 5)

Crime & Passion Series
Mysterious Lover (Book 1)
Letters to a Lover (Book 2)
Dangerous Lover (Book 3)
Lost Lover (Book 4)
Merry Lover (Novella)
Ghostly Lover (Novella)

The Husband Dilemma Series
How to Fool a Duke (Book 1)

Season of Scandal Series
Pursued by the Rake (Book 1)
Abandoned to the Prodigal (Book 2)
Married to the Rogue (Book 3)
Unmasked by her Lover (Book 4)
Her Star from the East (Novella)

Imperial Season Series
Vienna Waltz (Book 1)
Vienna Woods (Book 2)
Vienna Dawn (Book 3)

Blackhaven Brides Series
The Wicked Baron (Book 1)
The Wicked Lady (Book 2)
The Wicked Rebel (Book 3)
The Wicked Husband (Book 4)
The Wicked Marquis (Book 5)
The Wicked Governess (Book 6)
The Wicked Spy (Book 7)
The Wicked Gypsy (Book 8)

The Wicked Wife (Book 9)
Wicked Christmas (Book 10)
The Wicked Waif (Book 11)
The Wicked Heir (Book 12)
The Wicked Captain (Book 13)
The Wicked Sister (Book 14)

Unmarriageable Series
The Deserted Heart (Book 1)
The Sinister Heart (Book 2)
The Vulgar Heart (Book 3)
The Broken Heart (Book 4)
The Weary Heart (Book 5)
The Secret Heart (Book 6)
Christmas Heart (Novella)

The Lyon's Den Series
Fed to the Lyon

De Wolfe Pack: The Series
The Wicked Wolfe
Vienna Wolfe

Also from Mary Lancaster
Madeleine (Novella)
The Others of Ochil (Novella)

PROLOGUE

Autumn, 1851

S HE FIRST GLIMPSED him in the dark of night, looming out of a thick London fog.

They were in a narrow back alley, in the midst of a police raid. The light of wildly swinging lanterns flared for an instant across the most fascinating face she had ever seen—lean, dark, and aquiline. Strong, oddly beautiful bones beneath taut skin…a high forehead, black brows arched over deep-set eyes…full, sensual lips, a determined, slightly pointed chin.

Tall and lean, yet broad of shoulder, the man was both striking and handsome. When the mist swirled between them once more, she actually moved closer so that she could keep looking. He paid her no attention. He was gazing upward, at the roof of the tall building where the subject of the raid had fled, hotly pursued by several policeman and at least one gentleman.

She had only come here to provide protection for an old, somewhat naïve friend and her companion, the entirely surprising Lady Grizelda. Native curiosity had something to do with her presence too, as had the entertainment value. She found delightfully piquant that she, well known as a courtesan and a brothel madam, should be here in respectable, fashionable dress, escorting the daughters of a duke and a banker respectively, both in the unmistakable, gaudy garb of prostitutes. They imagined they were in disguise, which would not have saved them from the fury of the women whose territory they were invading.

All of which was great fun. But who the devil was this unusual and intriguing man?

He sprang upon her so suddenly that she barely saw him move. He slammed into her, and she staggered backward several paces. She would have fallen had his arms not held her up. Shocked, she could only stare as the body of a man tumbled past her eyes and crashed sickeningly onto the cobbles, almost exactly where she had stood the instant before. Surely the thief and murderer they had all come for.

The man who had saved her life blocked her view of the horrific sight. The commotion all around them seemed to fade. There was only this man who held her in his arms. He smelled of fresh soap and delicious spice, with just a hint of brandy on his breath, and other people's tobacco on his clothes. He was all muscle and sinew and power against her, his steady, dark eyes profound and compelling. She could not look away. Excitement swept through her. *Desire.*

Slowly, his arms loosened. "I beg your pardon."

Dear God. His voice, velvet soft and deep, melted her bones. Stunned, she could not even thank him with more than a slight inclination of the head in response to his graceful bow.

"Ah, you've met," said Lady Grizelda mischievously. "Mrs. Constance Silver, Mr. Solomon Grey."

CHAPTER ONE

S OLOMON GREY JOURNEYED to Greenforth Manor the old-fashioned way.

This was not through any mistrust of the railways but rather of his own restlessness. He disliked feeling trapped or dependent on either railway schedules or the goodwill of his hosts in supplying transport to the nearest station. So, although it took him two days rather than a few hours, Solomon traveled in his own comfortable, well-sprung carriage, secure in the knowledge he could come and go as he pleased.

He rather enjoyed the slow drive through the countryside to the soothing beat of his horses' hooves. He had shut himself up among the crowds and bustle of London for so long that it was lovely to see greenery again. There were no dramatic hills or lush forests here in Norfolk, but gentle undulation, glinting water-ways, and space to breathe. So far from the day-to-day concerns of ships and cargoes, staff, and money, he could have relaxed completely were it not for the pulse of excitement within him, the nagging hope that at last he might learn something, and inevitable fear of what that might be.

The carriage swept through ornate gates and along a drivea-way lined by beech trees, to a large, rather pretty manor house. In the afternoon sun, its stone glowed and the windows gleamed in apparent welcome. A shadowed side of the building hinted at another wing not visible from this angle.

He wasn't sure he liked the house—too neat and enclosed, somehow, in its manicured grounds. But it was old enough to be the keeper of many secrets. Like his hosts, perhaps.

The servants were certainly well trained and clearly expecting him, for two footmen ran from the front door, the first to hold the horses, the second to open the carriage door and let down the steps.

As he alighted in leisurely fashion, his hostess emerged to greet him, smiling in welcome. If she regretted inviting him, she gave no sign of it.

Deborah Winsom was a pretty, appealing woman, perhaps still on the right side of forty, neat in appearance and shy in manner, from his recollection. He did not know her well, just as an occasional presence on a hospital board of which he was a member.

"Mr. Grey!" she greeted him warmly. "How delightful to see you again."

He took her hand, bowing over it. "My thanks for inviting me, Mrs. Winsom."

She smiled, with a sudden, brilliant coquettishness that took him by surprise. Although dressed much as he remembered her from London—plainly and modestly, with none of the excesses of recent fashion—she exuded a slight feverishness that he had not noticed before. Perhaps she did not like parties and this was how she dealt with them.

Looking back, she had certainly latched on to him with something approaching relief when he expressed interest in meeting her husband, the Norwich banker. He had imagined she felt comfortable with him and was glad.

"Come to Greenforth!" she had invited him. "We are having a few close friends and family join us there for a week next month. My husband will be charmed to meet you. He often speaks of his time in the West Indies. I shall send you an invitation."

She had, and he had accepted for his own reasons, though

now he began to wonder if he had mistaken hers.

She took his arm in a somewhat proprietary grip, drawing him toward the house. "You are just in time for tea, so you will meet my husband and our other guests. How was your journey?"

Their polite small talk was interrupted as they entered the house to find a distinguished and handsome man striding across the hallway. He turned toward them saying, "Deborah, where—" then broke off, smiling in welcome.

Although he must have been approaching fifty, he had the demeanor and the energy of a man twenty years younger. He possessed a full head of dark hair, only graying slightly at the temples, and a firm-featured countenance with gleaming blue eyes. The man almost crackled with vitality—one of those larger-than-life characters who drove their own success.

He advanced on them, holding out his hand to Solomon. "You must be Mr. Grey. You are very welcome at Greenforth, sir, very welcome indeed."

"My husband, Mr. Winsom," Mrs. Winsom murmured. "And yes, Walter, this is indeed Mr. Solomon Grey, lately of Jamaica."

Mr. Winsom shook his hand vigorously. "Wonderful! I look forward to reminiscing with you. Come and join us for tea! Unless you would rather go to your room first and make yourself comfortable?"

"I am perfectly comfortable, thank you," Solomon said, and received another beaming smile.

Mr. Winsom led the way into a sunny room at the side of the house, from where French doors led out onto a terrace. Tea was clearly about to be served there, for a white cloth had been spread over a round table, with teacups, saucers, and plates awaiting distribution.

Two ladies in elaborate, wide-skirted gowns were chatting together. One stood with her hands on the balustrade, her back to the window. The other, seated at the table, was an attractive woman, who broke off her conversation to turn toward them.

"Ladies, meet our newest guest, Mr. Grey," Winsom said,

bowing his wife and Solomon through the doors ahead of him.
"Sir, Mrs. Bolton, one of our oldest friends."

"How do you do, Mrs. Bolton?" Solomon murmured, bowing
to the lady at the table.

"Delighted to meet you, Mr. Grey," Mrs. Bolton replied. She
did not offer her hand. More reserved than her hosts, she was
beautiful in a cool, detached kind of way. Solomon knew she was
the wife of Winsom's banking partner, Thomas Bolton.

"And this is Mrs. Goldrich, one of our newest," Winsom
added.

The second lady turned unhurriedly, and Solomon forgot to
breathe.

By any standards, she was dazzling. Thick, golden-blonde hair
with just a hint of red, like an early sunrise, framed a face of
distinctive yet delicate beauty. Large, direct eyes of an unusual
shade, more green than blue. Almost translucent skin, and sensual
lips that seemed to have an extra, delicious upward curve when
she smiled. Which she did now as she advanced on him,
stretching her hand gracefully toward him.

"How do you do, Mr. Grey?" she said in a low, perfectly
modulated voice. "A pleasure to make your acquaintance."

A lie. Two lies, in fact. She could not possibly have been
pleased to see him, and she was not making his acquaintance for
the first time, even if she had never actually spoken a word to him
before. Moreover, her name, to the best of his knowledge, was
not Goldrich, and she was a most unlikely guest in such a
respectable house.

She was Constance Silver, London's most notorious courtesan.

Did she know he could denounce her?

Oh yes. Her eyes were bold, and yet contained a spark of
something that might have been defiance or plea or some mixture
of the two. Without doubt, she recognized him.

Solomon did not need Constance Silver's favor. He did, however, wish to ingratiate himself with his hosts. Surely, Winsom

had not brought her here under his wife's nose?

Solomon took the courtesan's soft fingers and bowed over them. "Mrs. Goldrich. Enchanted."

Something in her eyes changed. Before he could analyze it, a quick, impetuous footfall interrupted them, closely followed by an irritable sound that might have been a growl.

Like a dog watching another cur steal his bone, Solomon thought with amusement. Releasing Constance Silver's hand, he turned to face the new arrival—a young man of surely no more than twenty years, black haired like his father and just as dramatically handsome, although his looks were somewhat spoiled by his sulky mouth, which veered toward petulance, and by the unfriendly glimmer of his eyes.

"Our son, Randolph," said Mrs. Winsom proudly. "Randolph, meet Mr. Grey, who completes our party this week."

Randolph nodded curtly, retaining enough manners to mutter, "Pleased to meet you," before almost barging between Solomon and Constance Silver and handing her into a chair beside the one he had clearly chosen for himself.

So that was it, Solomon thought cynically. Constance had found a gullible youth to sink her claws into. He wondered what the boy's parents thought of that. No wonder she had changed her name.

He was given no time to dwell on the issue, however, for the rest of the party arrived and had to be introduced before they sat down.

"I gather you are just come from Jamaica, Mr. Grey?" Mrs. Bolton said as everyone sipped their tea.

"Not *just*. I settled in London some five years ago."

"I understand the climate in Jamaica is insalubrious."

"To some. I was used to it, being born there. But I wished to spread my wings a little."

"Mr. Grey is modest," Winsom interjected. "He owns a large and successful shipping empire. I imagine London is the most obvious headquarters for you, Mr. Grey."

Solomon inclined his head.

"And are you happy there?" Mrs. Winsom asked.

"It suits me for now," Solomon replied, and casually turned the subject. "Is Greenforth your ancestral home, Mr. Winsom?"

"No, but it is my family home. My father was a man of the church, so I made my own way in the world. Acquiring Greenforth, almost fifteen years ago now, was my reward."

"Winsom and I are partners in banking and other business ventures," said Mr. Bolton, a slight, dapper man who appeared to have a quieter, less ebullient nature than his partner. "Both in Norwich and in London."

"I see," said Solomon, who was well aware of the fact, having made it his business to find out.

"Perhaps we may find a way to work together," Bolton said, "to our mutual advantage."

"Yes, but we shall not be discussing it at the tea table," his wife said tartly.

"Indeed, no," Winsom said, with a laugh that made sure his partner was not embarrassed. "Such bad form to bore the ladies."

Solomon caught a look, then, on Bolton's face that he could not quite read, but surely it contained a glint of malevolence, almost instantly smoothed into shared humor, and the moment passed.

The company was courteous and friendly, though he intercepted a few curious, searching glances in his direction as he drank his tea and conversed. He looked forward to getting to know everyone better—people interested Solomon—although it was Walter Winsom he really wished to speak to.

His biggest surprise, as the tea party was breaking up, was when young Randolph invited Mrs. Goldrich to "come and look at the garden."

"Not right now," she replied casually. "I'm talking to your sister."

Randolph, already on his feet, scowled in annoyance. "Oh, Ellen doesn't mind, do you, Ellie?"

Ellen's eyes danced with mischief—she was the Winsoms' youngest child, a very young lady, surely no more than sixteen summers.

Before she could speak, Constance said mildly, "I mind."

And across the terrace, Mr. and Mrs. Winsom's eyes met, very briefly, and parted.

It was another small incident, overheard by no one else, but interesting all the same. Solomon was almost sorry to leave the terrace and be shown to his bedroom by a most haughty and stony-faced butler called Richards.

He discovered his bags already unpacked by the Winsoms' well-trained servants. Dropping his smart morning coat on the bed, he went to the partially opened window and gazed out over the gardens and fields that rolled over a gentle hill toward a narrow, winding river. Pretty. Very pretty.

A knock sounded on the bedroom door.

"Come in," he said. Expecting a servant, he glanced around without much interest. But it was Constance Silver who whisked herself inside, closed the door, and leaned against it. She smiled, just as if she were delighted to see him.

"Well met, Solomon."

CONSTANCE WAS, IN fact, appalled by the arrival of Solomon Grey. Any faint hope she might have harbored of his failing to recognize her was dashed the moment their eyes met. Nor was she relieved by the fact he had not given her away. Yet. He could still do so at any time.

They were hardly on first-name terms. She had never even spoken to him. Their entire acquaintance consisted of one admittedly memorable evening in Coal Yard Lane, when a man had tumbled off a tall roof in dank fog and almost landed on top of her. That she still lived was due to Solomon Grey's hurtling out of the mist and shoving her to safety. It was hard to say which of them had been more shocked.

At the time, Constance had merely inclined her head in gratitude, too stunned by her narrow escape to speak. At least, she assumed that was the problem, although it persisted into the motley party that had then gathered at the house of Lady Grizelda Tizsa. There, Constance had continued to ignore Solomon Grey while being more aware of him than any of the other dashing, noble, and beautiful people in the house.

Strangely tense and off balance, she had left after only half an hour, in her own carriage, offering no one a seat.

She knew who he was, of course. And he clearly knew her. To ensure his silence, it did no harm to imply a fictional intimacy and the damage any hint of it could do him with her hosts were he foolish enough to give her away.

So she said, "Well met, Solomon."

Oh, but he was a handsome devil, tall and elegant and lean, with cheekbones to die for, eyes to drown in, and a mouth...

"Is it?" he asked mildly. "I can't imagine you are remotely pleased to see me."

"That rather depends on your discretion."

"I am notoriously discreet. When I choose to be. Is it your plan to marry Mr. Randolph Winsom?"

"God, no," she said.

"Then what the devil, Mrs. Silver, are you doing at Greenforth?"

"I was invited. You find me unworthy to mix with so respectable a family?"

"That might depend on whether or not there was ever a Mr. Goldrich."

"I feel sure there must have been, though fortunately never married to me. But then, you know, there was never a Mr. Silver either. My titles are honorary. Like the cook's."

He blinked, as if he didn't know cooks were always addressed as married women, whether single or not. "They're likely to be different titles with no honor at all if you are discovered in my bedchamber."

"While you could dine out on the story for years."

Amusement lurked in his eyes. "You think to make me more exciting than I am?"

"That rather depends on why *you* are here at Greenforth."

"I was invited, too."

"Solomon Grey, the great shipping magnate, obscenely rich philanthropist, associate of dukes and friend of baronets. What the devil do you want with such small players as the Winsoms?"

"You exaggerate," he said mildly. "Though again, I could ask you the same question."

His eyes were steady, his body still. He had poise of the kind she had seen in fighters, in people confident of their own physical safety in any environment. She had seen it that foggy night in the alley. And yet his long, shapely hands were smooth and manicured, belying the hardness beneath. She reserved judgment about violent tendencies. She knew people who liked him, who thought he was a good man. She wasn't sure she trusted her own judgment where he was concerned.

"I am not here to hurt anyone," she said. "My change of name is simply explained—I would never have been invited with my own."

His brow twitched, and for a moment, she thought he would question her further. She wondered how much to tell him, how much he would understand, if any.

He walked to the bed and picked up his coat, shrugging it on with easy grace. "I was about to explore the house. Perhaps you would care to join me?"

She watched him stroll toward her, lithe as a large cat and probably just as lethal. "Why?"

"Because I need to know my way around, and I would value your insight."

She chose to step aside, and he reached beyond her to open the door. Though even as she moved out of his way, she wondered if he would have taken advantage of her closeness, or just taken flight. Most men could be divided into one category or the other.

For a moment, he blocked the open doorway, then stood aside for her to precede him. If he was protecting her reputation by making sure she would be unseen, it was so subtly done that she could not be certain. She sauntered out, moving unhurriedly along the passage to the stairs.

"The public rooms are all on the ground floor," she told him as they descended the staircase. She pointed to the left of the front door. "I believe that is the reception room where callers are asked to wait, and along that little passage next to it is the billiard room. Do you play billiards, Mr. Grey?"

"I have been known to."

"Would you like a game?" She was teasing, but he answered without hesitation.

"Why not?"

However, the billiard room was already occupied by Ellen Winsom and one of the guests, a local entrepreneur called Ivor Davidson. They appeared to be enjoying a rather hilarious game. Ellen glanced up, and despite her recent confidences during tea, her smile died and her eyes held a hint of desperate doubt.

Davidson's expression, on the other hand, was one of unalloyed pleasure. He was a young-ish man, too well aware of his own attractions. He straightened, letting one end of his cue slip to the floor, while his eyes devoured Constance. His gaze barely flickered dismissively in Grey's direction.

"We shan't be long," Davidson said, smiling at her. "Ellen is beating me to flinders. Who wishes to play the winner?"

"Not I," Grey returned, already turning aside with an amiable nod. "Please carry on. I am merely looking around... Who exactly is Davidson?" he asked when Constance had led him out. She walked next into the garden room, which opened onto the terrace where they'd earlier had tea.

"Some business associate of our host's," she replied, walking across the room to the French windows. "Unpretentiously in trade, not interested in gentility. Or so he says."

"You don't like him," Grey observed.

"Not particularly. On the other hand, I don't truly dislike him either. Many of the rooms, as you will see, open directly onto the garden. Like the formal drawing room next door. Let me show you."

Mrs. Albright and Mrs. Bolton were discovered comparing needlework in the drawing room. This was a large, gracious apartment, also with a French window onto the garden, and containing a handsome piano and some elegant, older pieces of furniture. A glass cabinet displayed fine oriental porcelain.

The ladies smiled in welcome, clearly curious about Constance's companion. Constance knew how they felt.

But again, Grey merely bowed and, after a polite exchange with the ladies, declined to linger.

"Mrs. Albright is the Winsoms' elder daughter?" he said. "Married to the vicar, if I recall."

"To *a* vicar," Constance corrected him. "Not the local incumbent."

"Somehow, I imagined Winsom would be more ambitious for his children."

"Ah, well, Albright is an ambitious clergyman," Constance said wryly. "They tell me he will be a bishop one day."

He smiled faintly. "Did Mr. and Mrs. Albright tell you that?"

"Oh, no. I assure you, I have a vast array of sources."

"I don't doubt it."

She crossed the hall to the front of the house again. "This is the breakfast parlor, where breakfast is served from eight o'clock onward. Next to that is a very fine library, if you are interested."

"I am."

Mr. Winsom himself was discovered in the library, writing busily, although, the perfect host, he beamed at the interruption and immediately laid down his pen and rose to his feet.

As always on seeing him, Constance felt her heart give a little flurry of doubt and hope and possibility. There was never any warmth in his eyes, let alone recognition. He could not have liked his son's inviting her here, and yet since her arrival yesterday, he had shown her nothing but courtesy.

"Forgive the interruption," Grey said in his soft-spoken manner. "Mrs. Goldrich is being kind enough to show me around."

"I always find it helps to orient oneself in a new house," Mr. Winsom agreed. "Although at least Greenforth is hardly large enough to lose oneself in! You must feel free to borrow any book you wish from these shelves, Mr. Grey. I am rather proud of my collection, from the classics to the flora and fauna of the West Indies. And I have several very rare volumes which are my weakness. What is your greatest interest, sir?"

"My interests are catholic and depend largely on my many moods. I shall certainly be grateful to peruse such a fine collection. Thank you."

"Join us in the drawing room for a glass of sherry before dinner at seven," Mr. Winsom invited them. "You'll hear the gong."

It was an amiable dismissal.

Grey's eyes seemed to burn into her carefully serene face as they walked to the formal dining room.

"He intimidates you," he said.

She smiled. "No. He eludes me, which is unusual for a man."

"You expect us all to fall at your feet?" He sounded amused, damn him.

"No, I expect you to be easily read. Most of you are, you know. He is not. What is *your* interest in Mr. Winsom?"

The sudden attack was merely her form of defense, but unexpectedly, it struck home in this other unreadable man. His eyes pulled free and he shrugged as if he would not answer. Then, abruptly, he said, "Information."

She glanced at him, searching his serene, averted face. Curiosity prickled, but perhaps his quest deserved the same privacy as hers. Instead of asking what she really wanted to know, she said,

"Over there is Mr. Winsom's study, where he goes when he does not wish to be interrupted. No one but he and the maid who cleans are allowed in. Ever. Next to it is the gun room, I believe."

"And where does this lead?" he asked, indicating the stout, ancient-looking door on the right.

"To the old wing," she replied, "disused and strictly forbidden, since as a boy Randolph put his foot through an upstairs floor and fell through to the one below. It was a miracle he was not more badly hurt. He landed on a sofa, apparently. Now the doors are always locked, since the wood is rotten and even the masonry unsafe. Although it looks solid enough from the outside."

They walked on, past the baize door to the servants' quarters. "There is a ballroom right at the back of the house," Constance said, "together with a supper room, and an orangery. Shall we look? Mrs. Winsom is holding a ball at the end of the week. Do you enjoy dancing, Mr. Grey?"

"I do. Perhaps you will save me a waltz?"

"Oh, no," she said, just because it was so dangerously tempting to accept. She remembered the strength of his arms, his hard body... Why did only he have this effect on her? But at least now she was prepared. She opened the double doors of the ballroom and stood back to let him look. "I do not dance, Mr. Grey."

He looked at her rather than at the blank, empty space beyond the doors. "Whyever not?"

She smiled. "Because I am a widow, of course, and still in mourning." She curtsied, with more than a hint of mockery. "I shall see you at dinner, sir." And she flitted away from him, disappointed she could not see his expression. But his breath of laughter made her smile, and then his footsteps echoed into the distance toward the orangery.

CHAPTER TWO

S OLOMON CONTINUED HIS explorations alone. Constance had already given him valuable insight into his host, as much by what she did not say as by what she did. He would not think of what he had learned about her—if anything—except that somehow she surprised him. The silent, exquisite woman he had saved by instinct in Coal Yard Lane was today overawed by neither her surroundings nor her company. Now he wondered if she had been so then either.

She had said she was not pursuing Randolph, and yet she was clearly his guest here. What the devil was she up to?

It was, of course, none of his business. He had come to learn certain facts from Walter Winsom, things he might deny if asked by letter, simply through distrust and suspicion of a stranger.

The orangery was pretty and swelteringly hot. Enclosed as they were, the trees did not smell as they should to him, although they bore plenty of fruit. From there, he walked outside into a fragrant herb garden. Following the path he came on to a wider one that, judging by the horsey smell drifting on the air, led to the stables.

He paused to glance back at the house from this angle and was intrigued by the outside of the old wing. Although it must have been the other way round, it looked curiously tagged on to the main part of the house, the short leg of an L shape. There was no door that he could see, and the windows, though still glazed, did not gleam. They looked curiously blank, as if they had been boarded from the inside. It seemed a waste to him to leave such space unused, especially if the servants lived in the usual cramped accommodation in attics and basements.

But it was not his house.

He walked on, took a detour down another short path, and found dog kennels. A gaggle of hunting dogs were playing and sniffing in the paddock beyond their indoor shelter, although they suddenly started barking and streaming back inside.

The reason seemed to be the man trudging down the path with two pails. He nodded civilly to Solomon. "Afternoon."

Before Solomon could speak, a bark that was more of a thunderous roar startled him, and a black shadow reared up in a separate cage.

The man gave a crooked, almost malicious smile. "Don't mind Monster. He can't get out."

Monster appeared to be a bull mastiff with large teeth and slavering jaws.

"I'm very glad to hear it," Solomon murmured. "What does he hunt? Lions?"

"He doesn't get the chance. He's Mr. Randolph's pet."

"Pet," Solomon repeated.

"Nearly took the kennelman's throat out," said the man with some relish, opening the main kennel to pour the contents of one pail into the trough within. "He refused to have anything more to do with him, so now I have to feed the brute. I'm Hudson, the gamekeeper."

"Solomon Grey." He never minded introducing himself to servants. "Why doesn't Mr. Randolph feed him if the dog's his pet?"

"Oh, he does sometimes. Tied up with guests just now. Mr. Randolph's the only one he likes. Won't let anyone else near him."

The dog glared balefully at Solomon, drawing back its slobbering lips before transferring its attention to Hudson's pail. He barked again, vibrating the ground beneath Solomon's feet."

"Best leave me to it," Hudson advised. "He particularly don't like strangers."

THE VISITING LADIES at Greenforth made a virtue out of not bringing their personal maids with them, claiming they did not need them. Constance, who knew the real reason was the house's lack of accommodation for servants, could have used the practical help in hooking and unhooking her gowns—she had no husband to perform the task for her. But she had no real choice in her decision to come without the girl. Janey still looked and sounded what she was—Covent Garden ware, pulled from a life on the streets when she grew too ill to earn. While regaining her health, Janey was still loud, mouthy, and utterly indiscreet.

Constance, with her laughable dislike of a stranger's touch, had rejected the help of both the housemaid and Mrs. Winsom's personal maid. Now, contorting herself to fasten her evening gown of deep blue silk, she thought with longing of Janey, strident vulgarity and all.

At last she caught the final hook, blew a strand of hair out of her face as she straightened with relief, and eyed her reflection in the mirror. She had looped her thick hair about her head in the soft, artfully casual style she favored for evenings, and once the flush of exertion faded from her face, she would no doubt look well enough. The deep, V-shaped neckline of her gown exposed her creamy chest and shoulders no more than was strictly fashionable. A single, modest string of pearls encircled her throat. Her only other jewelry was the gold wedding band one of her girls had found for her in a pawnshop.

Mrs. Silver never bothered with a wedding ring. No one believed in the fiction of her marital status in any case. Mrs. Goldrich needed the illusion of respectability. If only to stave off Randolph Winsom, who was becoming a shade possessive. As a result, she was reluctant to go down to dinner too early, even though the first gong had sounded. She could probably rely on Randolph's mother not to place them together at the table, and in any case, she reminded herself, she was a past master of the art of avoidance. And of taking over-amorous young, entitled men down a peg or two.

In her own establishment, Randolph was someone she would have watched, at least initially. He was pleasant enough and not cruel by nature, but he did have a temper and a recklessness about the eyes that could cause trouble.

Constance drew on her gloves, glanced at the old fob watch on her dressing table, and decided it was time to go down.

Everyone else had already gathered in the drawing room. They probably thought she was deliberately making an entrance, and in truth, she didn't mind.

Solomon Grey stood by the mantelpiece, a glass of sherry in his long, elegant fingers. For an instant he looked curiously alone, almost vulnerable, and then the illusion vanished as he smiled at Mrs. Winsom and made some apparently amusing remark. She laughed, gazing up at him with sparkling eyes and *delicately* flushed skin.

So that is the way of it... At least from Deborah Winsom's point of view.

He did not appear to notice Constance. Why should he?

Mr. Winsom, the very definition of genial host, was leaning over the back of a sofa between Ivor Davidson and Mrs. Bolton. Utter charm combined with impenetrable respectability. Only, of course, she knew otherwise. At least in his younger days, Walter Winsom had been wild to a fault.

Randolph hurried up to Constance, bearing a glass of sherry, his eyes just a little too warm as they drank her in.

"You look even more beautiful every time I see you."

"You are kind, Randolph, but incredibly forgetful, for I look as I always do. Thank you," she added, accepting the glass from him. She barely had time for a sip before dinner was announced and she was escorted into dinner, rather to her surprise, by her host.

Perhaps he had decided it was time to discover her intentions toward his son, whose attentions were a little too marked for mere politeness. Well, she had a good deal of discovering to do on her own account.

Throughout the first courses he made mere small talk, at which she had learned to excel with just a sprinkling of humor to dispel the tedium. It seemed to work, judging by the slight softening of his eyes, the spark of pleasure that told her he was not immune to her. Part of his charm was that he at least appeared to give his full attention to whomever he spoke to, as though he were genuinely interested in even the most mundane of remarks. She recognized the technique, one she had learned early in life.

"How did such a charming lady come to meet my graceless son?" he asked teasingly, between mouthfuls of soup.

"Didn't he tell you?" Constance asked as though surprised. "We met at the theatre. A mutual friend introduced us—Lady Grizelda Tizsa. Perhaps you know her?"

"I do not," he said, still smiling.

"Oh, she is a most cultured lady. A daughter of the Duke of Kelburn, I believe, married to a most interesting Hungarian gentleman. He and your son share views on politics."

Mr. Winsom snorted. "I daresay they will both learn."

"Very probably," Constance agreed peaceably. Randolph affected a radical stance, probably to annoy his father. "At any rate, Randolph and I amused each other to the extent that he escorted me the following day to an exhibition of paintings I had long wished to see. We became friends, and he invited me to join you here. I hope I was not misled by his assurance that you and Mrs. Winsom would not mind."

"Mind?" he said, in apparent shock. "My dear lady, you are most welcome, as is any friend of our children."

"You have been such kind hosts that I would hate to take

advantage," Constance said with a straight face.

He smiled again, and while the servants cleared the soup and brought the fish, he turned to Mrs. Bolton on his other side.

A little later, during a lull in conversation, he returned to her. "Forgive me for asking, but have you been widowed long, Mrs. Goldrich? You seem very young to have known such tragedy."

"I am older than I tend to look, or so I am told. I have been widowed some five years now."

"What did your husband do?" he asked with unexpected bluntness.

"He was a gentleman of leisure," Constance said without a qualm. "A younger son, but with private means."

"Then you were fortunate enough at least not to be left destitute by the tragedy of his early demise."

"I do not struggle financially," said Constance, this time with perfect truth.

He smiled slightly. "Randolph tells me we may thank you for drawing him away from...the *excessive* pleasures one may discover in the capital."

Well, that was a first. "Oh, I don't believe he was so very bad. Young men have always sown their wild oats." She met his gaze with a conspiratorial twinkle. "Didn't you?"

He twinkled back merrily. "Perhaps."

And still did, she suspected, though perhaps with more circumspection.

He leaned closer, confiding, "Between ourselves, it was why my father sent me to the West Indies, where I discovered my gift for entrepreneurship. So perhaps it was no bad thing."

"How long were you there?" she asked.

"Two, almost three years. I left England in 1828 and took ship home from Jamaica in 1831 when the slave revolt broke out. I like to think I returned a better man. I settled down to marriage and worked hard and never looked back."

"What an uplifting story. Did you not work hard *before* you went to Jamaica?"

"No, I toyed with things. And with people," he said regretful-
ly.

Her heart gave a jolt. "In what way?"

The twinkle came back. "In ways I cannot talk about to a
lady."

She would have liked to dig deeper, but he was already turning once more to Mrs. Bolton.

Still, the conversation left her with much to think about. He
had owned up to bad behavior in his past, to *toying* with people.
And they had reached enough of a rapport that in a day or two,
she could refer back to it, and perhaps reach the truth.

More than that, she could not help liking him. He might have
been a thoughtless, selfish youth, but he had grown into a man
she might well grow to admire. And that filled her with warmth.

SOLOMON WAS A patient man. Quite aside from Constance Silver's
inexplicable presence here, Greenforth was a house of secrets. He
could feel it in his bones. But did Walter Winsom hold the secret
Solomon had come for?

At dinner, he was seated between Mrs. Winsom, who had
chosen him to escort her to the dining room, and her younger
daughter Ellen, who was clearly curious by nature.

"Have you truly just come from Jamaica, Mr. Grey?" she
asked, wide-eyed.

"I came five years ago from Jamaica."

"What did you do there?"

"I grew sugar and cotton and coffee."

She smiled. "With your own fair hands, Mr. Grey?"

"Sometimes, when we were short of laborers. I owned the
plantation. It was in my interests to make it work however I
could."

Her gaze was very direct and disapproving for so young a

lady. But then, her parents were still involved in the anti-slavery movement. "Even with slave labor? Did you own slaves, Mr. Grey?"

At least she didn't say, as many had, *Were you a slave, Mr. Grey?*

"No," he replied. "By the time I inherited, the slaves had been freed."

"But you received compensation from the government for the loss of your *property*?"

"My father did," he said evenly. "Was it helpful to us? Yes, to a point. Do I approve of slavery in any shape or form? No."

"And yet your fortune was founded on the practice."

"So was yours, most probably, in some part, shape, or form. One cannot change what was done in the past, only try to be better."

She blinked. "Then you pay your workers a living wage now?"

"Don't allow my daughter to catechize you, sir," Mrs. Winsom said on his other side, frowning direly beyond his shoulder at Ellen. "You are hardly responsible for the slave trade and all its ills!"

"There is an argument that we are all responsible," Solomon said mildly. By then, he was aware of others around the table listening in without appearing to. Opposite him, Ivor Davidson was smiling with rather malicious amusement.

"Did you mistreat your slaves?" Ellen asked with a defiant glare at her mother. "Before they were freed?"

"If you mean physical mistreatment, no, I didn't, though I know it happened elsewhere. But, of course, the whole practice was abuse."

She seemed to accept that, a frown tugging at her brow as she gazed at him searchingly. "You are sympathetic. Perhaps you have slaves among your ancestors."

He smiled slightly because she had, very probably, addressed the elephant in the room. His African ancestry was as obvious as his European, if one cared to look.

"Ellen!" exclaimed her mother, sacrificing the polite custom of only addressing one's immediate neighbors at the table.

"Indubitably," Solomon said. "My grandfather—er...freed himself, and farmed in the hills. My mother was very fiercely free, but still chose to marry my father."

"How romantic," Ellen exclaimed, her eyes shining.

Solomon let it go. It *was* romantic, after all. Recriminations and prejudices did not change that.

"Why did you leave Jamaica?" Ellen asked a little later.

"To see the world and to make money," Solomon replied promptly. "There is little profit in plantations nowadays, so I moved into shipping and other ventures. London is really the center of the world's trade."

"That's what Papa says."

It was what "Papa" had to say about his time in Jamaica that truly interested Solomon. His chance came after dinner, when the ladies had withdrawn and decanters of port and brandy were being passed around the table. The strong scent of cigar smoke filled the room.

Solomon had hoped for a more relaxed atmosphere without the distraction of the women, but despite the alcohol and tobacco, he still sensed an edge. Whether that was because Solomon was an outsider or because there was tension among the others, he did not yet know.

Opposite him, Ivor Davidson gazed broodingly up the table to his host.

Randolph, who had perhaps indulged in too much wine at dinner and was onto his second generous port, passed the decanter on to him. "Cheer up," he murmured. "He only does it because he can, you know. Once you're aware of his power, he might change his mind."

Davidson curled his lip, though whether at Randolph or the subject of his remarks—presumably Walter Winsom—was not clear.

At the other end of the table, Bolton was talking animatedly to his host, his posture both urgent and confiding, until abruptly, Winsom addressed the room at large on the subject of horse racing, leaving Bolton cut off in mid-sentence. It was the first sign of ill nature that Solomon had seen.

A little later, returning from the cloakroom, Winsom sank into the chair next to Solomon's and poured some brandy into a fresh glass before topping up Solomon's.

"Tell me about Jamaica," he said. "Do you miss it?"

"Yes," Solomon said truthfully. "I miss the sunshine and the colors. The sheer brightness. Do you?"

"I did at first, though I left in a hurry, and it was a good time to go."

"How so?"

"It was during the slave revolt of 1831. I don't suppose you remember it."

"I was ten years old. I remember it vividly."

"It must have been terribly frightening for you as a child. Was there violence at your estate?"

"Some. We were to the southwest of the island."

"I was mainly in the east and I did not own slaves, but yes, that was when I realized there was no money in Jamaica anymore. At least, not for me. Plus, the violence appalled me, both that of the rebels and of the men who put them down. I could not see my way to deal with such immorality. I joined the Anti-Slavery League as soon as I got home."

"Had you much to do with slaves when you were there?"

"In the sense that I was supposed to be learning to manage a plantation, yes. But I was young and foolish, and more interested in enjoying myself."

"In what way?"

Winsom winked. "Ladies, you know. I was sorry to leave them, but the violence was certainly a wake-up call to me. I had to think seriously about what was right and wrong. And about what I was doing, and what I wanted to do in the future."

"Which port did you leave from?"

Solomon's question was a bit abrupt, but he could feel hope draining away from him.

"Port Royal, in the autumn of 1831."

Solomon picked up his glass, holding Winsom's gaze. The date was all wrong, if it were true. "And your ship? It wasn't the *Gallant*, was it?"

Winsom frowned. "No, I don't think so. So long ago, I barely remember…It was a merchant vessel, some bird's name or other. *Hawk* or *Albatross* or something. *Cormorant?*" He shook his head. "Why do you ask?"

"Oh, just an old mystery. Around the time of the revolt, a boy was seen being dragged on to the *Gallant* against his will. I wondered if you had seen anything, that's all. It was something of a *cause célèbre* for some time."

"No, all the violence I saw was ashore. I saw nothing like that."

Solomon shrugged as if he didn't care. He still wasn't sure he believed him.

"Why was the boy being dragged?" Winsom asked, apparently thinking about the matter. "Didn't he want to leave?"

"I don't suppose he did. His family was still on Jamaica. It *might* have been a forcible rescue. Or the story might be made up. Either way, the boy was never seen again on the island."

"That is sad." Winsom smoothed his brow and leaned forward to clink glasses. "Too sad for an evening with friends. Shall we rejoin the ladies?"

IF CONSTANCE HAD not been aware of the approaching male voices, she would still have known from the sudden excitement of the other women that the gentlemen were about to join them.

It was like her own exclusive establishment when her salons

full of girls heard the ringing of the doorbell. In this situation, the agitation felt both odd and wrong, for apart from young Ellen, all these women were married and perfectly used to seeing their husbands. The reason behind the tension could only be anticipation of someone else's husband. Or one of the unattached men— the young, dramatic Randolph Winsom, the forceful Ivor Davidson, or Solomon Grey.

Interestingly enough, it was Grey that drew all female eyes without his having to try. So she was not the only woman attracted by his mere presence. And there was the novelty, of course. None of them except Mrs. Winsom had met him before today—just how had that meeting come about?

"What about some music?" Mr. Winsom said jovially. "Ellen, entertain us with the piece you were playing the other day."

Obligingly, Ellen went to the piano. Ivor Davidson followed her to turn her music for her. A brief spurt of irritation crossed Mrs. Winsom's face. Constance wondered if she had anything against Davidson, or just thought Ellen too young. Though a quick glance at the elder daughter, already married and apparently expecting her first child, reminded her that Miriam Albright must have been married when she was barely eighteen years old. She was younger than Randolph, who was still only twenty.

Ellen glanced up at Davidson a few times, but he did not appear to notice. He gazed at the music, turned the pages at the right time, and behaved with perfect courtesy.

Ellen played very prettily, though she shyly refused to sing.

"Good thing," said her brother with a grin as she stood up from the piano. "Constance, you sing for us. *You* have a lovely voice."

Although irritated—she wished to be free to listen and learn and ask questions—there was little Constance could do except comply gracefully. She had hardly been brought up with such accomplishments, but as soon as she could afford it, she had made it her business to learn them, part of her strategy to move into the higher end of the oldest profession, and it had been useful before now. Many Society hostesses might have envied the refined entertainment of Mrs. Silver's lower salons, to say nothing of her guest list.

To her own accompaniment on the piano, she sang a French air she had learned from a naval officer, remembering to alter the words subtly in case anyone understood. Only Solomon Grey showed a glimmer of amusement, but then, he probably spent a lot of time on the docks. Next, she sang a jollier English song that made everyone smile, then stood up to make way for Mr. and Mrs. Albright, who performed a duet they had clearly been practicing.

"You are a lady of much talent as well as charm," Davidson murmured, sitting down beside her. "What on earth do you see in poor old Randolph?"

"Is he poor?" Constance murmured. "He is certainly a gentleman."

Davidson, taking that to mean he was not, flushed. "It was a joke," he muttered. "I'm very fond of Randolph. Of all the Winsoms. What is your connection to them?"

"Oh, I have none but friendship," Constance said, smiling, and pretending to listen with pleasure to the Albrights' duet.

Loneliness washed over her. She was used to that—the feeling of being alone, even while the center of attention. *Especially* when the center of attention, because she was always playing a role. No one ever saw beneath her roles. She could not afford that they did.

But she despised the weakness of self-pity. With an effort, she threw it off like an annoyingly damp cloak and raised her hands to applaud the performance.

HER MOMENT OF weakness, brief as it had been, was a warning she did not ignore. The strain of keeping up her pretense, of trying to worm information without appearing to be more than politely curious, was beginning to tell. On top of which, Randolph was becoming embarrassingly attached, and now Solomon Grey's arrival, with his knowledge of her true identity, added to her stress.

In short, she was not sure she could keep up this nonsense for the full week. She had already been here two days. She needed to know one way or another, and she could no longer afford to be polite about it. Different methods were called for, after which she could invent some summons home, return to London, and be seen no more by the Winsoms.

Unless she discovered something that required a little more action on her part. She was no longer sure what she wanted the truth to be. Not that her desires mattered—the truth was absolute.

And yet, when everyone retired to their respective bedchambers, and Walter Winsom bade her goodnight, she thought his eyes were warmer than before, and just a little puzzled, surely as if he sensed some familiarity about her, wondering about the rapport springing up between them.

She could not take advantage of it. His family and friends stood close by, and she could not ask for privacy at this time of night.

Not that it was late by Constance's standards. Country hours were early. She smiled and carried on upstairs with her candle.

She did not undress, merely read a little, paced a little, gazed out of the window at the countryside, and waited for the house to quieten. In the distance, an owl hooted. A dog howled plaintively, probably Randolph's ferocious pet longing for another throat to bite.

It was after midnight when she crept out of her room with a single candle and flitted along the passage to the stairs. The whole house was in silent darkness, yet she had the feeling, as she sometimes did when she seemed the only person in the world who was awake, that it was alive and watching her, and ready to protect its own.

Perhaps I count as "its own."

Did she want to? She could decide that after she knew the truth.

In the large hall at the foot of the stairs, her candle flame did not penetrate far. She paused, peering into the blackness all around her. She could see no lights under doors, though gradually, she realized the darkness was not absolute either. Moonlight shone through the cupola above and through the windows on either side of the front door.

Somewhere in the house, a board creaked, and another. The old house was settling for the night. Or objecting to her presence. Ignoring both fancies, she turned and made her way toward the library.

What if he is in there? What if someone else is?

It was always a possibility, which was why she had her excuse ready. So she did not hesitate, merely opened the door, quietly, yet as if she had every right to be there.

The curtains were not drawn, and moonlight drizzled through the long windows, casting an eerie silver glow over the carpet and the armchairs and the shelves of books on either side.

Constance was already moving toward the largest desk, where she had twice seen her host at work, when she realized someone was already there.

Her free hand flew to her throat as though to stifle the rising cry of startlement.

A tall man stood very still behind the desk. The moonlight did not quite reach him, but a candle at his side illuminated him quite well enough.

Solomon Grey.

CHAPTER THREE

"MR. GREY," CONSTANCE drawled, walking toward him. "Looking for a little light reading before bed?"

Since one of his hands was inside an open drawer, her sarcasm was more than justified. He did not, however, look particularly put out, let alone guilty.

"Why? Are you?" he asked, with apparent politeness. He removed his hand from the drawer, though he didn't trouble to close it.

"I'm not the one caught with my fingers in the—er...pie."

"Only because I got here first."

He was still fully dressed, and quite as elegant as he had looked earlier in the evening. Even so, Constance was not foolish enough to go too close. He was too large, and his very stillness radiated danger. She had caught him prying, poking around in a private drawer that might even have been locked. The fact that she had indeed intended to do exactly the same did not stop it being crime against hospitality and gentlemanly conduct—a transgression quite as unforgivable as her own false pretenses.

He must have been well aware of that, yet the candlelight flickering over his face from both sides revealed no embarrassment.

She set her candle down on the desk. "What did you find?"

The tiniest spark of surprise glinted in his dark eyes. "Nothing of great interest to me. Perhaps it is to you. What are you looking for?"

"You first," she said politely.

His teeth gleamed in what looked like a genuine smile. "You have style, Mrs. Silver. Would you not prefer to join forces than work against each other?"

"Since I don't know what you are working toward, I cannot say. What is it you suspect of our host?"

"What makes you think I suspect him of anything?"

She lifted her brows. "Solomon Grey has no need to steal anyone's petty cash. You have already admitted you seek information. At least tell me if you have found what you are looking for."

There was a pause. "Not yet. You? Shall I move over?" He actually stepped aside to give her access to the open drawer, but even as she speculated whether or not to accept the improper offer—after all, so far, all the wrongdoing was his—his gaze shifted beyond her.

A frown flickered, and he brushed past her so swiftly she had no time to move aside. The echo of distinctive scent teased her senses, half remembered, wholly intriguing.

She found herself following him to the window.

"Did you see that?" he breathed.

"What?"

"Something glinted outside. Then a shadow vanished into the trees."

"I don't see anything," she said, truthfully. "No lantern lights."

He did not answer, merely strode back to the desk, snapped the open drawer shut, and snatched up the nearest candle—hers—before making for the door.

Intrigued, Constance fetched the remaining candle and hurried after him.

Without blundering into any furniture, they got to the French windows of the drawing room. Constance unlocked them as she had seen Mrs. Winsom do, and again he brushed past her, either from rudeness or for her protection. She reserved judgment as to which.

He set off purposefully along the garden path toward the trees. She hurried with him. Her candle flickered out, but it made little difference. The full moon seemed to flood them with light, making the familiar landscape new and different and more than a little uncanny.

Country noises were different to a town's. Constance had known both the dangerous, dark alleys of the London slums, and the street-lit, well-patrolled streets of Mayfair. She survived well in either, because the threats were always distinctly human. Here, her imagination ran riot.

The shadows were new. Night creatures scurried and called in the distance. Trees loomed, menacing from above, reaching out with their branches and whispering leaves. Hedges hid unknowable, lurking risks. The air seemed thick with generations of ghosts stretching back to a time beyond history. God knew she did not belong here.

She stumbled over a root. Grey, who had not appeared to be paying any attention to her, caught her hand to steady her, and she was rattled enough to grasp it as they moved on.

He seemed to be following his nose, entering a copse only briefly before reemerging at the other side of the house, beneath the terrace where they'd had tea that afternoon. The formal garden, whence Randolph had tried to entice her, smelled strongly of rosemary and pine and flowers she couldn't name—or perhaps it was the perfume of long-dead women.

And when did I become so ridiculously fanciful?

Pull yourself together, Constance Silver...

"I still don't see anyone," she breathed.

"Neither do I." His low voice seemed to vibrate through his fingers into hers, reminding her she still hung on to him. Nor was she ready to let him go.

He halted, peering ahead and then to either side. His breath hitched, and then he set off toward the swing beyond the pond and the weeping willow.

"What?" she whispered. "What do you see?"

"Something glinted again. Something that shouldn't be there..."

She saw it then, too, and he was quite right. The blade of a large, bone-handled kitchen knife should not have been in the garden, beneath the swing. It most certainly should not have been buried between the shoulder blades of a man.

The danger was human, after all. She walked forward quickly, barely noticing that her hand was freed. They crouched together by the fallen man and Constance seized his wrist, feeling for a pulse.

His skin was not warm, though it lacked the icy coldness of death. She searched frantically for any positive sign of life but could find none.

"He's dead," Grey said. "And not for very long."

Shifting position, he lifted the dead man's shoulder, enough to let the moon shine down on his face. Their host, Walter Winsom.

THE REVEREND PETER Albright strode into his marital bedchamber a worried man. The strength of his anger with his father-in-law made him doubt his calling, and he needed Miriam's gentle strength. In fact...

But Miriam was not in their room.

The lamp was still lit, but her nightgown was neatly folded on her pillow.

He felt deflated, let down, even jealous, that she should be with her mother or her sister rather than with him when he needed her.

Hastily, he changed into his nightshirt, flung his robe about him, and paced the room until she came back.

She entered quietly, as though afraid of disturbing him.

"Where have you been?" he asked.

She jumped. "Goodness, you startled me! I thought you must be asleep by now."

"I was waiting for you."

"Mama is a little distraught," she said carefully.

So am I! "You could have told me you were going to see her."

She blinked. "How could I do that, Peter? You left the room almost as soon as we got here. Where did *you* go?"

That was the thing about Miriam. She always did as he asked, never quibbled, was the perfect, obedient wife. Except when he was being unreasonable, which he was. He drew in his breath. "Sorry. I am a little on edge. I needed a few moments alone to calm down. I need to talk to you."

"Now?" she said, trying to smile. She looked tired and strained. Pregnancy was taking its toll on her.

He managed to smile. "No, tomorrow will do. You are too tired. Come to bed."

→≫≫≪≪←

SOLOMON STARED AT the dead man and lowered his head slowly back to the ground.

Walter Winsom lay on his front, both arms out as if he had tried to save himself from falling. He wore his evening coat, stained now with the damp, sticky darkness of blood, a small, irregular patch around the obscene knife sticking out of his person.

One side of his face was visible, his eye wide open in apparent surprise. Solomon sat back on his heels, inevitable pity and outrage mingling with his sense of frustration. Another door had closed, and in such a way that suspicion remained.

Who would murder a blameless man, and why?

A kitchen knife in the back was no accident, no act of self-defense.

Beside him, Constance Silver stared too. She had been feeling for a pulse that would never beat again and still held the dead man's right hand. With a strange, blind look, she touched it to her cheek. Her eyes glistened in the moonlight. Something very like a tear trembled at the corner of her eye.

"What is he to you?" he blurted.

She blinked, laying Winsom's hand back where it had been. Her smile was cynical, which somehow made it no less beautiful. "Not what you are thinking. I'll rouse the household." She rose quickly, and he with her.

He caught her hand. "Wait. Go back to your room. I'll wake the servants."

She widened her eyes at him. "Why? Afraid I'll implicate you?"

She could, too. The body was still warm, implying the murder was recent, probably occurring while they had blundered about the garden. Which made his blood run cold. All the same, the alternative was even more chilling—that it had happened before either of them entered the library. Constance could have killed him then. And in her eyes, if she were innocent of the crime, so could he.

"Yes," he said. "I'm afraid you will implicate me."

Their eyes met. There was no fear in hers, just speculation. "Guilt or chivalry?" she murmured. "And would I ever know?"

"Go," he said, before he changed his mind.

A moment longer she hesitated, then flitted away around the house to the drawing room window.

Alone, Solomon hastily rifled through the man's pockets, and found nothing at all. But his gold watch remained in his waistcoat pocket, and his jeweled sleeve buttons in his shirt cuffs. Unlikely it was a robbery.

Solomon rose. For the first time it struck him that the fingers of the dead man's left hand were curled. He walked around the body and crouched again to investigate. Winsom was clutching a square of fine, embroidered cloth—a lady's handkerchief.

Solomon pocketed it and rose once more.

On impulse, he walked toward the nearest side of the house, trying the locked side door and then the French windows of the dining room, which were also locked. As were the front door, the orangery door, and the kitchen door.

Constance had, fortunately, left the drawing room door slightly open for him. He went in, closed it, and set off for the kitchen.

He found a boy asleep on a makeshift bed, close to the kitchen stove, and roused him without fuss. "Go and wake Richards and the housekeeper and Mrs. Winsom's maid. Tell them there's an emergency and they must come to the drawing room immediately. They needn't bother about proper dress."

Fuzzy with sleep, the boy still jumped up to obey, pulling on his own clothes, and lurching off toward the stairs with the candle Solomon gave him. Solomon followed more slowly, back upstairs and across the hall to the drawing room. He paused only to light a lamp on the way, and then another in the drawing room.

It was going to be a long night.

ALICE BOLTON WAS surprised to discover she had been asleep, even if only for a moment. She had expected to lie awake for hours, yet she clearly hadn't, for her husband joining her in the marital bed actually woke her.

She kept her breathing even, so Thomas would not know he had disturbed her. She was not ready to talk to him, though she did wonder where he had been. Not quarreling with Walter, she hoped. More probably, he was answering a call of nature. Or poring over yet more figures from the wretched bank.

But then, it seemed Thomas was not the only member of the party up late. Alice could hear footsteps and whispers in the passageway, and then surely, distant hooves from outside, as if someone were riding away from Greenforth in the middle of the night. Unusual but not alarming.

She closed her eyes again, hoping her even breathing would carry her back into the arms of Morpheus. It almost had when the wailing started, a terrible, drawn-out shout of grief followed by an almost continuous howl.

"What on earth...?"

"It's Deborah," Thomas said irritably from the pillow next to her. "No one else would ever make a racket like that. Shouldn't you go to her?"

Alice tried to keep the distaste out of her voice. "Presumably Walter is there."

"Even Walter can't be expected to deal with a hysterical woman all by himself."

His words were petulant and uncharacteristically sarcastic. Oh yes, he knew something...

Alice rose with exaggerated patience. With an air of great generosity, he lit the lamp for her. She donned her dressing down, tying it at her waist with unnecessary force, before wordlessly snatching the lamp from him and leaving the room.

It was not difficult to trace the howling. Nor was she the only other member of the household up. Servants and guests milled uselessly in the passage in varying stages of dress and undress, wavering lights from candles and lamps flickering over white, frightened faces.

"What is it?" Alice demanded of Peter Albright, resplendent in a deep purple, frogged dressing gown. "What ails Deborah? Is Walter with her?"

"Walter is *not* with her," Peter said, his voice sad and rather self-consciously portentous. "He will never be with her again. Or with us."

She had to reach out with her free hand to grasp the wall, as though the world had tilted impossibly. "*What?* What do you mean? Speak plainly, for God's sake."

"It is my sad duty to tell you that the lord has seen fit to—"

"My father is dead," said Miriam Albright from her mother's bedroom doorway. Tears streamed down her cheeks. "My father is dead. Where is Ellen? Does she know?"

Alice moved forward blindly, mostly to get away from everyone else, even if it meant walking toward the dreadful noise of the widow.

Deborah's maid, Wilson, was with her, sitting on the edge of the bed, trying to talk calmly through the wailing while she held her mistress's hand and stroked it helplessly.

At least Deborah had the luxury of grief. Alice had not. She could not give in—she had to think through it, behave as she ought.

Deborah sat upright, eyes tight shut, thrashing her head from side to side against the positive froth of pillows behind her, her heels drumming rhythmically against the mattress. She was clearly oblivious to her maid or anyone else. Without compunction, Alice pushed the maid aside and sat down, taking Deborah by both shoulders and pinning her to stillness.

"My poor Deborah, you must stop that noise," she said firmly. "You have children who need you. What will Ellen think if she sees you like this? *Hears* you like this?" The whole house must be able to hear her, from attic to kitchen.

The howling cut off like a tap. Deborah opened her eyes and stared into Alice's. Abruptly, she fell on Alice's neck, weeping silently, and at last Alice too could give into tears. The two women held each other, united in grief, until Miriam came in with Ellen. Both girls were white with shock.

Quietly, Alice rose and left the room. At least the passage was now empty. She walked slowly back to her own room.

Thomas was standing by the bed in his nightgown. "What the devil is going on?"

"You had better get dressed," Alice said prosaically. "Walter is dead, and the magistrate—or at least a constable—is on his way."

"Don't be silly! He can't be—"

"I assure you he can," she interrupted in a small, hard voice she barely recognized as her own.

"Dear God, how? What—" He broke off, scowling. "In any case, no one will come out in the middle of the night unless it is the doctor—"

"I assure you they will when they hear he died with a kitchen knife in his back."

CONSTANCE FELT UTTERLY dazed, as though the floor had vanished beneath her feet and she was falling. Which was ridiculous. Although it was some years since she had witnessed violent death, tonight was hardly the first time she had done so. And she had known Walter Winsom a mere two days, so she was hardly entitled to grief.

Mrs. Bolton calmed the widow. The daughters clung to each other. Randolph stood alone in the passageway, staring at his parents' bedroom door. In his dressing gown, white and still, he looked suddenly much younger than his twenty years, like a child in need of comfort.

Constance was suddenly ashamed. She had lost a possibility that in the grand scheme of things meant nothing. Randolph and his sisters had lost their beloved father, and in such a brutal, incomprehensible way. Impulsively, she went to Randolph and took his hand.

He turned his head and looked at her, blinking.

She squeezed his fingers. "Bear up, Randolph," she whispered. "You must be strong now, for your family."

Being strong, taking on responsibilities, was the only way she knew how to cope with grief. And her words did seem to reach him, for a spark of determination penetrated the bewildered glaze of his eyes.

She left him and went downstairs to deal with the servants, one of whom was in hysterics and frightening the others. By the time she had settled them to make tea and be useful, a white-faced constable and a half-dressed footman had brought the body into the house and placed it on one of the long supper-room tables next to the ballroom. The local doctor was there, talking to Solomon Grey and looking as shocked as everyone else. Constance asked him to call on the widow after he had finished with his other duties.

She then returned to the servants' hall to send them back to bed for the few hours that remained of the night. Richards, the once-haughty butler, and Mrs. Farrow, the housekeeper, seemed to have wilted, which was probably scaring the lesser servants as much as the murder of their master. The pair sat silently together at one end of the table, the others in huddles whispering or weeping according to their natures.

At sight of her, the whispering stopped, and everyone looked at her in mingled hope and alarm. They were not used to their realm being invaded by those from upstairs, and yet they desperately needed some kind of direction.

"I think you should all retire now," Constance said to Mrs. Farrow. "The family will need you and the staff quite desperately in the coming days."

It seemed to be the right thing to say. Mrs. Farrow squared her shoulders and sent the maids off to bed. Richards blinked several times, then rose to his feet and jerked his head at the footmen.

On her way out, Constance heard movement in the kitchen and went in. To her surprise, the constable had not left the premises. He was with the stout cook and Solomon Grey, and in his hand, he held the bone-handled knife Constance had last seen in Mr. Winsom's back.

For an instant, she felt queasy, until she reminded herself sharply that she was not really a refined, delicate lady. Grey saw her first, but acknowledged her with no more than a twitch of the eyebrows before his attention returned to the cook, who made a grab for the knife in the constable's hands.

"Of course it's mine," she snapped, "and I'd like to know what it's doing in your grubby mitts, Johnny Barker!"

Constable Barker snatched it out of her reach. "Sorry, Mrs. Corben, but this knife is evidence. You can have it back after the coroner says so."

The cook grasped for the back of the nearest chair and almost fell into it. "You mean...the master was killed with my knife? Oh, dear God!"

"No one's suspecting *you* of such a foul deed, Mrs. Corben," the constable assured her. "But we will need to know exactly when and where you last saw it..."

The cook moaned, realizing for the first time that she might be suspected of this hideous crime.

Constance knew how she felt. If the knife had come from this kitchen, then surely it was someone in this house who had committed the murder.

Why had she not thought of that before? This was no random act of city violence, no opportunistic robbery by a passing stranger...

She realized Solomon Grey was gazing right at her.

She met his gaze, wondering what violence he had seen before, and what he had done.

And then she wondered about everyone else.

"I couldn't find it last night," the cook said hoarsely. "It wasn't in its usual place in that drawer right there with my other knives. I used it preparing dinner during the day, and when I went to carve the meat, I couldn't find it."

So the knife had vanished the day or night *before* the murder. The day everyone but Grey had arrived. The attack had been planned. Somebody, surely somebody in this house, had stolen the cook's knife from the kitchen in order to kill Walter Winsom with it.

Slowly, Constance turned and walked out to the stairs that led to the baize door separating the servants' quarters from the family's.

CHAPTER FOUR

I T WAS ONLY very gradually that the house fell back into darkness and silence.

Constance lay in the comfortable bed she had been given for the week under false pretenses and wished it was dawn, when she would have to stay awake. Instead, she drifted into uneasy sleep, full of dreams of blood and violence that were half nonsense and half memory. It meant that when daylight did wake her, she felt shaken and unrested and wanted to bolt for the safe home she had made for herself and her people.

Escape, however, proved not to be an option. When she joined the other subdued and uneasy guests in the breakfast parlor, she found the magistrate seated among them. He was an upright, elderly gentleman with a trim beard and whiskers who had the look of a retired army officer. And indeed, he was introduced as Colonel George.

"I'm afraid I must remove Mr. Winsom's remains for the coroner to examine," the colonel said. "And I have sent to London for the help we will need with so vile and serious a crime. I must ask you all to remain here at Greenforth until someone from Scotland Yard has spoken to you."

"That is something of an imposition on the grieving family," Mrs. Bolton demurred.

"Nonsense," said Miriam Albright, who, pale and red-eyed between her husband and her sister, seemed to have stepped up to her mother's role. Mrs. Winsom was understandably absent.

"My mother will be comforted by your presence especially, and by the support of all her friends." She tried to smile. "I am afraid you will be terribly bored, since there can be no question now of the entertainment that was planned."

Colonel George rose from the table and bowed smartly. "Thank you for your time and your understanding. Once again, my condolences."

Constance poured herself a cup of coffee and took a slice of toast from the sideboard, though she doubted she could eat it.

"What do they want with a parcel of strangers from London to find a madman in this neighborhood?" Randolph demanded. "Surely the local men will find the culprit more easily."

"Not necessarily," Solomon Grey said mildly. "It is certainly more comfortable to imagine a passing stranger did this…"

"*Comfortable?*" Ellen said in a choked voice. "If you imagine—"

"Forgive me, Miss Ellen," Grey said. "A poor choice of word, and yet imagining an insane stranger committed this crime is really an illusion. The weapon came from the Greenforth kitchen, and there is no sign that anyone broke into the house."

Ivor Davidson tugged at his collar. "You are saying someone *in this house* murdered Mr. Winsom?"

"It does seem the inescapable conclusion." Grey sounded almost apologetic, but his dark eyes were anything but submissive. They were bright with intelligence and perception. "I do not say this to upset anyone, merely to warn you of the kind of questions we are likely to be asked."

"Such as?" Davidson demanded.

"Such as where we were at the time the murder occurred, and"—Grey's gaze flickered over everyone, so it might have been imagination that it lingered on Constance—"and exactly what was our relationship with Mr. Winsom."

For several seconds, no one spoke.

"Who even found him?" Ellen asked into the stunned, awkward silence.

"I did," Grey said calmly.

Ellen's turbulent gaze met his. "And what were you doing in the garden in the middle of the night? Just taking a walk?"

Constance's stomach twisted. She should admit to being with him, only…

"Not *just*," Grey admitted. "I was in the library not long after midnight when I thought I saw something move outside. I was curious enough to go out and look around. I found your father but not the culprit. I'm sorry," he added gently.

Ellen's gaze dropped to her untouched plate of eggs and bacon. "So am I," she whispered.

Grey finished his coffee, set down the cup, and rose, excusing himself with a bow.

"Well," Mrs. Bolton said with some resentment, "if it *was* anyone in the house who did such a thing, we should look first at *him*."

"Why is that?" Constance asked.

"Because he was *there*, by his own admission," Mrs. Bolton snapped. "And let's face it, he is not one of us."

Constance was not entirely free of her own suspicions, but at this, her hackles rose in defense of her fellow outsider. and she could not be silent. "*Not one of us*? You mean because he might bear the blood of the slaves whose cause you support so loyally?"

Mrs. Bolton flushed, her nostrils flaring with dislike, and Constance knew she had made an enemy.

"No," Mrs. Bolton uttered. "I don't mean that at all. It has nothing to do with his ancestry but with the fact that none of us knows him. Poor Deborah invited him on very little acquaintance. Walter had never even met him!"

"But he had heard of him," Mr. Bolton said unexpectedly. "As had I. And Davidson, too, I imagine. He is, even I know, a sought-after guest."

Mrs. Bolton waved one dismissive hand, but she said nothing further. Constance forced herself to take a bite of toast. All around the table, people were taking surreptitious glances at each other.

"One of the servants with a grudge?" Davidson murmured to Randolph, who shrugged impatiently.

"Unlikely. But then, it's *all* damned unlikely, isn't it?" Randolph glared around the room. "We were all in bed at midnight. I daresay the married people may vouch for one another, but the rest of us cannot prove we were in bed when my father was murdered."

"Randolph!" Peter Albright said sharply.

"Well, Grey has a point! The police *will* ask such questions."

"Not of the family, surely," Miriam said, staring at him.

Such innocence, thought Constance pityingly.

"Oh, probably not," Randolph said, "but one must be prepared for unpleasantness... More unpleasantness."

Feeling the need for fresh air, Constance escaped from the breakfast parlor as soon as she could. She was fairly sure those remaining would speculate on the possibility that she had committed the crime, but she could not prevent that. What she did need to do was speak to Grey to decide what to tell the police.

Discovering from Richards that Mr. Grey had gone out, she ran upstairs to fetch her bonnet and change into walking shoes. As she left the house, she wondered seriously about the possibility of someone entering the house and stealing the kitchen knife before coming back the following night to murder Mr. Winsom.

"Constance."

Annoyingly, it was Randolph calling from behind her, striding rapidly along the path to catch up. She forced down her irritation with a smile, reminding herself of his very recent loss.

"Randolph. How are you?"

"Coping. It helps to be busy. Or to plan to be. Thomas Bolton and I will go through Papa's business papers this afternoon. It's my mother who worries me."

"Give her time," Constance said gently. "It has only been a few hours."

He nodded.

"Don't ask too much of yourself, either," she added. "As you say, it helps to be busy, but the grief will still be there."

"You know about grief," he said, gazing at her. "Because of your husband. Have you buried your own parents?"

"Yes." It was true, in a manner of speaking. "And several very good friends."

"I'm sorry." He drew a deep breath. "I did not mean the party to turn out quite like this."

"I know."

"And now we shall have police, detectives from Scotland Yard, down here, raking over our lives and his."

"I'm afraid that is unavoidable." She just hoped they did not look too closely into hers and discover her name was false. Which was another reason to speak to Grey.

"The thing is," Randolph said, "should one tell the truth?"

"I imagine it's generally best, if one has nothing to hide."

"Or if a friend has."

"A friend?" she repeated, looking around for any sign as to the direction Grey had taken.

"You, for example."

Her stomach jolted. Her eyes flew back to his face, though she managed—she hoped—to keep control of their expression. "I?"

"Where were you just after midnight, Constance?" he asked softly.

"In bed, of course, until I heard all the commotion."

His lips twisted. "You can't prove that any more than I can. In fact, I could, if I chose, tell the police that wherever you were, it was *not* your own bed."

She widened her eyes. "What do you mean by that?"

"I mean I knocked on your door at midnight and you did not answer."

"Of course I did not," she said virtuously. "And frankly, Randolph, I am surprised at you, particularly in your mother's house."

He flushed but snapped back, "Well, I was pretty surprised

too when I opened the door to discover you weren't there! Where were you?"

She leaned her head to one side, regarding him. It annoyed her unduly to be discovered in a lie, and as usual, she attacked. "Is this where you accuse me outright of immoral behavior? Or of murdering your poor father?"

"No," he said. "It's really where we agree to tell the police we were with each other. The story will go no further, I am sure, and it means I can protect you."

She almost laughed, though the disappointment was surprisingly deep. "You mean you can make sure *I* protect *you*."

He flushed. "You misunderstand me."

"No, I don't. And my advice stands. Tell the truth, Randolph. I will."

And she walked off toward the wood, raising one hand in clear dismissal, just in case he tried to follow her. She was striding along so furiously that she did not see the man seated on the tree branch among the foliage until he dropped right in front of her, landing lightly on his feet like a cat.

She stopped dead, glaring at Solomon Grey. He looked as elegant as ever in his well-cut clothes, even with bits of leaf clinging to his coat.

"Who has ruffled your feathers?" he inquired.

"You know perfectly well it was Randolph Winsom. I'm sure you had an excellent view of our encounter from up there." She brushed past him and strode on.

"Lovers' tiffs do not interest me," he said, falling into step with her.

"If you imagine that boy is my lover, you are quite laughably wide of the mark."

She expected him to ask, but he remained silent so long, merely ambling along beside her, that she turned on him. "Well, you are! Do you know he had the nerve to blackmail me into giving him an alibi? Of course, he pretended it was for *my* protection, but he had already told me he knew I wasn't in my room just after midnight. So I was to sacrifice my reputation in order to protect him!"

"Interesting," was all Grey said.

For no reason, that hurt her. She curled her lip. "I am well aware of my true reputation, but he is not. I suppose you think whores deserve to be treated like that."

He turned his head, focusing on her face. "No, I don't. I just don't see why you are so angry. He is young and frightened and might just have killed his father. You are older and wiser and you already know that when it comes down to it, you have me to prove your alibi."

"After midnight," she blurted. "Not before. *You* could have done it before you entered the library."

"So could you. Though I must point out that we probably saw the killer pass from the library window."

"I only have your word for that. *I* didn't see anyone. You could have made it up to get me out of the library and keep me busy while you carried on searching for whatever it was you sought there in the first place."

"I could," he agreed. "But I am not always quite that devious. I had no reason to kill him, you know. I wanted information only he could give me. And he didn't have time in the end."

"What sort of information?"

In silence, he walked three paces. Four. "He might have seen my brother when he was in Jamaica."

Whatever she had expected, it was not that. "Winsom left Jamaica more than twenty years ago."

"So did my brother. Maybe. Certainly, I have not seen him since."

Twenty years ago, he could not have been more than ten. How old was his brother? He gave her no time to ask.

He said quickly, "Has it struck you that as the outsiders at Greenforth, you or I might well be the preferred suspects?"

"Yes," she admitted. "To say nothing of my false pretenses. And your prying into drawers."

He did not look offended by the accusation. In fact, he might not have been listening. "I have been thinking about your friends, the Tizsas."

Dragan Tizsa, physician, refugee, and one-time revolutionary, had somehow married Lady Grizelda Niven, a daughter of the Duke of Kelburn. They were an eccentric couple, devoted to art, music, social justice, and mysteries—and to each other, which was rather endearing. Constance had met them the same night she met Solomon, and they had solved the mystery surrounding her old friend Elizabeth…

"We could use their help," she admitted. "But we can hardly invite them into someone else's house of mourning."

"No. But…we could try to solve this murder ourselves. If only we trusted each other."

"We don't."

"True." He walked on, then glanced back at her. "Do you want to try anyway?"

She didn't even think about it. "Yes." She drew a deep breath. "I hadn't learned what I wished to, either. I thought…"

"You thought what?"

She glared at him, daring him to laugh at her. "That Walter Winsom might be my father."

IT SEEMED SHE could always snatch Solomon's breath. He wasn't surprised that she had agreed so easily to his suggestion of working together to discover the truth—they needed each other's support in this house. But in all his speculations as to the reasons for her presence here, he had never even thought of anything so…sad.

The woman ran a bawdy house, albeit a very discreet and expensive one. He knew that beneath the beauty she used as a marketable weapon, she was hard as nails. She had to be. But she looked after her women. She had even looked after Elizabeth and Lady Griz. He allowed her curiosity and compassion. But this… This admission, if true, betrayed a yearning to belong to someone, to have roots and a family, a loneliness and vulnerability quite at odds with her outward character. Loneliness was something he understood only too well.

He too could be guilty of prejudice.

In the dappled sunlight of the woods, she glared up at him, daring him to laugh. Sympathy would be just as unwelcome. And for that reason, he believed her.

"Was he?" he asked, carefully indifferent.

"My father? Who knows? As a youth, he certainly raked around the stews of London. A friend who had dealings with Randolph told me she knew other whores who had known his father in the past. Also, that Walter had fathered an illegitimate girl, more than twenty-five years ago. That could have been me."

Her voice was too deliberately light, disparaging her own origins as well as Walter's character.

"Did you *want* him to be your father?" he asked.

She shrugged. "I don't even know if I liked him. I thought Randolph was quite sweet. I thought I'd quite like him as a brother."

"Only you don't."

"No. But you see why I laughed when you suggested a quite different relationship."

He inclined his head. "Randolph himself is clearly aware of no connection. How badly does he want to marry you?"

She opened her mouth to deny any serious intent on his part, and then closed it again. "You think he wanted me so badly he would kill his father for refusing to allow it?"

"I don't suppose he's the first man to commit murder for you."

She fluttered her eyelashes. "Why, Mr. Grey, you say the sweetest things."

"It was not a compliment."

"I shall still choose to regard it as such."

"Have you always had that accent?"

"Wot, vis old fing? Bless yer, guv, no. I 'ad to buy the pebbles for me mouf special like."

His lips twitched.

"Would that accent make you feel better?" she asked politely.

"It was never about the accent. One day, I would like to hear your life story."

"No, you wouldn't." She glanced up at him. "I might like to hear yours, though."

"Imagine how the long winter nights would fly by."

"Well, hopefully, we'll have solved the crime by then and not be in prison awaiting execution. Who do you think did it? Apart from me."

"At the moment, I suspect everyone has a motive—except the servants. I haven't considered them at all yet. I do have one clue." He fished in his pocket and brought out the embroidered handkerchief. "I found this in Winsom's left hand last night."

Constance took it. "I don't recognize it. It's probably his wi—" She broke off, her gaze on the embroidered initials. *A.B.* "Alice Bolton…"

She halted and raised her gaze to his. "Then they *were* having an affair."

"Perhaps." He shrugged. "And perhaps not. He could have found it somewhere in the garden."

"He could. But it's odd he should have been wandering in the garden, holding on to it. Unless he'd only just come across it, surely he'd have put it in his pocket? No, I think there's something between them. But does it help us?"

"It might. At the moment, it's just another mystery. What do you think about the servants, and Mrs. Corben's missing knife?"

She shook her head. "Servants have little motive to attack the hand that feeds them. The Winsoms are not cruel to their staff. Let's leave them until later. What of Randolph? He is Walter's heir and stands to inherit what I gather is a substantial fortune."

"Much of it tied up in business," Solomon said, "largely in the bank with Bolton. I doubt Randolph has taken the trouble to understand the workings of that. Still, he will have a much larger allowance to play with—or will do when he is of age."

She sighed. "Then you discount his love for me as a motive? I am crushed."

"No, it just adds to the general greed. Then there is the grieving widow."

"Seriously?"

Solomon raised his eyebrows. "She is angry with him about something. I may be self-obsessed, but I got the impression she was trying to rile her husband by inviting me."

"By flirting with you," she corrected him.

Annoyingly, he felt heat rise into his face. He hoped she could not see it. "In a very sedate way, perhaps. But it would surely have the same effect."

"No, flirting is better, and she definitely was. Perhaps she had only just discovered Walter was unfaithful with her friend Alice Bolton."

"But was he?" Solomon asked.

Constance considered. "It always struck me that he was a little friendlier than he should be with Alice. They exchange a lot of looks and are quite often discovered in private conversation. But then, the Boltons and the Winsoms are old friends—the husbands are business partners."

"An affair could certainly be motive for Bolton or Alice or Deborah Winsom herself to kill him." If it were true and if they had been found out. Or if he had ended the affair. Solomon frowned. "Could things really be so fraught amongst the two couples? Don't they appear too…"

"Smug?" Constance suggested.

"I was going to say *contented*, but perhaps there are elements of smugness. If Alice and Deborah are rivals in love, I've seen no signs of hostility between them." In fact, he had seen them through her bedroom door, clinging together. "Have you?"

"Not really, but then, I never observed them before I came here, so I don't really know them or how they were before. The four of them must be very close. On the other hand, Bolton seems to me to be very much the junior partner, overshadowed by Winsom, at least in personality."

"And in business," said Solomon, recalling that brief flash of something very like malevolence he had imagined in Bolton's eyes as they rested on his old friend. "Perhaps Bolton had simply had enough of being second fiddle. I certainly caught an expression that was neither friendship nor admiration."

"Perhaps," Constance said, clearly unconvinced. "But would you kill a man simply for outshining you?"

"I wouldn't, no. But perhaps I should dig a little deeper. If Bolton is the brains behind their success and Winsom took all the credit—along, perhaps, with the bulk of the money and Bolton's wife…"

Constance nodded. "It would help to know such things. But Randolph is right about one point—the Boltons share a bed. There are no dressing rooms in the guest bedchambers. They would know, surely, if one of them got up, committed murder, and came back to bed?"

"Not necessarily. And even if they did, would they say? A married couple tends to rise or fall together. Even if they're unhappy, they would cover for each other."

Constance waved her hand dismissively. "Then to the devil with them. Who else might have done it?"

"Randolph. To get his hands on the money or on you."

"Would he, though? He's not yet twenty-one. Would he not have a trustee or someone acting for him? To say nothing of Bolton."

"Yes," Solomon allowed. "But he would certainly have more clout, more access to money, and he could probably get around everyone else but his father where you are concerned."

"I really don't think he is so desperate for me that he would murder his father! He just tried to blackmail me."

Solomon stopped suddenly. "If he planned the murder, perhaps you were only invited to supply his alibi."

Constance regarded him with dislike. "Now that really is insulting. Although it might well be true. If the knife were taken from the kitchen in advance, then the murder was surely planned. And we know Randolph was up and wandering at the time it happened."

"Had he ever come to your room before last night?"

"Mr. Grey," she drawled. "What a question to ask a lady." She sighed. "Which, of course, I am not. On the other hand, I've just told you I suspected he was my brother!"

"I didn't ask if you let him in," Solomon said mildly, "only if he knocked at your door."

"No, he treated me with a great deal of respect," she admitted. "It was a bit of a balancing act, if you want the truth, but I very much had the upper hand in our relationship."

She was used to manipulating men. For her own possibly ridiculous reasons, she had decided to come here and callously picked on young Randolph as her means. Solomon could almost see the situation in his mind's eye—Constance, all womanly temptation, twisting the boy around her little finger, while maintaining all the proprieties of a tolerant if indulgent sister, a respectable widow, a few years older and wiser than the infatuated young man.

He didn't like the images. The very idea was distasteful. But then, she had probably learned very early in life to be all things to all men. He didn't like that notion either. It involved too much pity as well as disdain. And God knew he had never been immune to her undeniable charms.

For an instant he remembered her beneath the hazily flaring torchlight in a foggy back alley, incongruously well dressed and the most beautiful creature he had ever seen. Unaware of him, she had been watching other people. She had not seen the man falling backward off the roof directly above her.

Instinct had propelled Solomon into her, pushing her to safety, holding her upright. No woman ever had felt so wonderful in his arms, even in that tiny moment that had nothing to do with lust. She had stared up at him, startled, confused, only just absorbing the knowledge of her narrow escape. And yet, just for a moment, she had seemed frightened. Not of death but of him.

Was it not that odd vulnerability as much as her beauty that ensured he remembered her? Whatever, the attraction was strong and unique. But he would never allow her the upper hand.

"Davidson," he said abruptly, dispelling her image from his mind. "Why is he here? Who invited him?"

"I don't know," she admitted. "He has done business with Winsom and Bolton, but I don't know what. He is very attentive to young Ellen."

Solomon kicked broodingly at a couple of dead sticks on the path. "What does a thirty-year-old, self-made man of the world see in a sheltered schoolgirl?"

"Money," Constance said cynically. "And it does no harm to his business to be the son-in-law of Walter Winsom."

"Did her parents approve of such a courtship?"

"I'm not sure they noticed," Constance replied. "Which was why she spoke to me."

He was turning back toward the house, but at that, he glanced at her. "What did you tell her?"

"To take her time, spread her wings, and keep her options open. And that she is a route to money and influence for unscrupulous men. I assure you I am quite the champion of moral rectitude and sensible advice."

All things to all people... And she imagined Ellen might be her little sister. "Does it give him a motive?" Solomon wondered. "Or her, come to that. Can you see her murdering her father?"

"Not without a much better reason than Ivor Davidson. Davidson wouldn't risk it either—except in a temper, perhaps."

"Like Randolph? *He* has a temper, has he not?"

"Yes," Constance allowed. Her voice was flat, deliberately unconcerned. Even she, mercenary and independent, had wished for a family, and not just for material gain. "I don't suppose the vicar has, though."

"Albright? Why not? Because he is a man of God?"

"Please," Constance said. "I cannot tell you the number of so-called godly men who pass through my establishment. I had to ban one of them for reasons that would make you blush. I would not tar Peter Albright with that particular brush, but he is an ambitious career churchman. I cannot think murder in his family would improve his chances of preferment."

She had a point. "And Miriam?" he asked, for the sake of completeness.

Again, she surprised him. "Miriam is an interesting character. Quiet, almost submissive, she is clearly proud of her husband and as obedient to him as she was to her parents. Yet she took charge last night, looked after her mother—as far as she could—and her siblings."

"Then she is stronger than she appears?" Solomon said with new interest.

"I think she must be. She does not love her husband."

He blinked. "Then her marriage was to please her parents? Does that not rather imply weakness, since she would not stand up to them?"

"I didn't say she did not want the marriage," Constance pointed out. "But it takes a certain kind of strength to submit to a man one does not love."

"I suppose you would know," he replied.

There was the smallest of pauses before she said, "Yes, it is something of a specialty in my profession."

He looked at her quickly. She appeared unconcerned, gazing straight ahead of her, and yet something in her had changed. Was she angry? Hurt? He could not tell.

She turned her head to meet his gaze. "Never imagine I am submissive, Mr. Grey. Our partnership would come to grief."

He widened his eyes in amusement. "Are you warning me off?"

"Oh, I don't think I have any need of that with you," she said affably. "I am just telling you in a general kind of way. Women, like men, are generally more than they seem. Are we any further forward in discovering our murderer?"

"No." It was an effort to adjust his mind away from her once more. "Though I thank you for clarifying a few matters for me. We need to ask some questions. And look again, perhaps, at the scene of the crime."

The shadow of a frown flickered across her brow, as though she were annoyed with herself for not thinking of it herself. He wondered what crimes she had been involved in before this, whether as victim or perpetrator.

She certainly walked back toward the garden at breakneck speed, and in very few minutes they stood by the swing, close to where they had found the body. Solomon had already been here this morning, before breakfast, but he hoped she would notice something he had missed. He kept his gaze on her face, not on the churned-up lawn.

She swallowed audibly. "Do you think he was running away when he was stabbed?"

"Impossible to tell. The grass is certainly depressed and churned up in places, but not enough, I would think, to show any kind of struggle."

To his surprise, she bent down and touched the patch of mud in front of her, then glanced back toward the house. "The quickest way back to the house is not by the paths but through that flowerbed." She rose unaided and walked over to it. The plants had been trampled, and the earth clearly walked on. "Too many feet to see any in particular."

"They brought the body back into the house this way. And I daresay the constables poked around here too. If the murderer left his footprint, it's well obliterated."

"Mr. Winsom's, too," she said, "though I can't imagine his barging through flowerbeds and trampling the plants. Was he sitting on the swing, and the murderer waited for him to move before he attacked?"

"Where would he hide? The moonlight was bright enough."

"Perhaps he didn't need to hide," Constance said slowly. "Perhaps Winsom was waiting for someone. He would not fear his own guests."

"True. We already know it was a planned crime, so the murderer is unlikely to have hidden here on the off chance of Winsom passing this way."

"He could have followed him from the house... Only, wouldn't Winsom have heard him? Turned to face him?"

"It must have been sudden," Solomon said. "I think he was with someone he trusted. Perhaps they were walking together, and the killer fell back just a little and attacked."

"There wasn't much blood," Constance said. "He died quickly. By luck or design, the knife must have gone straight though his heart. Then the killer bolted back to the house through this flowerbed?" She shivered and looked up at Grey, sudden anguish in her face. "Perhaps he even heard us coming. A minute or two earlier and we might have saved him."

CHAPTER FIVE

I VOR DAVIDSON WAS shaken. Probably for the first time in his life, he found it difficult to think straight, to concentrate.

He had never expected the London police to be involved, and he had heard enough rumors of their privacy invasions to realize that he would soon be cast in a very poor light, if not clapped up and hanged. There was more involved here than just convincing a gentleman magistrate that he was a fellow gentleman and watching him deliver some poor ne'er-do-well to the Assizes for trial and hanging.

Everyone's life would be turned inside out, and the state of Davidson's once-promising business revealed. He could not bear the sight of Ellen's tragic face—which perhaps was fortunate, since she seemed to avoiding his.

On the other hand, she must be an heiress, bound to inherit a good part of Winsom's hoard...

But there was a time and place for everything, and this was not it.

Escaping the unbearable atmosphere of the house, Ivor let himself out of the garden room door with a sense of relief and was quickly buoyed up further by the sight of the delectable Constance Goldrich gliding toward him.

She had clearly been in the company of Solomon Grey, who walked on toward the stables with his loose, confident stride. Now there was a man Ivor should most definitely cultivate, only at the moment he did not feel remotely clear enough in his head.

To lose himself in a little light flirtation—or even blind lust—seemed a much better short-term plan. And widows missed the physical comfort of their husbands…

"Mrs. Goldrich." He bowed. "Have I timed my walk badly? You look as if you are returning from your own exercise."

"Yes, but I am happy to keep you company," she said with unexpected friendliness.

So he had hope. "I must apologize for my words last night," he said as she turned and they set off together along the garden path. "I did not really mean to disparage Randolph to you. I was merely trying to make you a compliment, and it came out a little wrong." He smiled winningly. "That is, very wrong."

"Well, it's not a technique I would advise in courting Ellen," Mrs. Goldrich said wryly. "She seems rather fond of her brother."

"When they aren't teasing the life out of each other. Then you forgive me?"

"There is nothing to forgive on my part, Mr. Davidson. I am, after all, guilty of wondering much the same thing about you."

"About me?" He didn't know whether to be flattered she thought of him, or worried.

"Ellen is sixteen years old, a mere schoolgirl, however lively and pretty. You are a mature and successful man of the world. I cannot imagine you lack female admiration."

"She is bored. Practicing flirtation in a safe environment."

"I imagine you are very happy to help. After all, none of your other flirts have the felicity of being Walter Winsom's daughter."

He raised his eyebrows. "My, but you are sharp, Mrs. Goldrich. But then, I suppose none of the other gentlemen at your feet are Winsom's son and heir."

"Touché, Mr. Davidson. Touché. But are you not already in business with Winsom and Bolton?"

"They lent me money for a successful venture last year. Successful for them, too, I might add. I am offering them partnership in a new project… Or I was. I was very glad to be invited this week to discuss the matter."

"I see. I suppose that must all be up in the air now, with this tragedy."

"Yes. It is."

She was watching his face with sudden intensity. He liked that. There was something exciting about her, something that went way beyond mere physical beauty. When she smiled...

"You do not seem cast down," she observed.

He shrugged. "About business, why should I be? Thomas Bolton will be amenable, too."

"And Ellen?"

He did not want to think about Ellen. "She is a child, as you say. Frankly, so is Randolph. I would rather talk to you, look at you. What do you say, ma'am? Should we not look for a little delight in each other?"

To his pleasure, she was neither outraged nor dismissive. Instead, she appeared to consider.

"We *could* look," she allowed. "But would we find it? Considering the circumstances."

"We could try."

"I never *try* in such matters, Mr. Davidson. It takes all the fun out of them. Will you be able to tell the policemen where you were around midnight last night?"

"I shall have no problem telling them. They may have a problem believing, though frankly, where else would they expect me to be but alone in bed? Like you, I imagine."

"You have no valet to vouch for you?"

"I don't keep a valet, and if I did, there is little room for guests' servants at Greenforth." He smiled down at her. "I might wish I had stayed up late playing billiards with Randolph, or even enticed that pretty maid to my room, but sadly, I did not, since I can only think of you."

"You are a poor liar. The police are not idiots, you know."

He regarded her with open amusement. "What do you know of the police, Mrs. Goldrich? Don't decent people avoid them like the plague?"

"Most, perhaps," said the surprising widow. "I happened to be present one evening—along with several other, er...decent people—when the police captured a thief and a murderer. Unlike many, I believe London is safer for their presence."

"Then you will be able to prove where you were around midnight last night?"

"I will," she said tranquilly.

IT WAS ONLY after they had agreed that she should be the one to talk to Davidson that Solomon realized he too was using her charms to entrap a man. No wonder there had been a gleam of wry laughter in her eyes as she inclined her head.

"By the same token, you will appeal more than I to the ladies. See who you can seduce into telling the truth."

He didn't know whether to be amused or ashamed, so elected for neither, merely tracked Miriam Albright to the stables. When he glanced back, Constance was strolling in the sunshine beside Ivor Davidson.

Was he putting her in danger asking for her help? If Davidson had murdered Winsom...

Equally, Constance could have murdered him. She was strong enough and brave enough. He reserved judgment on whether or not she was wicked enough. The trouble was, she did not seem wicked in the slightest, which was a dangerous conclusion to reach about someone in her profession.

No, he was far from immune. But even allowing for that, her distress seemed touchingly genuine when she considered how the murder had been committed, and how close they might have come to saving him. She *felt* the tragedy.

At the stables, he waved the grooms away, assuring them he was only visiting his own horses. Inside the stable, he found Miriam Albright, her arms around the neck of a plump chestnut mare, her face buried in its neck as it nuzzled her like a foal.

It was an oddly touching moment, and for an instant he contemplated creeping back out again and coming in more noisily. Before he could, however, Miriam jerked around and saw him. The mare lifted her head and huffed.

"Your favorite horse?" Solomon asked lightly.

"Yes. She was my first adult riding horse, and now she is my sister's."

"She still loves you too."

"They do love, you know. Papa used to laugh at me for believing so."

"I expect he was teasing," Solomon said diplomatically. He approached the mare and idly stroked her nose. "I'm sorry you have all this mess to put up with. It is bad enough mourning a parent without having police prying into everything."

"Do you think they will?" she asked naïvely. "My father was not nobody, you know."

"I do know. So do the police, which is precisely why they are bound to fully investigate what happened and why."

Miriam shook her head, closing her eyes as if that could prevent her from seeing the inevitable images scored across her mind. "Who would do such a thing? I cannot believe anyone in this house is responsible. It *must* be an intruder."

"Perhaps the police will find it is so," Solomon said. He didn't believe it, but it seemed kinder, and the girl looked so lost, her safe world turned upside down. She could only have been nineteen years old. "Did your father have enemies beyond these walls?"

"Enemies?" she said, startled. "I was thinking more of a disturbed burglar, a madman…"

Since Winsom had been stabbed in the back, he had clearly not disturbed whoever killed him. Unless he was running for help…? No, that made no more sense than the madman theory.

"We must help the police consider all possibilities," Solomon murmured. "Your father was a successful man. It is difficult to achieve what he did without making some enemies—however inadvertent. I speak from experience here."

She regarded him, frowning, her eyes unexpectedly direct. Slowly, she nodded. "Then I must take your word for it. I do remember a man swore at him in the street once—it must have been a year or so ago—because Papa had dismissed him from the bank. But to commit murder…"

"It would need to be a powerful grudge," Solomon agreed. "That is why I ask about known enemies."

"Mr. Bolton would know more about such things. He would not discuss them with us."

"Mr. and Mrs. Bolton must be a great comfort to your family," Solomon said. "You will have known them a long time."

"All my life. Or, at least, all I can remember of it. They are family friends as well as Mr. Bolton being Papa's partner in the bank."

"I wonder which came first?" Solomon said. "Were they friends before they formed the bank?"

"Yes, since they were at school. Papa made a sizeable sum on imports and on the stock exchange. Mr. Bolton is a genius with figures and accounting. According to Papa, he had the money and the imagination, Mr. Bolton the necessary financial skill, which was how they came to found the bank."

"It has an excellent reputation. I'm sure your brother will continue the fine tradition."

For an instant, Miriam looked doubtful, then she smiled. "He will."

"I don't suppose," Solomon said apologetically, "that there were any quarrels with neighbors? Tenants? Anything like that?"

She shook her head immediately. "Not while I lived here, and I never heard of anything after I married. I'm sure Mama would have told me."

Solomon nodded. He had thought she would say that, though he would still ask around. "I am only a new friend," he said, "but if I can help in any way, know that I will."

"Thank you," she said huskily.

Solomon inclined his head, beginning to move on toward his horses, who, hearing his voice, were whinnying at the far end of the stable. By way of a parting shot, he said, "Your father must have been very proud to see you settled so happily with such a fine man as Mr. Albright."

It took her by surprise. She blinked several times. "Yes. It was what he wanted for me." She tried to smile, a trembling effort that steadied under his gaze.

He merely smiled back and moved on, but he had already seen more than she had intended, more than he had.

Constance was right. Miriam did not love her husband, but she was strong enough to live with the choice. Just for a moment, her determination had wobbled, as if she were acknowledging that her father had only had a year to enjoy her appropriate marriage. Miriam had a lifetime. And if she had waited a year, she probably would not have married him at all.

How angry did that make her under the surface of her gentle demeanor?

JUST BEFORE LUNCHEON, Constance found the Reverend Peter Albright in the library. She had cause to dislike clergyman as a species, so she had to remind herself that her experience was not everyone's. On top of which, when she had first come across Walter Winsom's name in connection with her mother's, she had set about discovering all she could about his family. No one had a bad word to say about Miriam Winsom's husband.

The scion of an old, landowning family, he was well educated and ambitious. If a few people found him "holier than thou," and a one-time fellow student described him as "a dull stick," he was generally regarded as a good man who practiced what he preached. His parishioners liked him, praised his charitable efforts and his way with a sermon. An amiable if slightly debauched bishop of Constance's acquaintance told her Albright was earmarked to replace him in the diocese in a few years. Albright had certainly never frequented Constance's establishment, although she knew he visited the capital frequently, and no other madams or girls she had spoken to knew anything about him.

It was all in his favor. She might even have liked him had he not regarded her with quite so much suspicion in his eyes. And even that she could forgive, in theory, since he was, presumably, only looking out for his young brother-in-law.

He sat now at one of the smaller desks in the library, busily writing. A Bible was open beside him, and another book shoved to the edge of the table. He glanced up at her entrance, and his brow twitched before he set the pen in its stand and rose politely to his feet.

"Mr. Albright," she greeted him with feigned relief. He was a man who appreciated modesty in women, so she made no effort to gain his admiration. It was probably a lost cause in any case. "You must be in a great deal of demand in such terrible circumstances. I hope you don't mind my interrupting you?"

"Not in the least," he said. "Is there some way I might assist you?"

"To be honest, I was hoping there was some way I might be of assistance to the bereaved family. I thought you would know best what needed to be done, any small service that a stranger might perform? Would any of the family be comforted by company, or should anyone be left in peace for now?"

"That is very thoughtful of you, Mrs. Goldrich." He could not quite hide his surprise. "Everyone is still somewhat numb from the shock, but I shall pass your kind offer on to my wife and my mother-in-law. As for company... Only my mother-in-law seeks the privacy of her own rooms at the moment."

Constance allowed her nose to wrinkle with distaste. "It will be so difficult once the police arrive from London with all their intrusive questions. I was thinking—particularly of Mrs. Winsom and her daughters—if we could present the police with the clear facts, there would be fewer questions for them to disturb the family with." She felt like crossing her fingers as she said this, for she had no idea if it was true and rather suspected not. "I would be happy to collate what information we have?"

Albright blinked, wary but open to suggestion. She suspected this was how he conducted most of his life. "Such as?" he asked at last.

Constance sat on the chair by the next desk to his, and he sank back on to his own.

"Such as," she said delicately, "who can be confirmed as in bed around the time the murder occurred, and if anyone saw or heard anyone else still up and about. For example, I imagine you and your wife would be able to confirm each other's whereabouts very easily."

"Of course," he said stiffly. "We were in bed, as, I imagine, was everyone else."

"Not everyone else," she pointed out. "Not Mr. Winsom, for one. Was it his habit to take a walk so late?"

"Not to my knowledge, but I have known him to walk after dinner."

"Did you hear him go out?" she asked. Seeing Albright's nostrils flare, she added quickly, "If we knew when he went out, it might help keep the innocent out of the investigation."

He mulled that one over. "Perhaps," he said at last. "But no, I did not hear him go out. Nor anyone else."

She assumed a puzzled, helpless expression. "What time did you retire, sir? I believe we all left the drawing room and went upstairs around eleven of the clock?"

"I believe we did."

"Did you go straight to bed, or were you in a position to see anyone else moving elsewhere? The servants to lock doors or clear up downstairs? Someone looking for a book or a game of billiards, or a drink, perhaps?"

"I did not notice," he said after a few moments. "But I can see those are sensible questions we can easily answer among ourselves." He rose suddenly. "Shall we join the others for luncheon?"

CHAPTER SIX

A GAIN, EVERYONE WAS present except Mrs. Winsom.
As Constance sat down, Albright said, "We have been talking, and it would make a great deal of sense if we could present these London policemen with the basic facts that will prevent them prying too disturbingly. I have asked Mrs. Goldrich to collate this information."

Constance, discovering Solomon Grey seated next to her, met his hooded but admiring gaze with limpid good nature.

"Clever," he breathed.

"I thought so." She looked apologetically around the table. "Of course, I shall write it all down, so that we may all see it,"

"With what purpose?" Miriam asked.

"That of saving your family as much discomfort as possible. I cannot imagine you want the police hanging around you any longer than they need to. You all have enough to bear."

"Why don't you begin, Mrs. Goldrich?" Grey said, with a glint of amusement in his eyes.

"Very well. I went upstairs when we all did, just before eleven o'clock, and went to my room. Once there, my mind would not settle to sleep, so I went in search of a book."

"What time was this, Mrs. Goldrich?" Grey asked with apparent interest.

"Not long after midnight. I definitely heard the clock in the drawing room chime the hour before I left my room. I went straight to the library—where I saw Mr. Grey."

"I can confirm that," he said solemnly to the company. "She left again when she saw me there. Did you see anyone else moving about the house, Mrs. Goldrich?"

"No, I did not."

"And how long were you in the library?" Randolph asked. There was a certain sulkiness in his face because she had accounted for not being in her room. But he would hardly want to say in front of his sisters that he had been there.

"Just a few minutes. The curtains were not drawn, and Mr. Grey thought he saw movement outside. He went off to investigate."

"And why were you in the library, Mr. Grey?" Mrs. Bolton asked.

"For the same purpose as Mrs. Goldrich. I must have been there for about five minutes before she came in. She did not linger. I decided to investigate what I had seen from the window and left the house via the French window in the drawing room."

It was Constance's turn for an admiring glance. He had preserved them both without telling any direct lies.

And yet he could still have committed the crime before she entered the library. She could be complicit by her silence as to what he had been doing there. She acknowledged it again. There was a hardness about him. She did not put killing past him, but killing in such a way? A knife in the back? And why on earth would he do such a thing? He wanted information from Winsom about his missing brother—which was a whole different mystery. Could Winsom have told him something that had inspired ungovernable fury?

Going to the kitchen for a weapon first?

Hardly a moment of rage, and she doubted he was subject to those anyway. He was far too self-controlled. And in any case, the knife had vanished before Grey got here. That surely proved his innocence.

She thought.

"And you, Mr. Grey?" she asked. "Did you see anyone else

apart from me in the house or garden, between the time you left your bedchamber and when you roused the household after discovering Mr. Winsom?"

"No, I did not. Only the shadowy figure outside, whom I could not identify."

"And which may not even have been real," Ivor Davidson drawled. "Tree branches move. Cats, foxes, swooping owls—all cast shadows that can fool us."

"You are right, of course," Grey said, inclining his head. "And yourself, Mr. Davidson? Did you go straight to sleep?"

"I did not. I wrote some letters first. It must have been just before midnight that I prepared for bed, for I had just closed my eyes when, like Mrs. Goldrich, I heard the clock chime downstairs."

"Did you hear or see anyone else in that time?" Grey asked.

"I heard quiet footsteps in the passage," Davidson said, a hint of malicious amusement in his eyes as they found Randolph, who blushed furiously. Davidson knew exactly whose footsteps he had heard and where they had gone. "They retreated again almost at once. That was all I heard before the household was aroused."

Constance inclined her head and turned to Alice Bolton next to him.

"Mrs. Goldrich," Thomas Bolton said suddenly, "how do you propose to remember all of this in detail?"

"Oh, I remember everything, sir," Constance said amiably. "Whether written or spoken. I find it both a gift and a curse."

"I find the whole thing an impertinence," Mrs. Bolton snapped.

"It is," Constance agreed at once. "But I think we will all find it less impertinent than answering the police."

"Disingenuous," Grey said to her later. "The police will ask exactly the same questions, whatever detailed notes you give them. Unless they are entirely incompetent or far too easily intimidated."

"I'm sure you are right," Constance admitted.

They sat alone in the morning room, where they had agreed to meet to compare notes. Grey lounged on the window seat, his long legs stretched out in front of him, crossed at the ankles. Constance sat at the little bureau, drawing up a table on a sheet of paper. She had the names of everyone in the household written down the left-hand side and was recording their answers under various columns.

"However," she added, setting her pen in its stand, "it gives us a head start, and still might prove useful if someone gives the police different answers to the ones they have given us."

"There could be any number of reasons for that."

"There could. But we can still learn from them. What do you make of our suspects so far?"

"No real surprises," Grey said. "The Boltons and the Albrights both claimed to have been in bed with their spouses all night until the household was roused. No one heard anything except Randolph's footsteps to your room, and I don't even know if that was true or if Davidson said it just to annoy Randolph. Or you."

"No one heard *our* footsteps," Constance observed.

"You walk very quietly for a woman."

She glanced up at him in surprise that he had noticed. Was that a hint of darkness creeping along the fine blade of his cheekbone?

"Most woman rustle," he said, a little too quickly. "Particularly in such ridiculously wide skirts."

"*Fashionable* is the word you are looking for. Not ridiculous. And in my profession, as you may know, a woman learns to move quietly."

She said it to annoy him, just to see the effect, now that she suspected he observed her more than he appeared to. It worked, too, though not in any way she had expected.

A frown tugged down his brow. "Why do you do that?" he demanded.

"Do what?" she asked, genuinely bewildered. Idly, as though she had no interest in his words, she picked up the rather ugly statuette on the table beside her.

"Remind me constantly of your profession."

"Hardly *remind*," she said, turning the figurine in her hands. It felt too smooth and cold. "I'm sure you never forget it."

His gaze held hers, unreadable but curiously...turbulent. "Why do you still continue with it? You must be wealthy enough to retire or invest in some legitimate trade."

"Why should I?" She kept her voice carefully amused, though her fingers tightened on the ornament. "In order to be invited to respectable houses such as this under my own name? If you believe that would *ever* happen, Mr. Grey, you are considerably more naïve than you look."

"You could travel, live anywhere, do whatever you want."

"I *am* doing what I want," she said. How could such meltingly dark eyes pierce so sharply it was an effort to meet them? "I happen to enjoy my work."

Mockery was her best weapon, but he didn't rise to it. Neither embarrassed nor angry now, he simply held her gaze until it became damnably difficult to withstand.

"Do you?" he asked deliberately, just as if he had seen or guessed the truth.

"Of course," she said, smiling. "I am good at it. You are welcome in my establishment any time you choose."

Surprising her again, he quirked his lips into a half-smile, but at least he released her eyes. "I do not care to pay for such favors."

"And yet you do. One way or another. One always does."

"Who has hurt you, Constance Silver?" he asked softly.

The figurine fell into her lap, and his eyes followed it before lifting slowly to hers once more.

She laughed. "Oh, no one hurts *me*, Mr. Grey. One needs a

heart to be hurt. Contrary to popular belief, it is my mind that is my strength. Women do think, you know. Many of us are good at it."

"I know."

She replaced the ornament on the table, appalled by the slight tremor of her fingers. Picking her pen back up, she returned to her notes.

"Ellen," she said, determinedly writing the girl's name. "She claimed to be asleep and to have seen and heard nothing."

"You don't believe her," Grey observed after only a very short pause.

"Do you?"

"I think she's much too curious by nature to go tamely to sleep when other people are still wandering about the house and grounds. People such as you and I, Randolph, Winsom…"

"And whoever killed him." Constance, tranquil once more, replaced her pen in the stand.

"And whoever isn't telling us the truth," Grey added. "Which is probably all of them."

"And we still need to talk to Mrs. Winsom. And the servants."

"The servants won't talk to strangers like us—not about the family, at any rate. They'll have seen nothing, heard nothing, and know nothing. We might be better leaving them to the police."

"Perhaps," Constance said noncommittally.

IT WAS DIFFICULT, Solomon thought with rueful amusement, to win any encounter with Constance Silver. Just when he thought he had found a chink in her armor, she saw through his own. His other suspicion, that she had been hurt, should not have surprised him. Many women lived with abuse, and prostitutes were in more danger of it than most. Constance had taught herself ladylike refinement, but she had dragged herself out of the stews—she would not otherwise have admitted to having been born there, the illegitimate child, presumably, of another prostitute and, possibly Thomas Winsom. Or someone considerably less savory.

He did not want to think of what had happened to her, then or now. It angered him, hurt him, even. Worse, somehow, was the idea that she could be hurt in less physical ways. *Hard as nails...* He doubted his previous assumption now.

The woman who had sat so silently beside him in the Tizsa house had not been hard but overwhelmed. The woman searching naïvely for her father was not hard either, whether or not she had been looking for financial gain from the fact.

But she was damnably perceptive, and he must never forget that she could read him like a book. Or at least like any other man.

"Mr. Grey, sir." He turned to face a red-eyed maid in a plain dress without an apron.

"Yes?"

"Mrs. Winsom is asking for you. If you could spare the time."

From second nature, he hid his excitement. "Of course."

"Please follow me, sir."

She led him upstairs to the large bedroom he had glimpsed last night through the open door. Although it was dominated by the large, velvet-curtained bed, Mrs. Winsom was not reclining there. This afternoon, she sat in an armchair beside the fire, which made the room uncomfortably warm, a shawl about her shoulders as though her very bones were chilled. She looked ten years older than yesterday, and indescribably frail.

"Mr. Grey!" Her face lit at the sight of him as he followed the maid inside, and then immediately, tears started in her eyes. "Oh, Mr. Grey, forgive me."

"Forgive you?" he repeated, startled. He moved toward her, and the maid closed the door softly. "For what, dear lady?" He took her outstretched hand.

"I have brought this suspicion upon you," she said brokenly.

He kept the same gentle expression on his face. At least, he hoped he did. "How did you do such a thing, ma'am?"

"By bringing you here! And now Wilson—my maid—has heard gossip among the servants that my other guests are blaming you for Walter's death. I would not have had this happen for the world."

"They are merely shocked, ma'am, and latching on to the next best thing to a stranger."

She looked unconvinced, so he smiled, releasing her hand, and sat in the chair close to hers.

"What possible reason," he asked lightly, "could I have for so attacking a man I had known only a few hours?"

"Me," she said tragically. "To be rid of my husband and marry me yourself."

It certainly took his breath away. "No one could truly think such a thing," he said, and then, seeing the added hurt in her eyes, he added hastily, "The world knows you as a virtuous lady and a loyal wife. How could anyone mistake your kindness to a stranger for that kind of encouragement? Besides, a man with such designs upon you would hardly accept an invitation to meet your husband, especially not one issued in public at a hospital board meeting. Seriously, you have enough to distress you without imagining you owe me any apologies."

"And so I told her, sir," the maid said roundly from her place by the door.

Mrs. Winsom scowled at her. "Go and find something to do in the dressing room, Wilson."

Obediently, the woman opened the door on her right and went into the room beyond. Solomon glimpsed a fully made-up bed with an opulent, masculine dressing gown laid across it, and a mirrored dressing table with a man's hairbrushes and other accoutrements laid out. A quick glance about the much more feminine outer room showed him only feminine accoutrements. Mr. and Mrs. Winsom had slept apart.

He wondered how recent that was. Only since she had

learned about his affair with her friend Alice Bolton? Or had she? Did it even exist in more than Constance's imagination?

He refocused his eyes on the widow. She looked terrible, her skin somehow shrunken and pale, her eyes red with weeping.

"How are you?" he asked gently.

"I don't know." She tried to smile. "I don't know what to do."

"Remember all the good things about him and your time together."

"Yes," she said eagerly. "He was a good man, generous and kind. And such fun. Everyone liked him, you know! Didn't you?"

"Indeed I did," Solomon said honestly. How could he question this fragile creature about her husband's murder? About where she was, and who had hated him?

"And yet someone killed him," she whispered, gripping her chair arm so fiercely that her knuckles were white. "Do you think the police will find the terrible person who did this?"

"I sincerely hope so." He leaned forward. "You know they will ask you questions that seem both intrusive and impertinent?"

Her eyes widened. "Me? Questions such as what?"

"Such as the state of your marriage, who were your husband's friends and enemies, why he would be walking in the garden so late, what time he left you—that kind of thing."

Her mouth opened and closed in silence. She dropped her hands into her lap, gripping her fingers together, and gazed at them. "And must I answer?"

"I think so. It is their duty to find out everything they need to in order to discover the culprit. We have all been cooperating downstairs in order to tell the police where we were at the crucial time."

A surprisingly cynical smile flashed across her face and vanished. "Have you?"

"Sort of. Mrs. Goldrich has written it all down."

"Mrs. Goldrich," she repeated. She lifted her eyes suddenly to his face. "Does she want to marry my son?"

"I don't believe so. Her feelings seem to me more...sisterly.

Do you not approve of her?"

"She is a widow, several years his senior, and he is too young to be married."

"I don't believe you need to fear it. Nor has she any need to marry anyone for money."

"Perhaps she is lonely, being a widow." She closed her eyes. "Like me."

"It might help to talk to her," Solomon said, not entirely to pave Constance's way to a more intimate conversation. When she chose, Constance could exude an unjudging understanding that was both soothing and beguiling. And probably a professional skill. Knowing that, he had still told her about David's disappearance. Sort of. He had never told anyone that. His many exhaustive, fruitless inquiries had always been impersonal.

"I shall think about it," Mrs. Winsom said. "I have been thinking about so many things… It must be terrible for everyone to be trapped here with this awfulness."

"Everyone is concerned for you and would help if they could. Mrs. Winsom, did your husband discuss his business ventures with you?"

"Not really. Ladies do not have a head for business, you know. Why?" Her expression changed. "You think someone was in such a dispute with Walter that they—"

"I don't know," he said quickly when she struggled for breath. "I'm sure the police will look into it. I can't imagine anyone here had such a dispute."

"No," she said a little doubtfully, but did not elaborate.

"Were your husband and Mr. Bolton in broad agreement about the running of the bank?" he asked.

"Oh yes," she said, without any real thought. "Thomas always so admired Walter…and Walter was quite in awe of Thomas's head for figures, his knowledge of the markets…whatever they are. It was a perfect partnership. Thomas will be lost without him."

"He will have your son as his partner now."

"I suppose so. Though I am not sure banking is quite Randolph's forte…"

Solomon rose to his feet. "I should leave you to rest… Just before I go—for Mrs. Goldrich's records, did you happen to see or hear anyone after we all retired? You followed the rest of us upstairs, did you not?"

"I did. Wilson looked after me. Walter came up, but only for a little before he went out again."

"Was he going to meet someone else?"

"He didn't say." Her voice was very small. Because she suspected her husband of going to meet Alice Bolton? Or was she covering for someone? Her son? One of her daughters?

Either way, Solomon could not ask more just now without losing her good will. He smiled, bowed, and left her.

CHAPTER SEVEN

I N THE LIBRARY with Randolph, going through Winsom's
business papers, Thomas Bolton missed his partner. Which
was odd, because he had resented Walter for much of his life,
even while he admired him. But at least Walter would concentrate on the matter in hand. Randolph showed little interest and
less understanding.

"Do you actually *want* the burden of the bank, Randolph?"
Bolton asked, abandoning the pile of papers in front of him.

Randolph refocused on his face. "Of course I do. It's mine."
He rubbed at his forehead with one hand. "I'm sorry. I find it
difficult to concentrate. I keep thinking of my father."

"So do I," Bolton said, more gently. "Perhaps we should have
given ourselves more time before we begin on this. It is just that I
want everything to be in order so that there is no interruption to
what you and your mother receive. And to be honest, I thought it
would help to be busy. For both of us."

"I railed against the bank a bit," Randolph confessed. "I
thought it dull and was desperate to pursue my own path." He
grimaced. "But of course I never found one."

"You are young," Bolton replied.

Randolph gave a slightly crooked smile, so reminiscent of his
father that it caught at Bolton's breath. "But no longer privileged
enough to despise the business that feeds me, my mother, and my
sister. I am the head of the family now."

"And of the bank," Bolton said lightly. "But to be honest,

your father never got to grips with the day-to-day running of it. He trusted me to see to that while he concentrated on our most important clients and investors. That was his forte, and it could well be yours."

Randolph had the sense to look doubtful. "I hardly have my father's gravitas! Or his knowledge, let alone yours. How on earth would such wealthy men trust *me*, let alone rely on me?"

"They wouldn't, of course, not quite yet. They must grow used to you. It will be hard work to reach the position your father occupied. You have to be sure it is what you want."

"I want to do the right thing," Randolph said determinedly. He gave a quick smile. "I just hadn't envisaged doing it just yet. But needs must."

"Don't feel overwhelmed," Bolton said kindly. "I will help you. Everyone at the bank will." It was not the time to add that Randolph could simply step aside to pursue his own interests, leaving Bolton to guide the bank in the direction it needed to go. Walter had been far too high-handed, taking them down much-too-risky paths, and Bolton didn't miss that side of his partner at all.

Randolph regarded the piles of papers and ledgers spread out on the desk and looked overwhelmed.

"Perhaps a glass of brandy would help," Bolton said. "Your father found it aided his concentration from time to time!"

That wasn't quite true, but the poor boy had lost his father, and in such a way.

As he poured, Bolton felt excitement surge within him. Being in sole charge of the bank was exhilarating, releasing a thousand new and wonderful opportunities. And yet the grief took him by surprise by rising just as fast. He would have no one to share his successes with. No one who understood. Only those who saw the results in terms of new gowns and servants and houses—like Alice, whom he could not afford to think about right now. Or Walter's son, who gazed at him in such bewilderment, who really wanted money and position without working for it.

Bolton handed one glass to Randolph and raised his own. Tears prickled. "To your father," he said huskily.

"HOW DID SHE know?" Constance asked, when Grey had told her about his somewhat surprising encounter with Deborah Winsom, including the interesting fact that Walter had been banished from the marital bed to the dressing room.

They were once more alone in the morning room, both dressed for dinner. Constance wore burgundy silk, since it was the darkest evening gown she had brought with her. While she paced back and forth across the floor, Grey sat in the window seat, apparently fascinated by the rain on the glass. He could not have seen much through it.

It struck Constance that he was avoiding looking at her because he could not bear to be in alliance with such a distasteful person. That would have hurt, if she had let it. Instead, she concentrated on admiring his lean, handsome profile whenever it was within her line of vision. She enjoyed his stillness, even if she wondered intensely what went on behind that closed, private face of his.

But at her last question, a puzzled frown tugged at his brow. He even glanced away from the window. "How did she know what?"

She halted and turned fully to face him, letting her skirts settle with the distinctive, delicious rustle of silk. "That you didn't kill her husband. From what you say, she was concerned the others were accusing you, not that you might have done it."

"I don't think she believes anyone she knows could have done it."

"She doesn't know you," Constance pointed out. "She has met you twice."

Solomon opened his mouth as though to make some derisive

reply before he acknowledged the truth with a slight inclination of the head. "You think she did it herself? Is she that good an actress?"

"Perhaps," Constance said. "Like most of us, she is used to playing a role in public. And her state of upset *could* be due to guilt as much as grief. Or perhaps she knows who did do it and is protecting them for some reason. In which case, we should probably watch over her quite carefully. Or…" She eyed him speculatively.

He sighed. "Or what?"

"Or she fancies you and now feels guilty about it because her husband is dead."

Of course, he regarded her with disapproval. "Do you read a lot of novels?"

"In between the pamphlets that the reforming ladies leave on our doorstep. Trust me, those things give my girls more nightmares than the most lurid novel you can imagine."

"I am sure you are made of much stronger stuff."

"I am. It's the laughing that keeps me awake. Don't you want to know what I learned this afternoon?"

"Yes."

"Absolutely nothing," she said, scowling with discontent. "Alice Bolton looks down her pointed nose at me, as if I dropped off the sole of her dirty boot. Her husband was far too busy in the library with Randolph all afternoon, and Ellen is avoiding me. Which is interesting, I suppose, but hardly helpful."

Grey at last left off gazing at the rain trickling down the glass and rose from the window seat. "Then let us join the others before dinner and see what else we can learn."

They entered the drawing room together. Unsurprisingly, all conversation halted as everyone looked toward them.

"Mrs. Goldrich," Ivor Davidson greeted her, his eyes both challenging and mocking. "Do you have all our movements recorded?"

"I wrote down what you all told me," Constance said, as

though she didn't notice his hostility, "and left the results on a table in the library for you to see. If I have made mistakes—or you have—please tell me."

There was no time for more, for Mrs. Winsom tottered in on Miriam's arm.

"Mama!" Randolph went to her at once, which made Constance feel slightly better about him.

"How brave of you to come down, Deborah," Alice Bolton said warmly. "We are all cheered by your presence."

Constance rather doubted that. The most severely bereaved tended to be an embarrassment and were hardly the life and soul of any party. But perhaps Mrs. Winsom's appearance was a welcome sign that she had not disintegrated altogether. Constance thought it probably helped the widow more to be among her family and friends, although surely she must be aware that one of them had murdered her husband.

Unless Deborah had done it herself.

Watching her with fresh eyes as she clung to Randolph and then to Thomas Bolton, Constance could still not quite believe in her guilt. Like everyone else, she had a motive, and, once her maid had left her, she had the best opportunity of whisking about the house and grounds unseen.

But would she even know where her cook kept the knives?

Perhaps she had seized it in passing one day, while consulting about menus...if such business was conducted in the kitchen rather than in Mrs. Winsom's territory.

The company was even more subdued than at luncheon. No one wished to say anything to upset the widow further, which made for long silences and brief, awkward conversations.

Until Deborah herself said suddenly, "When should we expect the policemen from Scotland Yard?"

Strict table manners had fallen by the wayside as though the burden of one single, general discussion was easiest. Even so, there was a short silence following this question, some of it dismayed, or simply blank.

"Tomorrow sometime, I imagine," Thomas Bolton said reluctantly. "The inquest will be held then, too."

His wife added, "Mrs. Goldrich has taken it upon herself to write down where everyone was and who can vouch for whom. Apparently, the police might be interested in such matters."

"I imagine they will be," Mrs. Winsom said unexpectedly, looking straight at Constance. "Thank you, Mrs. Goldrich. You will wish to add me to your list, though I retired immediately and saw or heard no one after Wilson, my maid, left me at half past eleven." She frowned. "I suppose you have included the servants in your list?"

She seemed quite unaware of the footmen currently standing on either side of the dining room door.

"I thought it might have been presumptuous," said Constance, who had actually thought it would be useless. "But I did ask Richards and Mrs. Farrow to write down what they could."

Mrs. Winsom nodded. "Very sensible. Most of the servants are together, after all. The maids share a room in the basement, where Mrs. Farrow has her own room, and the menservants are in the attic under Richards's watchful eye…"

"Apart from the grooms and the coachman, who sleep above the stables and the carriage house," Randolph pointed out.

"And the gardener has his own cottage," Ellen added. "Of course, he has a wife to vouch for him. So does John Coachman, and the grooms may vouch for each other too."

"So we can account for all of them," Miriam said. She didn't sound happy about it, probably because it cast the likely guilt back to the family and guests in the main house.

"Apart from the boot boy," Mrs. Winsom said vaguely.

"What?" Randolph frowned at her.

"Owen the boot boy," his mother said patiently. "He sleeps in the kitchen because he is up so early collecting shoes to polish and building up the kitchen fire for morning tea and breakfast."

"He was certainly very fast asleep when I woke him at half past midnight," Grey said.

Davidson laid down his spoon. "Then he would have plenty of time to steal the knife while was alone!"

"What, a child of ten who is up at four polishing your boots before he wakes the maids?" Ellen scoffed. "Where do you imagine he finds the time, let alone the energy, to steal knives and murder his master? For what conceivable reason?"

Davidson blinked at this attack. A hint of color stained his cheeks. "I'm not accusing the boy, merely stating a fact. I'm sure Mrs. Goldrich will pass it along to the police along with everything else."

"Mrs. Goldrich is not a police spy in this house, Mr. Davidson," Mrs. Winsom said with mild disapproval. "She is a guest like you, and trying to be helpful." She smiled faintly. "Like you."

Constance regarded her with surprised respect. So the widow had claws after all. An interesting time to use them when she was so clearly bowed down by grief. Even more surprising, she had been defending Constance. What on earth had Grey said to her this afternoon?

Without the presence of Mrs. Winsom, the company might well have scattered after dinner. But the widow gamely led the ladies out of the dining room to the drawing room. Constance found it hard to believe that it was only twenty-four hours since she had last done so. How different the atmosphere was now. Grief, suspicion, and regret seemed to shimmer in the candlelight.

There was no entertainment, unsurprisingly, apart from more stilted conversation. Tea and the gentlemen arrived promptly, and after one cup, Mrs. Winsom excused herself and departed, leaning heavily on Miriam's arm once more.

Randolph looked relieved.

Ellen watched, her expression troubled. "I can't bear to see her so...diminished."

Was she diminished? Constance wasn't so sure. No one answered, and in time everyone drifted off, including Solomon Grey.

When Ivor Davidson followed, Ellen stood up too. So did

Constance. There was no sign of Grey following her. But she was in time to see Davidson leaping up the stairs two at a time, and Ellen, somehow disconsolate, wandering away toward the library.

Constance caught up with her there. Since the room was empty apart from them, she closed the door and said bluntly, "Are you avoiding me, Ellen?"

Ellen smiled ruefully. She did not seem unwelcoming. "I think I'm avoiding everyone."

"As long as I have not offended you somehow."

"No, of course not." Ellen settled on the sofa, and Constance sat on the chair opposite.

After a moment or two's silence, Constance asked, "How are you?"

"I don't know. Sometimes I forget and feel fine. And then I remember and feel guilty for having forgotten, even for a moment. How can I?"

"Protection. You have to look after yourself as well as your family."

"It's all just so...beastly. For him to die like that. I cannot believe I know anyone who would do such a thing to anyone, let alone to Papa."

"I know. It should be unthinkable."

Another silence while Ellen fidgeted and stared, frowning at her hands in her lap.

"Do you think Ivor did it?" she asked in a rush.

Aware of an incipient confidence, Constance forced herself to remain calm. "There is nothing to suggest he did. Except that, like many of us, he cannot prove he did not."

Ellen plucked at her skirts. *"He is avoiding me."*

"And you think that is because he is guilty?"

"Do you think so?"

"I have no way of knowing," Constance said. "What reason could he have for committing so heinous a crime?"

To her surprise, a somewhat cynical smile flitted across Ellen's face. "Don't worry. I know he would not do such a thing simply because my father repelled his suit. Things between us had never reached such a pass."

"He was flirting," Constance said. "Which is hardly appropriate now."

"And I am not worth a deeper friendship? You ask me how I am. He has not asked me once."

"I suspect he is feeling guilty about you, and looking after himself at the same time. Did you know he had asked your father to invest in his latest venture? And your father refused?"

Ellen met her gaze. Her lips twisted. "I see. He flirted with me to annoy my father. And now my father is dead, and he has two motives to have killed him."

"That would be an extreme response to two minor setbacks. And you know, if he truly wanted whatever money will come to you now, he would be haunting your every step."

"That is a good point," Ellen allowed.

"Do you care so much?"

Ellen thought about it. "I think I dislike the idea of being used as a pawn. I don't think I care for *him*, though the flirting was fun."

Good. Constance stayed a few minutes longer, and then they both retired to bed. After the disturbed night last night, the whole household seemed to retire early. As she closed her bedroom door, Constance felt suddenly exhausted. Somehow she managed to unfasten her gown without tearing it and then climbed out of it.

Bed, she thought with longing. *Bed...*

She blew out the candle and lay down with a sigh.

An animal howl rent the silence and chilled her spine— presumably Randolph's huge dog, who rejoiced in the appropriate soubriquet of Monster. Inevitably, her brain began to wake up again. She was in a house with a murderer, openly trying to discover his or her identity. It could be anyone, even Solomon Grey, whom she appeared to be trusting.

Why was she trusting him?

Because she liked the way he looked? She knew better.

Because she liked the way he sounded? That deep, soft voice, like warm, melted butter in her veins... Soft voices could hide as much malice as strident ones.

Because she sensed someone as self-sufficient and yet as totally alone as herself? A foolish basis for friendship, even if it were true.

Was that what she wanted? When she teased him and challenged him and flaunted her trade in front of him, was she really trying to be friends? She knew better than that too. Solomon Grey would never be her friend. He might treat her with a degree of courtesy, but he was a man who "did not care to pay for such favors." However loyal she might or might not be, she was too soiled in the eyes of any decent man for true friendship. He would never be seen with her, never introduce her to his friends. He would be ashamed. And he would find it distasteful.

And yet he notices me. Her mind seemed to be pleading with itself.

Yes, he noticed her, but he didn't want to. He was ashamed of that, too.

Constance had never whined over the hand that life had dealt her, or the paths she had chosen. She had just done her best with them and made them work. She would not be ashamed. And she would never be friends with Solomon Grey, who might or might not be a murderer.

Her instincts said he was not. So did her brain, which reminded her the knife had vanished before he arrived. But where he was concerned, she could not trust her instincts. They were already urging her into unprecedented temptation.

If Grey did not kill Walter Winsom, who did?

She went over the possibilities, so deep in thought that it was a moment before she registered the faint sounds beyond her door.

A whisper of soft footsteps, the creak of a floorboard.

Did she imagine they halted at her door?

She stared toward it, though she could see nothing in the darkness. She wished she had not closed the curtains. And just in case someone was at the door, listening, she was afraid to sit up and make noise lighting the lamp at her bedside. Instead, she listened intently.

The footsteps moved on, barely heard above the beating of her heart.

At once, she leapt out of bed, lit the lamp, turned it down as low as it would go, and threw on her dressing gown.

She eased open her door, peering into the darkness, straining to hear and see. Surely a dim light moved, somewhere in the well of the staircase?

Picking up the lamp in fingers that were not quite steady, she set out to follow, keeping the lamp shaded as much as she could with the wide lapel of her dressing gown. From the stairs, she heard the swinging of the heavy baize door that led to the servants' quarters and the kitchen.

Perhaps she had only heard a servant, Mrs. Winsom's maid, perhaps, returning to her own quarters? Only the footsteps had not come from Mrs. Winsom's room, but from the other direction. Though perhaps a servant would risk using the main staircase instead of the back stairs in the middle of the night.

Had the murderer gone to the kitchen for another knife? Her blood ran cold. Heart thumping, she listened at the baize door. Hearing nothing, she pushed it open warily. A dim light shone from the foot of the stairs. She leaned over the banister and saw the still figure, lamp in hand, with perfect clarity.

Solomon Grey.

CHAPTER EIGHT

W *HAT ON EARTH*...? By the light of his own lamp, he moved across the kitchen as if he knew his way. Silently, Constance set down her dim lamp on the table at the top of the stairs, where it was shaded by the wall, and peered over the banister toward the light.

In the corner beside the stove, it shone down on a small, still figure, sound asleep on a thin mattress roll. Owen the boot boy.

Fear clawed at her stomach so hard it hurt. But before she could move or make any sound at all, Grey moved away from him again. With one hand, he picked up a hard chair and carried it silently some distance from the boy and set it down against the wall. Then he sat in it and blew out his lamp.

From sheer instinct, Constance straightened and blew hers out too. Darkness closed around all of them. But it had finally come to her what Grey was doing. From his chair, he would be able see the sleeping boy. If there were any light.

He could not, however, see her, at least not when she wasn't stretching over the banister.

He was watching over the boy, not harming him.

Why?

Because Mrs. Winsom had announced to everyone at dinner that Owen the boot boy slept in the kitchen. He might very well have seen who stole the knife that killed his master.

Constance lowered herself to the far side of the first wide step, where the table and her useless lamp now resided. With luck, no one would see her either. She thought with longing of her warm, comfortable bed as she drew up her feet, laid her head against the wall, and closed her eyes.

She did not rate her chances of sleep as very high, and yet the movement of the baize door definitely woke her with a start.

Dear God, she was right. *Someone is coming to kill the boy!*

She shrank against the wall, her heart hammering.

An indistinct figure eased through the door in the paler darkness. He—or she—carried no light but seemed to need none, almost gliding sure-footed down the stairs into the kitchen.

Constance extended her legs till her feet touched the step below then grasped the spar of the banister and hauled herself to her feet. Whoever this was would be desperate, quick, and quiet. Did Grey even know he was here?

Holding the skirts of her dressing gown off the floor in one hand, and clinging to the banister with the other, she crept downstairs. As she reached the bottom, she released the banister and felt warily around for a weapon. She should have thought to bring her lamp from the table at the top...

Her fingers had just closed around a heavy candlestick when all hell seemed to break loose.

SOLOMON HAD JUST begun to think that he was wrong to worry about the boy's safety. In any case, he was likely to fall asleep soon and be worse than useless to him. He stretched one leg to ease it, then the other—which was when he heard the swish of the baize door and froze.

Though there was very little light coming through the un-curtained windows, for the night was cloudy, the intruder did not seem to need it. It appeared to be male, for he heard no rustling skirts, only the faintest of footfalls as someone moved down the stairs into the kitchen.

A patch of blacker darkness showed him moving from the foot of the stairs directly toward the stove and Owen. Solomon waited, poised, until the figure stood at the foot of the boy's bed, then rose to his feet. It struck him that only an hour or so earlier, he must have looked very like that threatening figure as he gazed down at the sleeping lad to make sure he was still breathing.

Judging by his swift movement, the attacker probably had the advantage of knowing the kitchen better. He certainly moved fast enough. But Solomon dared not take the time to relight his lamp.

He advanced with more speed than caution. The figure jerked around and immediately lunged at him. Solomon staggered back under the force of the onslaught, knocking over his chair and the lamp he'd left on the floor. At the same time, the attacker let out a roar of rage or fear. Solomon, expecting fists or blade to strike him, regained his balance and shoved his attacker aside, springing between him and Owen, who woke up with a yell of "Who's there?"

Solomon threw up his fists, ready for the next onslaught. He could hear the wild, heavy breathing of the attacker. Or perhaps it was own. Then the figure spun around and bolted—not toward the back door but to the stairs.

Solomon tore after him, but his foot slid, no doubt in the spilled oil from his lamp. He lunged onward, and the attacker let out a sudden cry, falling backward as though he'd been struck. A candle flame flared, illuminating the man, hunched and clutching at his eye. It wavered, raised in the hand of Constance Silver.

"Richards?" she said in disbelief.

Solomon knew how she felt.

The butler straightened, dropping his hand from his eye and blinking rapidly. "Mrs. Goldrich," he said hoarsely. "What are you...?"

"What are *you*, more to the point?" Constance drawled. She seemed to speak like that when she was shaken or defensive.

In the candlelight, she was breathtaking. Her thick hair gleamed like burnished gold, falling loose about her face and shoulders. She wore a finely embroidered dressing gown of some thin, luxurious material and apparently very little else. Without a crinoline, her figure was everything he had imagined, sweetly curving hips and...

Solomon caught his breath. "What the devil did you hit him with?" he asked.

With her free hand, barely glancing at Solomon, she lifted the knotted cord that tied her dressing gown. "Effective in the short term. Richards, we need an answer."

At that moment, Owen, in his shirt and unfastened trousers, tried to hurtle past Solomon toward the butler. Solomon grasped his shoulder and stayed him.

"I was protecting the boy," Richards said hollowly. "I'd have come earlier, only I fell asleep."

"I was trying to protect him too," Solomon said.

"I wasn't," said Constance. "I was watching *him*." She flicked her hand carelessly in Solomon's direction.

So, she suspected him. Or pretended she did. Either way, it should not have hurt.

Also, he had not even heard her enter the kitchen. He was not so good at this kind of task as he had imagined.

"I don't need protecting," Owen said, affronted. "I'm eleven."

"Not quite, you're not," the butler retorted. "And you'd better get back to bed, since you'll be up again in a couple of hours."

"But—"

"Owen!"

The boy swung his arm and turned reluctantly. "Am I in trouble, Mr. Richards?"

"No, boy, you're not in trouble," Richards said roughly. He straightened his shoulders, suddenly the haughty butler once more. "Perhaps you would like a tot of brandy for the nerves."

"Perhaps *we* would," Solomon said. He tried not to look at Constance, who was lighting another candle from the one she held.

The three of them sat on stools at the scrubbed kitchen table, drinking generous tots of brandy poured by Richards from a bottle he's produced from the top shelf of a tall cupboard.

"Why did you fear for him?" Solomon asked quietly, setting down his glass and enjoying the heat of the brandy trickling through him.

Richards sighed. "I heard what Mrs. Winsom said about Owen sleeping in the kitchen. It struck me that whoever killed the master might not have known that when he stole the knife. He's a good lad, is Owen. Got no one to look out for him."

"So you did," said Constance.

"Perhaps we should have spoken to you first," Solomon said.

"Perhaps you should've, sir." Richards drained his glass in one swallow. "I apologize for attacking you. I was pushing you away from the boy. I didn't realize you were protecting him too until you got between him and me. I'd no idea who you were."

"We seem to be no further forward," Constance observed. She glanced from Richards to Solomon. "Do you think he is safe for the rest of the night?"

"I shall stay here until he rises," Richards said.

It seemed safe enough. Even if Richards was lying, to kill the boy now would be to give himself away beyond doubt. Solomon stood. So did Constance.

She bade Richard goodnight and sailed upstairs ahead of Solomon, leaving him to bring one of the candles. At the top of the stairs she took a lamp from the table and held it for him to light. When he had replaced the cover and opened the baize door, she again walked out in front of him, as though used to the gentlemanly courtesies.

"Do you believe him?" she asked low as soon as the door swung closed behind them. Without waiting for an answer, she glided across the hall and into the morning room. He hesitated, then laughed at himself and followed her.

"I think so," he replied, closing the door and setting down the candle. "Do you?"

"It's plausible. We already agreed the servants were unlikely.

None of them that I spoke to or observed appeared anything but shocked by Winsom's death, and there's no whisper of discontent below stairs, either against the family or Richards. I can't see that he has a motive."

She dropped onto the sofa. Perhaps because she was dressed as she was, she lounged more than usual, more than was ladylike. She looked graceful, lovely, and utterly seductive. He dragged his eyes away, moving past her to hide his discomfort.

"Do you still think Owen is in danger?" she asked suddenly.

"Nothing has changed since dinnertime. Perhaps the murderer has decided that if no one knows who he—or she—is, then Owen never saw him. He does sleep pretty soundly."

"He's shattered, poor child... The family would surely all have known that he slept in the kitchen."

"Well, the girls might have, but can you imagine Randolph's taking an interest in domestic matters?"

"No," said Constance thoughtfully. "But I can imagine his plaguing the cook for snacks between meals. I think he'd know. The Boltons wouldn't necessarily, nor Ivor Davidson, nor Peter Albright."

Solomon turned and glanced at her. "Nor I?"

"You woke him the night of the murder," Constance reminded him. She met his gaze but did not elaborate.

"Why did you not tell me you were in the kitchen?" he asked. "You didn't follow Richards, did you?"

"No. I followed you. I didn't know who you were at first. I just heard stealthy footsteps in the passage and crept after them." She laughed suddenly, not the silvery yet full-throated amusement he was used to, but something very like contempt. "Don't curl your lip at me, Solomon Grey. We already agreed not to trust each other. But I saw you were watching him, not murdering him. I was curious."

A reluctant smile tugged at his mouth. "You are, aren't you? Curious. Well, having achieved little, shall we retire?"

"Mr. Grey. I thought you would never ask."

"My father would have called you a minx."

"I don't suppose I want to know what you call me."

"Trouble," he said, and held out his hand to her.

For an instant she didn't move, the laughter fading from her eyes. But he could have sworn he had surprised her. She took his hand and rose fluidly to her bare, dainty feet. They must have been frozen on the kitchen's stone floor, but her fingers were warm, soft, and strong. He knew an urge to hold on to them, though with what purpose, he had no idea. He released her and turned to pick up his candle and light her to her room.

They did not speak, but her quick smile when she left him at her door pierced straight to his loins. God help him.

DESPITE ANOTHER DISTURBED night, Solomon felt full of energy the following morning, and was first to the breakfast parlor at eight o'clock. He helped himself to some bacon, eggs, mushrooms, tomatoes, and toast and sat down with his heaped plate and a cup of coffee to consider what he knew about Walter Winsom and his death.

An ebullient man of strong character whom everyone had liked—or if not liked, then wanted as a friend or business partner. Or lover. Or father, in Constance's case. His family clearly loved him, although Randolph had rebelled somewhat against the path chosen for him. He had been eager, too, to ensure he was not blamed for the murder. Was that a normal first reaction to such a tragedy?

Perhaps. No one knew how they would behave in any fraught situation until it happened.

Solomon laid down his fork and reached for his coffee cup. Thomas Bolton walked into the room. He blinked in surprise to see Solomon there, but made no effort to bolt.

"Good morning, Grey."

"Good morning."

When he had filled his plate to his satisfaction, Bolton chose a place on the other side of the table, not quite opposite Solomon, but close enough to avoid any accusation of avoiding him.

Solomon carried on with his breakfast, curious to see if the man would ask him anything or confide anything. He didn't.

"What do you think of this whole business, sir?" Solomon said at last. "You knew poor Winsom well, knew his character, his family, his business. Did he really have no enemies?"

"It would appear," Bolton said dryly, "that he had *one*. But I cannot agree that anyone in this house could have done such a terrible thing. We must have had an intruder, someone who knew the house and grounds and how to gain access."

Solomon raised his brows. "Can you think of such a person?"

Bolton sighed. "I have been racking my brains, but no, I can't think of anyone, certainly not anyone with the malevolence and wickedness to—to…to do what was done."

"What about someone from the bank?" Solomon asked.

Bolton blinked. "From the bank? Who?"

Solomon shrugged. "A disgruntled employee, perhaps?"

"Our staff are all well treated and well paid. We provide opportunities for advancement. Everyone, I believe, is happy to work there."

"But not, perhaps, to be dismissed? Mrs. Albright recalled someone swearing at her father in the street, someone lately dismissed from the bank."

Bolton frowned in a clear effort of remembrance.

"Are there so many that you have difficulty remembering who it was who swore in public at Mr. Winsom in front of his family?"

Bolton's frown turned into a scowl. "No. I merely could not remember the case at all, since the man had no possible grudge. He was fortunate not to be prosecuted."

Solomon set his cup down in its saucer. "He committed some crime?"

"Framley? Oh yes. Fraud. We dismissed him at once. We had no choice. Though in consideration of his previous exemplary service, we did not charge him. At the time he was too angry at being discovered to be grateful."

"What happened to him?" Solomon asked.

"I have no idea." Bolton's eyes widened. "You do not think he can have broken in here? Murdered poor Walter in revenge?"

"I think it highly unlikely," Solomon said. "Was he ever invited to the house when he worked at the bank? Either as a guest or for bank purposes?"

Bolton finished chewing and swallowed. "I believe he was, once or twice. Carrying messages or books, that sort of thing."

It was, Solomon supposed, something else to think about, but it seemed an unnecessarily elaborate way for an employee to take revenge. On top of which, when could he have stolen the knife? And Winsom would have been far too wary of him to walk with him in the moonlight!

Solomon sat back in his chair and regarded Bolton, who seemed both tense and morose. There were no servants in the room, and he might not have a better opportunity.

"I believe you do business with Ivor Davidson," Solomon said.

"We shared a successful venture."

"Not successful enough to risk any further ventures with him?"

"I wouldn't say that."

"Oh? Then you didn't know Mr. Winsom had refused to invest in his latest scheme?"

Bolton barely paused. "Then he must have had good reason. Or..."

"Or?" Solomon encouraged him.

Bolton sighed. "Sometimes Walter would refuse initially in order to obtain a more favorable agreement."

"Did he mean to do so in this case?"

"I'm afraid I have no idea. Walter died before we could discuss it."

"Then you think Davidson is a reliable man?"

"I think he has flashes of brilliance but is overambitious. He wants too much, too soon."

"Does his business thrive?"

"I believe so, but really you must ask him that."

"I imagine the police will," Solomon said.

A spasm crossed Bolton's face. "This is going to be most upsetting. Have you ever had anything to do with such people before?"

"Some years ago, I had some diamonds stolen en route to their buyer and one of my men was killed. I had a somewhat mixed experience with the police."

"Meaning they were incompetent?"

"Meaning some of them were. Some of them were extremely competent. Let us hope for the latter in this case."

"Indeed." Bolton looked unhappy. "I suppose if they find the culprit we must forgive them for all the upset they will cause the ladies. I cannot like such interference in a gentleman's house. It almost smacks of revolution."

"I wouldn't go that far," Solomon said mildly.

It was only a few years since 1848, when revolutions had sprung up all over Europe. Britain had escaped any serious disorder, but the threat still hung over the wealthy and the powerful. Political revolution was not, however, quite the same as a professional force investigating crime, which had to be a good thing in Solomon's book, providing the individuals in question investigated properly.

He finished his coffee and, since no one else had entered the breakfast parlor, excused himself and left the room.

In the hallway, Richards was directing a footman to the porter's box by the front door. Presumably, the family were expecting condolence calls from neighbors. Constance Silver was descending the staircase in a dark blue gown, the crinoline of comparatively modest proportions.

Solomon bowed in her direction and sauntered into the morning room, where he hoped she would join him. He wondered what she would make of Bolton, and his view of Ivor Davidson.

A few moments later, she whisked into the room, in a teasing mood. "Are we having an assignation, Mr. Grey?"

"In front of the servants?" he said in shocked tones, and was curiously warmed by the glimmer of laughter in her eyes. Annoyed with himself, he immediately told her about his conversation with Bolton.

She listened without interruption until he stopped. "Do you believe him about Davidson?"

"That Winsom would have changed his mind? He did invite Davidson here. Why would he do that if he did not mean to invest with him? I don't know. My feeling is that Bolton is suspicious of the state of Davidson's business, even if he won't say so. Perhaps that was what he quarreled with Winsom about."

"And Davidson knew it and was desperate..." She met his gaze. "Desperate enough to kill Winsom and marry his daughter?"

"It seems a large leap," Solomon replied.

"Also, Davidson seems to be leaving Ellen alone," Constance pointed out. "Though I suppose that could be to make his plan less obvious. He has certainly incurred her notice, and could probably pick up where he left off once things have settled. Or imagines he could."

"Is he that brutal?"

"I suspect he is ruthless. But a cold-blooded, premeditated murder...?"

Solomon sighed. "Also risky. He would have to be very desperate indeed, and I'm not convinced he is. On the..." He trailed off, for Constance had suddenly darted toward the half-open door and was peering through the crack.

His lips twitched. "I saw a farce like this once at Drury Lane."

She glanced back over her shoulder. "It's the police from Scotland Yard," she said, and sallied forth to meet them. Solomon, giving up on discretion, followed her.

CHAPTER NINE

T HE FOOTMAN, CLEARLY under orders as to how to treat the
police when they arrived, was instructing them in a very
superior manner to go to the tradesmen's entrance.

Constance heard a voice arguing indignantly from the front
step, until another voice interrupted. "Oh, for the love of—" And
abruptly, the footman fell back as the door flew wide open,
almost knocking him off his feet. A man in a worn overcoat
walked into the house, a younger man trotting at his heels.

"You may inform your mistress that Inspector Harris and
Sergeant Flynn are here," the first man said briskly. "I shall be
happy to see her as soon as she is able. In the meantime, you had
better take my sergeant to your superior, a butler or a housekeeper—" He broke off, blinking, as his roving gaze landed on
Constance and Grey.

He groaned, though his dismay was nothing compared to her
own. "Oh no. Please tell me the Tizsas are not here too?"

"The Tizsas are not here," Constance said kindly, advancing
on him. She might as well brazen it out. "How do you do,
inspector?" She glanced at the footman, whose mouth had fallen
open. "Perhaps you could arrange for tea and some breakfast for
these gentlemen? I suspect they have had a long journey."

Inspector Harris was not a man who revealed his own
thoughts easily, but even he was looking slightly dazed by the
easy way the notorious Constance Silver ordered the servants of a
respectable lady—and was immediately obeyed, too. The young

sergeant strode off with the outraged footman toward the servants' quarters.

"Good morning, inspector," Grey said in his quiet, imperturbable way. "Perhaps you would care to come to the morning room for the moment? I am not sure what plans have been made for you, if any."

Constance led the way, almost surprised by the strength of her desire to stay at Greenforth and solve the mystery. Though once Harris revealed her identity, she and her baggage would be on the front step. Or in the backyard, more likely.

Harris rarely minced his words. He swung on Constance at once, even while Grey was closing the morning room door. "Him, I can understand. But I've been led to believe that this is a highly respected family. Why are you here? *How* are you here?"

The jibes did not hurt Constance. How could they, in the circumstances? The inspector was merely looking for information. And she could not think how to make him keep the secret of her true identity. Allure would not work. He had all a law officer's disapproval of her trade. Nor could she tease him— he was too serious about his profession.

Perhaps she could persuade him of an ambition to reform? Only, how would that play to the outraged Winsoms when he spoke to them about it? She shrank from admitting the humiliating truth, that she was searching for her unknown father...

Grey cleared his throat. "Mrs. Silver is here at my request, inspector. I have been conducting an investigation of my own— not a criminal one, of course—and I asked for her help. Naturally, she is not known to these people by her own name, but as Mrs. Goldrich. I would be grateful if you kept that to yourself."

Constance gazed at him in wonder. He had lied for her, so that there was at least the possibility of her staying. Whether from reluctant friendship or simply because she was useful, she did not mind. Either way, she was warmed.

Grey did not so much as glance at her. He was holding the inspector's stern gaze without difficulty or embarrassment. He even smiled, very faintly. "You may regard her as my employee, in a strictly business sense."

Harris's face cleared. Of course, if she was being paid, that explained everything to him. Though he still snapped, "I am conducting a murder inquiry in this house. If necessary, you will both be investigated like anyone else."

"If she is guilty, of course I release you from any obligation to me," Grey said smoothly. "But the truth is, Mrs. Silver and I found the body of Mr. Winsom together. The family and the guests believe I was alone."

Harris's lips twisted. "Preserving the lady's reputation, Mr. Grey?"

He didn't even smile. "Yes. Mrs. Goldrich is a respectable widow."

"Of course she is. So respectable you obtained an invitation for her."

"I obtained the invitation," Constance said, growing irritated with being discussed as though she weren't present. "Through Mr. and Mrs. Winsom's son, Randolph."

Harris's gaze flickered to her. "That, I believe. Well, you had better tell me what happened here."

"Mr. Grey will tell you," Constance said. "I'll fetch my notes from the library."

The hallway was almost eerily empty as Constance crossed to the library, where she discovered her notes where she had left them. The two sheets bore signs of being well thumbed, as though everyone had been making sure they were accurate and she had not slipped in anything to make their positions appear worse.

There was still no one in sight as she returned to the morning room, not even the footman who should have been guarding the door. A vague hum of conversation did seem to emanate from the breakfast parlor, so presumably everyone was gossiping in there about the arrival of the detectives from Scotland Yard.

In the morning room, Grey had clearly described the discovery of the body, and was just handing Harris the handkerchief he had discovered clutched in Winsom's fingers.

Harris spread it out on the arm of his chair. "A.B.?"

"Alice Bolton seems likeliest," Grey said, "the only person I know of with those initials. She is a guest here, a family friend and wife of Winsom's partner, Thomas Bolton."

"Why would he have her handkerchief?" Harris wondered.

"I suppose he might have found it in the garden and just picked it up," Constance said, dropping her notes onto the inspector's lap. "But we think there may have been an affair between them. We have no proof."

Harris grunted and picked up the notes. He read quickly, flipping over to the next page, and then back again. "You don't expect me to take all this as gospel, do you?"

"No," Grey said.

"Good." Harris glanced up at Constance. "However, it's a good place to start, and lists, you might say, all the *dramatis personae*. Excluding servants, I notice. What do you make of them?"

"Most seem to have been with the family for at least two years, considerably more in the case of the butler, Richards, and the housekeeper, Mrs. Farrow. Less, perhaps, for the boot boy. Which reminds me, he might have seen who took the knife, for he sleeps in the kitchen. It worried us and Richards enough for us all to keep watch on him last night."

Harris stiffened. "Really? And *did* anyone attack him?"

"No. But I still think he should be looked after."

"You're probably right," Harris said. "Well, thank you. That will be all for now."

Constance met Grey's amused gaze, but neither chose to quarrel with the inspector's dismissal.

"I'm going to breakfast," she announced. "I shall sing your praises, inspector."

Grey, though he held the door for her, did not announce his intentions, merely followed her out.

"Thank you," she murmured as they walked toward the breakfast parlor.

He didn't pretend to misunderstand her. "We agreed to do this together. And I believe he will keep your secret—for now, at least."

His cool matter-of-factness did not upset her. She was happy to allow him it. She parted from him with a sunny smile, and he walked on to let himself out of the front door.

Constance entered the breakfast parlor. Everyone else, apart from Mrs. Winsom, was around the table, though their clearly earnest conversation cut off at once. They all stared at her.

"I have met the police," she confided with an air of triumph. "The man in charge is one Inspector Harris, and he seems to be both polite and intelligent. Mr. Grey knows him," she added, walking to the sideboard and collecting a warm plate.

"How?" Mrs. Bolton asked with distaste.

"Oh, something to do with diamonds that were stolen from him some years ago."

Bolton sniffed. "Then let us hope this Harris is one of the competent policemen he dealt with."

"He *seems* very competent," Constance replied, helping herself to some eggs and a slice of toast before walking over to the table and sitting beside Ellen. "And there is a sergeant called Flynn, who is talking to the servants."

Miriam jumped to her feet. "Without any of us present?" she exclaimed in outrage. "I don't think so!" She marched off, a surprisingly martial glint in her eye.

"Richards and Mrs. Farrow will be there," Randolph called after her. "There is no need—" But she had already gone. Randolph shrugged and exchanged meaningful glances with Albright.

Ellen sighed.

Constance poured herself some coffee from the pot on the table and ate her breakfast.

IN THE LAST year, Inspector Harris had grown used to expressing dismay whenever he ran in to either of the Tizsas during any of his cases—which happened with alarming frequency. Not that he truly objected. Though they tended to complicate matters, they had too often supplied the insight and imagination that solved those cases for him to be truly angry. Transferring the same *almost*-banter to the man he had last seen in their company had seemed natural, but in truth, Solomon Grey was a very different kettle of fish.

Cool, wealthy, and inherently intimidating, he was unique in that Harris did not know quite what to make of him.

Or of Constance Silver, if the truth be told. His days of arresting women of the streets were behind him, and in any case, she was more of an expensive brothel keeper. Although for some reason, that disparaging description made him uncomfortable, too. Not because it was inaccurate, but because he was all too aware of the poverty and the risks surrounding prostitution. As far as he knew, the police had never had cause to go near Constance Silver's establishment. Perhaps because she greased the right palms. More likely because there had been no complaints from neighbors or clients. She kept her own order and had even moved into discreet premises in Mayfair. Rumor said one could meet more aristocrats in her salons than in the queen's drawing room. Harris didn't doubt it.

But it did not make her immune from his investigation. At this stage, any in the house could be guilty. Any of them vouching for each other could be lying, and from this he did not exclude either Silver or Grey.

Goldrich. She had a sense of humor. He gave her that.

The victim's widow was the first person he interviewed. Pale and stiff, she bristled with outrage at first, then drooped when her son stormed into the room, glowering. Since Mrs. Winsom had already told him the same story he had learned from Grey and from Constance Silver's notes, he left her to it for now, and, with permission to use the dead man's study for his interviews, he asked Mr. Randolph Winsom to join him there.

The study had clearly never been used as such. Though it contained a small desk and an equally small bookcase, it smelled faintly of old cigar smoke and was given over to masculine comfort—leather armchairs, a footstool, a tray of glasses and well-stocked decanters. This, Harris suspected, was where the victim had come to be alone and to relax, uninterrupted.

"Your father didn't do much work here, did he?"

Randolph flared his nostrils. "We have other rooms. If he chose to work at home, he did so in the library. I can show you that if you prefer."

"Perhaps later," Harris said amiably. He had met Randolph's type before—young, superior, overconfident in his privileged birth, education, and wealth. Harris sat down at one side of the desk and began by taking the wind out of his sails. "My sincere condolences, sir. An appalling thing to have happened. I know you will wish to give us every assistance in discovering who murdered your father."

Randolph could only say, "Of course I will."

"I understand you have all discussed it among yourselves. Mrs. Goldrich gave us your list of everyone's whereabouts that night, which is most helpful."

Randolph tried to look gratified. Harris gathered that he despised the list and had contributed to it only under the pressure of his peers.

"It's a very useful starting point for us," Harris explained, "but I've found over many years that people will often say one thing in public and another in private, where they will be guaranteed discretion."

Randolph regarded him with blatant disbelief. "Discretion? Seriously?"

"Providing it does not affect the case." Harris smiled very

slightly. "And providing the secret is not the murderer's. If someone does not tell me the truth, it means he has something to hide. So forgive me when I ask you where you were from around eleven of the clock on Thursday evening."

"I went to my room just before eleven and prepared for bed."

"But you did not go to bed, as you told everyone else?"

Randolph shifted in his seat. He seemed about to lie, then said abruptly, "No. Just after midnight I walked along the passage to see if Mrs. Goldrich was as wakeful as I."

"Mrs. Goldrich being a particular friend of yours?" Harris asked genially.

The boy blushed, bless him. "I'll not deny I admire her," he said. "In fact, it was I who invited her to Greenforth when I was introduced to her in London. I don't normally like the country. I don't like country hours, and I suspected she didn't, either. So I knocked on her door."

"At what time, sir?"

He shrugged impatiently. "I don't know precisely. Not long after midnight. The drawing room clock had chimed the hour a few minutes previously, and the house was quiet."

"So you knocked on her door," Harris prompted him.

"She didn't answer, so I knocked again as loudly as I dared, then pushed open the door to see if she were asleep."

"You're lucky she didn't scream the house down," Harris said.

"Constance is not so chicken-hearted. At any rate, she had no chance to because she was not in her room. I learned later she had gone to the library to find a book to read, but by the time she came back, I was in my own room and probably sound asleep. For I definitely woke up to my mother's screaming."

"That must have been very harrowing."

Randolph shuddered. It seemed genuine. "Thank God it wasn't she who found him. Grey did. He claims he saw someone in the garden and went to investigate."

"Your father was a banker, was he not? Did he do business

with Mr. Grey?"

"Not yet, but I know he had it in mind."

"Is that why he invited Mr. Grey here?"

"Oh no, my mother invited him. She thought he would entertain her guests, being widely traveled and very successful. She might even have thought he was a former slave in the West Indies—anti-slavery is one of her causes. But my father certainly didn't object."

"Hmm. Do you know anyone, anyone at all, who might have wanted to harm your father? Or had some kind of quarrel with him that just went too far?"

"A quarrel that went too far," Randolph repeated, staring at him. "He was stabbed in the back with a kitchen knife! I call that *much* too far."

"So you don't know of anyone who hated him that much?"

"I don't know anyone who hated him at all!"

"Then there were no quarrels within the family? I expect you butted heads with him occasionally."

Randolph's eyes fell. "Never in a major way. He wanted me to settle down to the business, but I wasn't ready to do that. I wanted to spread my wings a little. He understood. Mostly."

Harris nodded, as though he hadn't seen the tightening of Randolph's fist on the table. "Exactly how much did he understand?"

"I had to put up with the odd lecture, but he never stopped my allowance," Randolph snapped. "And I don't see how that is relevant."

"Oh, I think you will see it if you think about it. This is an unpleasant duty of mine, but I do have to ask. I'm told your father was well thought of in banking circles. Winsom and Bolton was pretty successful. Did Mr. Bolton and your father always agree?"

"You will have to ask Mr. Bolton," Randolph said haughtily.

"I'm asking you."

"Then yes, so far as I know, but I wasn't involved in their

business."

If Randolph was this defensive of his father's partner, Harris doubted he would react well to questions about his mother or his father's affair. There were better ways to find out about that. Instead, he asked, "Who inherits your father's estate?"

Randolph stiffened in his chair. For a moment he seemed about to refuse an answer, or perhaps direct him to the family solicitor, to whom Harris certainly intended to speak anyway.

"I get the bulk of it," Randolph muttered at last. "The house and the business. But my mother and my sisters will all receive sizeable sums. Enough to make them wealthy women, I believe, but I don't know the details. I never expected him to die so soon."

There was a tragic, almost childish note of loss and regret in his voice. Harris encountered it all too often in his work, but he never got used to it. Nor did he let it weigh too much with him. Many killers regretted what they had done.

AFTER BREAKFAST, CONSTANCE invaded the kitchen in search of Owen the boot boy. Inspector Harris's underling, Sergeant Flynn, was seated at the kitchen table, his notebook on his lap while he drank a cup of tea and ate biscuits with the cook and her assistant. Since he didn't glance in Constance's direction, she paused for a moment to observe him.

Although not a particularly handsome young man, he had the kind of face one noticed, strong and full of character. And he was clearly personable, for he had somehow overcome the servants' prejudice against the police far enough to be fed biscuits with his tea. Moreover, the cook and her assistant looked perfectly at ease with him.

Constance walked unchallenged toward the doors off the far side of the kitchen. In one room, she found the laundry maid up to her elbows in steaming-hot water. Her mouth fell open at sight of Constance, who merely smiled and left her to it. In the next room, Owen sat on a high stool at a workbench between two rows of shoes, energetically polishing a large black boot that he dropped in alarm as she walked in. He almost fell off the stool onto his feet.

"Sorry, Owen," she said with a smile. "I didn't mean to startle you. I just wanted to make sure you were well after we disturbed you last night."

"Oh yes, ma'am. Very well," he said fervently.

Constance bent and picked up the fallen boot. "My, that's a fine shine you achieved."

"It's Mr. Richards's own recipe, ma'am. Brings leather up a treat."

"I can see that. You must have learned your job very quickly."

"I do all the shoes, ma'am," he said proudly. "*And* I keep the fire stoked."

"You must be kept very busy. Please, don't let me hold you up."

Gratefully, he took the boot from her and hauled himself back onto the stool.

"How long have you been here at Greenforth?" she asked idly, eyeing the separate lines of dull and shiny footwear.

"Nearly a year now. I'm going to be a footman in a couple of years, and maybe learn to be a valet after that."

"Good for you. Then you like it here?"

"Oh yes, ma'am. *Much* better than the orphanage. I'm never cold or hungry here."

A twinge of pity shook her. She remembered the cold and the hunger, too. She remembered them without a roof over her head. There had been a time when she would have welcomed an orphanage, only she had never been an orphan. She hauled her mind back to the boy in front of her.

"No, and you have that cozy bed next to the stove, too. Must be lovely in winter."

He grinned. "It is. It's cold up in the attic, sometimes, and through there where the maids sleep. I wonder if I can still sleep here when I'm a footman?"

"You would have to ask Mr. Richards."

He nodded, moving on to the shiny boot's partner, which had already been wiped clean of mud.

"Do you ever wake up and find someone else in the kitchen?" she asked.

"Only when I sleep in, and I haven't done that for months."

"Then last night was the first time?"

"I never saw anyone take Cook's knife."

So he'd thought about it. And he was studiously avoiding her gaze, focused entirely on the boot.

"No, I know you'd have told Mr. Richards or Mrs. Farrow if you had," said Constance, who knew no such thing. If he were afraid, it was not of a murderer, though. It was probably of teasing by the other servants. She gazed thoughtfully at the boot in his hands. "Do you collect all the shoes for cleaning?"

"Yes. I look outside all the bedchamber doors and bring them all down first thing. At four or five in the morning. And then I put them back before the ladies and gents get up."

"When did you collect these ones, then?"

"They're the family's. Sometimes Miss Wilson, the mistress's maid, or Mr. Laird, the master's valet, bring me their things at all sorts of odd times."

"Did you have to scrape a lot of mud off them?" she asked, picking up an elegant lady's shoe and examining the sole.

"Not bad. These boots had a fair bit."

"Were they Mr. Winsom's?"

The boy's face fell as he remembered what had happened. But he shook his head. "No, these are Mr. Randolph's. He likes his boots kept shiny. I did his other pair yesterday. They were filthy."

"Were they?" Constance said, trying to keep her voice light and casual. "Dirtier than everyone else's?"

"Except for the mistress's. She must have been gardening in them. She loves her garden, does Mrs. Winsom."

"It is beautiful," Constance said, her mind racing. "Then even the morning after Mr. Winsom died, you were up early collecting shoes and boots?"

"No one told me not to," he said defensively.

"Even though you were up in the middle of the night waking Mr. Richards and Mrs. Farrow?"

He shrugged. "People still need clean shoes, and Mrs. Corben's still got to cook breakfast on a decent fire."

"Very true, and you are clearly a very conscientious worker." She decided to risk a question further. "The night your master died, who else left their shoes for cleaning?"

CHAPTER TEN

"I VOR DAVIDSON," SHE crowed to Grey when she tracked him down in the garden. "He, Randolph, and Mrs. Winsom all had muddy shoes the night of the murder."

Grey sat on the swing, trailing one foot with him across the grass as he moved gently back and forth. Although his gaze remained on her face with polite interest, he did not look particularly excited by her discovery.

"Don't you see the significance?" she said impatiently. "You must have felt the dampness of the ground when we found Mr. Winsom! It had rained early that day—before you arrived—but all the paths and most of the ground dried quickly. *This* patch..." She swept her hand from beyond the swing to the trampled flowerbed and the area around where Winsom had died. "This patch was still wet in the evening. The sun doesn't shine directly on it except first thing in the morning, before it rained, so it took longer to dry. At some point, Davidson, Randolph, and Mrs. Winsom must all have trodden on this ground."

"Not necessarily at midnight," Grey said, "and since the shoes are cleaned, we can't compare the kinds of soil attached to them to be sure it definitely came from this area. Also, have you considered that the murderer would not leave such evidence for the servants to find? Wouldn't he—or she—be more likely to clean the shoes themselves? Or hide them until the opportunity arose to do so?"

Deflated, she scowled at him instead. "Damn. Do you have to

be so *pernickety?*"

"Yes."

She sighed. "I thought I had made a vital discovery."

"It's possible you did," he said. "It just doesn't really rule anyone out. Though it might yet prove another nail in the murderer's coffin, as it were."

"You needn't try to make me feel better. I shall get over the disappointment in time."

His lips quirked. She liked to see him smile, however faintly.

He stopped the swing and rose to his feet. "I don't suppose Owen saw anyone in the kitchen during the night? Or taking the knife at any other time?"

"He says not. But I'm sure the sergeant is asking all the servants such things right now."

"Did you believe him?" Grey asked.

"Owen?" She frowned. "Actually, I'm not sure. I don't believe he's lying, precisely, but he sounds more certain than he actually is. I think. He's a growing child up before dawn and worked hard until he's sent to bed. The other servants are often still up, calling across the kitchen to each other, or laughing in the servants' hall nearby. I doubt he gets enough sleep. I think he might have known someone was in the kitchen but was too sleepy to look and doesn't want to think about it."

Grey nodded thoughtfully, beginning to walk back toward the house. "All the same, for Owen's sake, we should make a point of saying in front of everyone that he saw nothing and no one. That's the best safety we can give him."

ELLEN, LATCHING ON to any emotion that was not unbearable, was glad to feel indignant when she received the inspector's summons to the study. No one had ever gone in there without her father's express permission.

Accordingly, she fumed as she marched downstairs, prepared to give the inspector a piece of her mind on the subject of his inferiority in general and insensitivity in particular. From the foot of the stairs, she saw a complete stranger open the morning room door.

"Who on earth are you?" she demanded, stalking haughtily toward him. How many of their rooms did this wretched policeman wish to overrun?

He turned quickly to face her, and she saw that he was ridiculously young. She had imagined the inspector would be closer to middle age, and far too stolid to blush at the sight of her.

He bowed a little awkwardly. "Flynn, miss. Sergeant Flynn. I was looking for Inspector Harris."

"It doesn't give me much hope when you people can't even find each other. I believe the inspector is the study."

Deliberately, she turned her back on him.

"Er...where is that, miss? Might I trouble you to show me the way?"

He had caught up with her, so she favored him with a glance of disdain. To her surprise, he did not look bashfully away. Instead, he met her gaze directly, his eyes uncomfortably penetrating. It jolted her, somehow. Because he clearly did not regard himself as inferior? Or because she knew she was in the wrong to treat a stranger with such discourtesy, whatever her own grief?

Or just because he was too intelligent to have the wool pulled over his eyes?

She said nothing, merely strode across the hall to her father's study. Sergeant Flynn actually opened the door for her, which she chose to find impertinent rather than courteous.

She sailed in before him and, with a fresh spasm of pain, saw an older man in a worn but decent coat stand up from behind her father's desk.

"Miss Winsom? I am Inspector Harris."

"So I gather. This person is looking for you."

"My sergeant, Flynn." The two men exchanged looks over her head, which irritated her yet further. The inspector jerked his head to one side, and Flynn closed the door before sitting on a chair by the window and taking out his notebook.

Inspector Harris had the nerve to indicate the chair opposite his at her father's desk. Clearly it had been put there for the purpose. She sat on the edge of it, her back ramrod straight, and regarded him with dislike.

"My sympathies on your grievous loss, Miss Winsom."

To her horror, her eyes prickled. Here with these policemen, she could not possibly break down.

"Would you like to have one of your family present?" Inspector Harris asked. "I prefer to speak to the bereaved alone, but if you would be more comfortable—"

That word again! "It is not possible to be comfortable," she interrupted. "And I am not a child to need my hand held. What is it you wish to know, inspector?"

"When was the last time you saw your father?"

"When we went upstairs to bed. He gave me a candle." Her voice wobbled, and she swallowed fiercely. "We said goodnight, as normal."

"Then he did not seem worried or excited about anything?"

She frowned. "No, I don't think so."

"Happy or unhappy?" Harris pursued.

"Happy. He was always happy when we had guests. He is— was—a very sociable man."

"And I suppose he liked all his guests."

"Of course," she said.

"They are all old family friends?" the inspector asked.

"Yes! That is, no, not really all. The Boltons are, of course. Mr. Davidson is of more recent acquaintance, only about five years, I believe."

If she had hoped to put him off with sarcasm, she was disappointed. He did not even appear to notice, which made her slightly ashamed. She never treated people this way. Why was she behaving so badly?

"My mother met Mr. Grey in London last month," she added, by way of recompense. "But they knew him by repute. Mrs. Goldrich is a friend of my brother's. I don't know when he met her, but she is very kind."

"I see," Inspector Harris said without expression. "Was your parents' marriage a happy one, Miss Winsom?"

"Of course," she said coldly.

He smiled faintly. "But you will not tell me they never disagreed or quarreled? That would be unnatural."

"I shall take your word for it, inspector. If my parents disagreed, they did so in private. She always supported him in my hearing."

He nodded, as though he believed her. "To return to the night in question. You took your candle from your father and went up to bed. Did you go straight to your room?"

She glanced at Mrs. Goldrich's list, which lay on the desk in front of him. "You already know I did."

"I know what you told everyone else," he said pleasantly. "I am concerned with the truth."

"I am not in the habit of lying!"

"Then that is the truth you would be prepared to swear to in court?"

Her restless gaze flew back to his. "In *court*?"

"If necessary. Miss Winsom, we are trying to discover the person who killed your father, not searching for salacious gossip. Do you know of anyone at all who would want to hurt him?"

She shook her head miserably. "No."

She was never so glad to escape from anywhere, not even as a child being scolded or punished for misdemeanors. Vaguely aware that the sergeant held the door open for her, she glanced up at him and imagined she saw a trace of sympathy in his piercing blue eyes.

"Thank you," she muttered.

She went immediately in search of Miriam and found her

writing letters in the morning room.

"I'm surprised you can face writing to anyone," Ellen greeted her. "What on earth can you find to say that anyone will want to read?"

"Nothing," Miriam said flatly. "I am writing to inform family and friends of Papa's death. Mama is in no state to do it."

Ellen flew at once to her sister and rested her head in her lap. "Oh God, Miri, I'm sorry. I want to hurt someone, something. This is unbearable."

Miriam touched her hair. "I know. It helps to be busy."

"Can I write some of them for you?"

"Do you want to?"

With a sound that was half laugh, half sob, Ellen shook her head. "No, not really. I've just been interviewed by the police."

"They spoke to me earlier. What did they ask you?"

"Where I was that night, and a lot of questions about Mama and Papa and the state of their marriage. I told him they were happy."

"So did I."

Ellen lifted her head. "Were they?"

Miriam hesitated. "Mostly. More than most."

Ellen swallowed. "When was Papa banished to the dressing room?"

"A few weeks ago."

"Why?" Ellen asked, baffled. "Did he snore?"

Miriam smiled unhappily. "No. She was just angry with him."

"Why? What had he done?"

Miriam shrugged. "He flirted, I suppose."

"Flirted," Ellen repeated. Miriam blushed. "You know, you've turned awfully mealy-mouthed since you married Peter. Who was his affair with?"

Miriam hesitated, but she must have known she could not keep it to herself now. "Mrs. Bolton."

﹥﹥﹥✄﹤﹤﹤

AT THAT MOMENT, Harris was facing Alice Bolton across the small desk in the study. Flynn, having left the servants to their duties for now, resumed his notetaking by the window.

"How is Mrs. Winsom?" Harris asked, causing the lady to blink at him in surprise.

"Devastated," she replied. "Utterly devastated. Yet coping better than I imagined she would. She will recover more quickly without policemen in the house, if you will forgive me for saying so."

Harris raised his eyebrows. "She does not want to know who killed her husband?"

Mrs. Bolton frowned. "Well, of course, but it won't bring him back, will it?"

"Sadly not. And how are you coping with the grief, ma'am?"

For an instant, her gaze was piercing, though Harris knew she wouldn't learn much from his expression. "I? My husband and I have been close friends of the Winsoms for twenty years. We are naturally shocked and terribly saddened. But we are hardly chief mourners."

"How close?" Harris asked pleasantly.

"I beg your pardon?"

Harris took from his pocket the handkerchief Grey had found and spread it on the desk. "Do you recognize this, Mrs. Bolton?"

"It looks like mine," she replied without much interest. "It has my initials on it."

"Can you remember when you last saw it?"

She regarded him as though he had sprouted horns. "Of course I can't. I have a dozen like it."

"Then you didn't lose one?"

"Clearly I must have, since it is in your possession, inspector, but I was not aware of having done so."

"Would it surprise you to know that it was found in the hand of the late Mr. Winsom?"

It obviously did surprise her, for she stared at it in silence for several seconds. Color seeped into her face, which had been almost unnaturally pale, mottling her neck and leaving red spots on her cheeks.

"Of course it surprises me," she said at last. "What on earth was it doing there?"

"I was hoping you could tell me."

She shrugged elegantly. "Clearly, I must have dropped it somewhere. He found it and picked it up to return to me."

"In the garden at midnight?"

"He could have found it at any time," she said impatiently.

"And kept it clutched in his hand?"

She was glaring at him now. "What exactly are you implying, inspector?"

"I am asking if you met with Mr. Winsom that night after the household had retired."

"No, I did not, and I resent—"

"Mrs. Bolton, were you and Mr. Winsom conducting an affair?"

For the tiniest instant, fear stared out of her eyes, quickly veiled. He had his answer. But almost at once she sat back in her chair, her lips curled in contempt. "You nasty, grubby little man—how dare you? My husband has friends among your superiors who will see that your insolence is curtailed." She rose to her feet, causing both Harris and Flynn to stand also. "This interview is at an end. If you object, you may take that up with my husband too."

She swung away from him and marched to the door.

"Does he know about the affair?" Harris asked.

Her back remained rigid. She neither answered nor hesitated in her step. At the last moment Flynn reached the door ahead of her and opened it for her. She did not so much as glance at him.

"Go and find the husband, Flynn," Harris said, "before she gets to him first."

CONSTANCE HAD STATIONED herself in the library beside the study, so that she could see those who emerged from Harris's interviews. Alice Bolton stalked out in high dudgeon, but more than that, she was trembling, and something glistened at the corner of her eye. She marched blindly down the hall to the side door and let herself out.

Constance sprinted to catch the door before she closed it behind her. "Are you well, ma'am?" she asked.

"I'm fine," Alice gasped. "I just need some air."

Constance had never really cared for the superior Mrs. Bolton, but she suddenly felt a wave of genuine sympathy for the woman's distress. Her breath came quick and shallow, and she seemed to be holding herself together only by a precarious effort of will.

"Please..." Alice gasped. *Please leave me* was the clear command, but Constance could no more abandon her to her torment than she could one of her own girls.

She walked along beside her in silence.

"Insufferable man!" Alice burst out.

"Who, the inspector?"

"Wicked little man, poking and prying, making everything *grubby...*"

"I suppose they see a lot of grubbiness in their line of work. They don't always understand."

A strange sound escaped Alice's lips, half savage laugh, half sob. "Neither do I!" She stopped in the middle of the path and closed her eyes. "And dear God, I've made it worse. I should never..."

"What on earth did you say to them?" Constance asked.

"I denied it, of course..." Alice swung on Constance, the words bursting out of her as if they could no longer be contained. "He accused me of an adulterous affair with Walter!"

Constance touched her arm. "It was bound to come out sooner or later."

Alice stared at her, color rising and fading from her cheeks.

"I don't judge," Constance said, finding her way. "We all fall in love."

Alice dashed her hand across her face. "I didn't mean to. I suppose I always did, though. He was so different from Thomas, so…*alive.*"

"I know."

"I didn't intend anything to come of these feelings. I merely harbored them for more than a decade. But I knew he was not always faithful to Deborah, and I would not be one of many… Yet somehow it happened, once we were both old enough to know better."

"And now you grieve as his wife does."

"Worse," Alice whispered. "Because in the end, he chose her."

Understanding washed over Constance, along with pity for the strong, flawed woman brought low.

"Mrs. Winsom found out," Constance said slowly. "And he ended the affair. The night he died?"

Alice nodded miserably.

"You met him in the garden, at the swing…"

Alice nodded again, then her eyes widened. "How do you—"

"What time was that?" Constance asked urgently.

"What does it matter?" Alice demanded with a spurt of more characteristic impatience.

"You must see, it all depends on time."

Alice looked frightened. "You mean, he will think *I* killed Walter? Stabbed him in the back with a kitchen knife? Dear God!" But already the calculation was back, the careful mask. The moment of weakness and honesty had gone. "I met him not long after eleven. A quarter past the hour, perhaps. Not long after we all went upstairs to bed. We must have parted before half past. I'm not sure. I was upset."

Upset. Not angry. She was choosing her words much more carefully now.

"Did you walk back to the house together?" Constance asked.

"No. I left him in the garden and went to bed."

"Did you walk over the flowerbed to the house?"

Alice frowned. "Of course not. Why would I do that? I went along the paths."

"Was Mr. Bolton in bed already?"

"He was in our room."

Constance gazed at her until she looked up and met her eyes. "Did he know?"

There was a moment's pause, and then Alice nodded.

Well, that explains the look of hatred Solomon saw on Bolton's face. And when did he become Solomon to me...? "You should tell the inspector. If he asked you, he already knows."

"And I have already lied."

"People lie to the police all the time for all sorts of reasons. I'm sure he will understand your reluctance to admit adultery."

A spasm of outrage crossed Alice's face. The softness of misery had vanished from her eyes, leaving them defensive and hard. "And in any case, you will already have told the rest of the household, so I have no choice. Why did I even speak to you?"

"Because you needed a friend," Constance said mildly. "A confidante who can keep secrets."

Alice searched her eyes. "Can you?"

"Yes, but not from the police."

A moment longer, Alice stared, then nodded once before she turned back to the house. It might have been gratitude.

CHAPTER ELEVEN

"**I**'M NOT CONVINCED she did it," Constance said, when she was finally alone with Grey.

They had just finished tea with everyone else, during which Grey had told the company in tones of disappointment that the police did not believe that any of the servants—including Owen the boot boy—knew who took the murder weapon from the kitchen. Though Constance had surreptitiously observed the expressions around the table, she saw nothing out of the ordinary. If the killer sat among them, he probably knew perfectly well that no one had seen him—or her—steal the knife.

Now they were taking a walk, since Miriam was using their previous meeting place to write her letters.

"Not convinced that she did it," Grey repeated. "That is not quite a ringing endorsement of her innocence."

"No," Constance allowed. "You see, she has the strength and all that emotion churning below the surface. She was hurt enough and angry enough, possibly even tipped over the edge of sanity... And yet she did not *feel* guilty. Of adultery, yes—of the greater crime, no."

He regarded her quizzically. "Do you always know when your own girls are guilty of something?"

"Yes."

"Because they confess?"

"Usually, they do. They are not afraid of me, you see. But that's not how I know."

"You know because they *feel* guilty?"

"You are laughing at me," she said without heat. "But they do. Sometimes, you just have to ask the right questions to bring it to the surface."

"Perhaps you did not ask Mrs. Bolton the right question."

"Perhaps," she agreed with reluctance. As they emerged onto a well-trodden path, she caught sight of Inspector Harris and Sergeant Flynn striding ahead. "Aha!"

Without thought, she grasped Grey's arm and sped after them. He, after a startled resistance, just lengthened his stride and kept up easily with her trot. No doubt hearing the charge, both policemen turned and then paused for them to catch up.

"Something to tell us?" Harris asked.

"Something to tell *us*?" Constance countered.

"No," Harris said bluntly.

"Pity. Did Mrs. Bolton confess to her affair with Mr. Winsom?"

Harris stared through her.

Grey sighed. "You have Mrs. Silver to thank for that, you know. She sent her back to you when Mrs. Bolton confessed to her."

Harris scowled. The sergeant grinned before composing his face more seriously in response to Harris's glower.

"Do you know who committed the crime?" Grey asked.

Harris cleared his brow with apparent effort. "Not yet. They all seem to have a reason, and whatever their spouses say, they all had opportunity."

"Except the youngest girl," Flynn said. "I don't see what her motive is."

"Because you're not looking beyond her pretty face," Harris retorted, and Flynn blushed.

"Thank you for ruling us out," Grey said.

"I haven't," said Harris. "I was just being polite."

"I like you, inspector," Constance said, smiling at him. He looked more alarmed than gratified, but before he could say anything, she asked, "Where are you going? Surely not back to London?"

"No, we have rooms at the village inn."

"Excellent. Then we'll walk with you and compare notes."

"No, we won't," Harris said. "How many people do you think will talk to me if they know I'll tell everyone else?"

"How many are talking to you now?" Grey inquired. "With any semblance of truth?"

"Oh, there's truth in what most of them say. They just don't tell me everything."

Harris did not object any further to their presence. The brisk walk was pleasant, and as the sun came out, Constance realized she had no desire to return to Greenforth just yet. It was going to be a lovely evening. She liked the warmth on her face and the scent of grass and wild rosemary and a hint of roses on the breeze. And the gentle countryside was pretty. She felt oddly comfortable in this motley company.

It sounded like a joke one of her clients would tell: *A gentleman, a policeman, and a madam walked into an inn…*

"What happened at the inquest?" Constance asked. Grey hadn't got around to telling her, although he had attended to give his evidence of the body's discovery.

"Nothing unexpected," Harris said. "Murder by person or persons unknown."

"Seems pointless to go all that trouble to state the obvious."

"Procedure must be followed," Harris said sternly.

The path led into the village up the side of the inn. Flynn opened the gate, and Grey stood aside for Constance to precede them, just as though she were a lady.

"Back door," Harris said abruptly. "Right."

Constance could not help glancing left toward the front door. Randolph and Ivor Davidson sat together at the outside table, glasses of ale before them. Obediently she turned right. Harris led the way through the back to a pleasant coffee room where they were the only customers.

Grey ordered ale for three and a glass of rather good French wine for Constance.

"Well, *Mrs. Goldrich*," Harris said with faint mockery, jerking his head in the general direction of Randolph and Davidson, "what do you make of those two? Plotting together?"

"Only up to a point," she replied. "Davidson, you know, is young Ellen's possible motive."

This time it was Flynn who frowned. *Interesting.*

"How so?" Harris demanded.

"He was flirting with her—possibly to annoy her father, who had just refused to invest in his latest venture, or perhaps he fancied an heiress for a wife."

"Sounds more like Davidson's motive to me," Flynn said. "She's little more than a child."

"True, but don't be fooled. There is hidden steel behind that sweetness."

"There *is* sweetness?" Flynn asked in a slightly odd voice, as though he doubted it and believed it at the same time. Or wanted to.

"Oh yes. She is struggling and somewhat lost. I doubt you have seen her at her best."

Harris pounced. "Meaning she's protecting someone?"

"They're all protecting someone," Grey said broodingly. "Not necessarily the same someone, either."

"Who's your money on, then, sir?" Flynn asked, and received another scowl from Harris.

"I don't have enough information," Grey said.

"Evasion," Constance accused him.

"What about you, ma'am?" Flynn asked.

"Davidson," she said. "He's still sucking up to one of the Winsom children. And you, inspector?"

Harris hesitated, turning his glass on the table. Then he said decisively, "Mrs. Bolton. She had the best motive and opportunity. She admitted being with him during the time he probably died." He met Constance's gaze. "You don't agree with me?"

"I don't think I do," she replied. "The knife was stolen from the kitchen the night before, before Mrs. Winsom had delivered her congé. And besides, she didn't return to the house over the flowerbed."

The policemen looked baffled until Grey explained her theory of the trampled flowerbeds and the mud on the shoes of Davidson, Randolph, and Mrs. Winsom.

"The other reason I suspect Davidson," she said.

"Not Randolph, who inherits everything?"

"He doesn't really want to inherit the business," Constance said, her voice just a little too defensive. She didn't want the killer to be any of the Winsoms.

"I expect he'll like the money, though," Flynn said.

Grey looked at him. "Do you know much about the precise state of the bank and Winsom's other businesses?"

"Do you?" Harris countered.

"Doing well, by all I could learn," Grey said. "The bank—and Winsom himself—were well thought of."

"But?" Harris asked with interest.

Grey shrugged. "But I'm going by hearsay, not by the books."

"Flynn is going to the bank tomorrow to make general inquiries," Harris said.

"Ask about a former employee who was dismissed for fraud," Grey suggested. "Name of Framley. Apparently he bore a grudge, swore at Winsom in the street when he was in town with his family."

"What for?" Flynn asked. "We're looking at someone who was in the house at the time."

"I know. It just nags at me."

Flynn glanced at Harris, who nodded curtly.

"And what will you do tomorrow, inspector?" Constance asked.

"Look around. Speak to the widow again. And to Mrs. Bolton."

"Not to Mr. Davidson?"

Harris regarded her over the top of his glass and said nothing.

"I could do that," she offered.

Harris lowered his glass, scowling. "This is a police investigation. We are dealing with someone who committed premediated murder on a man he knew well. Stay away from it. Besides, we haven't ruled you out as a suspect. Or Mr. Grey."

Constance smiled. "Yes, you have, Mr. Harris, or you wouldn't be talking about it to us at all."

"DO YOU THINK that's true?" Grey asked as they walked up from the village, where they had left the policemen to a hearty inn dinner. Randolph and Davidson had vanished, presumably back to Greenforth. "That Harris has ruled us out as suspects?"

"If he has, it's because of you, not me. Neither of us has an alibi before midnight. On the other hand, neither of us has a motive in his eyes. If he knew my presence here had nothing to do with you, I'd leapfrog Mrs. Bolton to the top of his list."

He looked down at her. The incongruous conviviality of their drink with the policemen seemed almost to have relaxed him. "I doubt you have a previous record of violence."

"I learned early on to employ threat by proxy, namely that of large men."

He lifted one eyebrow. "Are they kept busy?"

"No. But they are there."

He looked away. She couldn't tell if it was distaste or concern. But she had felt the hard muscle of his arms the first time she met him, when he pulled her from under the falling man in Coal Yard Lane. His kind of poise spoke of...preparedness.

"Are you a violent man, Solomon Grey?"

"What do you think?"

"I think you try too hard not to be read. But I would admit you to my salons."

His gaze flew back to her, veiled as always, and yet she thought he was not pleased.

"It is a compliment," she drawled. "Whatever you think."

His lips twisted. "Probably one I don't deserve. I am not a violent man, though I have always looked after my own. But what makes someone kill in one situation and not in another? If our culprit was easily spotted as a murderer, no one would have gone near him."

She looked behind the words, behind the elegance and self-confidence, and still saw a man too much alone and too self-reliant. Like her, only he let no one near at all.

"What situation would it take for you to have murdered Walter Winsom?"

He met her gaze. "If he had harmed my brother."

Her heart thudded. "Did he?"

"No. I had already found the proof before you entered the library the night he died. He was aboard the wrong ship at the wrong time."

"And now you feel so guilty for your suspicions that you want to solve his murder."

"Perhaps. Partly."

"What was your brother's name?"

He looked startled. "David."

"Does he have to have been harmed? Couldn't he have run away and lived his own life? Was he older than you?"

"Why else would he not have contacted me? He was a child, no older than me." He glanced away from her. "He was my twin."

She felt it then, the wave of bewildered grief and unbearable loneliness that never left him. Where there had been two, there was suddenly one. Still one. There was nothing she could say to ease that. Nothing she could do, not for him. Even an understanding touch of his hand would be intolerable. Especially, perhaps, from her.

And yet he had told her.

She walked along beside him in silent solidarity. After a while, he turned his head toward her once more.

At the narrow stream, easily crossed with a large step, he took her hand to help her. He didn't like what she was, but he always treated her as a lady. At the other side, he placed her hand on his arm and they walked on to the house together. She felt almost...close to him.

CONSTANCE WAS TIRED enough to fall asleep almost as soon as her head touched the pillow, but she woke up early, disturbed by dreams of moonlight, blood, and threatening shadows that lunged into life, straight at her.

She lay still in the darkness, the dreams fading, even as she tried to grasp them. Unpleasant or not, there could have been something buried there that she really needed to know.

The first hesitant chirps of waking birds brought the same relief they always had, the promise of daylight after another night survived. A door to lock was a gift beyond price. She had locked her bedroom door here since the murder. She suspected everyone did—except perhaps the murderer.

She had told Inspector Harris her money was on Ivor Davidson, as though he were some promising horse in the next race at Newmarket. And in truth, she had as little faith in her choice. She knew nothing against him except her dislike of a mature man flirting with a girl almost young enough to be his daughter, and the fact that his shoes had been muddy, which could have had any number of reasons.

Harris, who had more experience of murderers, thought it was Mrs. Bolton. Winsom had carried her handkerchief like an accusation, and she could have guessed long before their last meeting that he was going to end their affair. There could have been some slow buildup of pain and rage in her, culminating in that lethal lunge… Like Constance's dream.

She shivered. The lovers had met in moonlight, in the garden where anyone could have seen them. The swing was not visible from most of the bedchamber windows, but the attic ones were probably high enough. Besides, anyone could have walked that way. Had someone else seen them? Mrs. Winsom, perhaps. What if she had mistaken a final parting for an assignation?

How did one conduct such an affair, in any case? Surely the two couples had met together often, frequently at Greenforth, from what she had gathered. So where did they tryst? None of them had separate bedchambers here, and she could not imagine the dignified Mrs. Bolton being tumbled in the barn or tussling in the woods.

She rose and pulled back the curtains, looking for outhouses that might be more comfortable than they appeared. But what caught her eye was to the left, the old, crumbling stone of the disused wing, a place where the Winsom children had played before Randolph fell through the ceiling and it was blocked off.

Why had they never renovated it? The Winsoms were surely wealthy enough, although Grey had thought much of their money was tied up in the bank.

On impulse, Constance turned away, seized yesterday's morning dress, and dropped it over her nightgown. She didn't trouble to fasten it, merely whisked a shawl around her shoulders. Without the crinoline, she had to gather up the skirts over one arm. If she ran into anyone she would look damned odd, but it was still better than being caught in her nightgown. Although it was beginning to get light, she lit the lamp. After all, the old wing's windows were boarded up.

With her feet in her soft slippers, she made little sound as she walked to the door. Unlocking it carefully produced only a slight click. She slipped out into the dark passage and crept swiftly to the end, past Grey's room to the ancient door facing her that led to the old wing.

She found the old-fashioned latch more by feel than sight, but to her surprise, the door was not locked like the downstairs one. Nor did its hinges creak. It must have been recently oiled. Oh yes, this *must* have been where the lovers met...

Not quite sure what she was looking for, she slipped through the door and pulled it almost closed behind her.

She was glad of the lamp in this pitch darkness. Barely any dawn light found its way around the dusty window boards, but by the light of her lamp, she saw she was in a large, well-proportioned room that must once have been lovely once. Now it was bare and soulless.

She walked forward warily. On the left side of the apartment, she made out the rough floor repair—new boards nailed crosswise across the rotted patch to make an obvious warning. Presumably, this was where Randolph had fallen through. Though she peered carefully in front before every step, the floor beneath her felt solid enough.

The room was empty of all furniture, hardly an enticing love nest. It only had one door, and on her right, away from the rotted area, so she pushed it open.

Aha.

It was a different world. Even in the pale lamplight, she could see that the floor and the surfaces were clean. A dressing table with a mirror stood against one wall. A large mattress lay on the floor, made up like a bed with an embroidered coverlet and crisp cotton pillowcases. There was another door at the far end, leading perhaps to a passage or a landing. This must once have been a dressing room or a sitting room attached to the larger bedchamber.

She moved into the cozy space, noticing the comb and hairpins on the dressing table. Oh yes, this was where Walter and Alice had trysted. It almost looked romantic, until one considered the spouses on the other side of the latched door. Had that made it more exciting for them? Until Walter had been found out and was not prepared to defy convention and leave his wife. Or perhaps he had simply chosen his wife over his peccadillo. In his own way, he had probably loved her.

Constance knew only too well how men—some men—regarded their adulterous pleasures, as if they were entirely separate from the respectable lives they lived with their wives and children. This room was, essentially, Walter's brothel.

She felt a twinge of distaste, which she never felt in her own establishment. Cut off from the rest of the house as it was, this was still Deborah Winsom's home. For an instant, the dream figure who lunged across her mind's eye was Deborah, hurt and furious beyond sanity, and wielding a long, sharp kitchen knife.

And Deborah had muddy shoes.

A loud creak jerked Constance out of her speculation.

Deborah, coming to torture herself, to assuage her guilt? Or did she somehow know Constance was here? Her heart hammered, because quite suddenly she had more to fear than the mere embarrassment of being caught where she had no business being.

The footsteps were not even particularly stealthy, merely slow and deliberate. Someone ascending a staircase, beyond the closed door. She only had one way out. She had backed silently into the outer room and turned down the lamp before curiosity overcame her once more.

Who else was braving the ban on this forbidden part of the house? And why?

She halted, trying to overcome her uneven breath, straining to hear over the sounds of her own heart, then began to move forward this time, once more toward the trysting room. This would surely tell her something, perhaps even solve the mystery of the murder…

She heard nothing. Surely she could peer around the door and glimpse whoever it was.

Without any warning at all, a dark figure filled the doorway between the rooms. A well-dressed man whose features were unrecognizable in the gray, shadowy light—until he moved a step inside with his own lamp.

CHAPTER TWELVE

"RICHARDS!" CONSTANCE GASPED, with no idea whether she should be relieved or not.

"Mrs. Goldrich." His voice was cold, and he did not bow. "Do you not know that this part of the house is dangerous?"

"Why, yes, Mr. Randolph told me when I first arrived. But I woke early, and I suppose curiosity got the better of me." Was she talking too much? "You have duties here?" It never did any harm, after all, to turn accusations around.

"Of course," he said. "I make certain there has been no further damage and carry out repairs where necessary. Like that one." He nodded toward the rough repair over the rotted floorboards.

That repair had clearly been done years ago, probably as soon as Randolph had fallen through. But it did not seem wise to argue with Richards. Nor, for some reason, did it seem wise to bring up the subject of the well-used room beyond. He probably thought she was heading toward it for the first time, and she chose not to change his mind.

She had never thought of him as a large or threatening man before, but her stomach lurched as he advanced upon her now. Her instinct was to back away from him, but it had been so long since she'd let anyone intimidate her that she couldn't bring herself to do it. She merely raised her eyebrows, and he halted again.

"If you please, ma'am," he said, nodding toward the latched

door she had closed over. "For your own safety."

The words chilled her, even though he made no overt threat. She was hampered by bunched skirts that would trip her if she let them go. She had no defense.

She smiled. "Of course, you are quite right."

She turned and walked in front of him to the door. Her neck prickled with fear. She could almost feel the blow, the shove, the pain. She had to force herself to take her time and pray he did not notice her shaking hand as she reached out and opened the door.

She stepped over the threshold, back into the main part of the house and the empty passage. She kept walking. Behind her, the door closed softly and a key turned. At last she could stand it no longer and glanced back.

Her knees almost gave way with relief, because he had remained on the other side of the door.

She stumbled back to her own room, closed and locked the door, and leaned against it. Slowly, she slid down until she sat on the floor. She could not remember the last time she had been so frightened.

Of Richards? The butler?

Had they been looking in the wrong place all the time?

DEBORAH WINSOM WAS roused from her torpor of horror and misery by outrage at the police inspector, who wanted to search Walter's room.

"You want to *what?*" she said, drawing herself up to her full height.

"Look around his private chamber," Inspector Harris repeated. "We may find some clue there as to why he died and who is responsible."

"If you imagine my husband *knew* anyone who could do this to him—" Only he had. Thomas and Alice and Randolph all acknowledged that it must be the case. She would only look foolish to suggest otherwise. "I suppose I cannot stop you," she said tragically. It seemed she had no control over anything anymore. Had she ever?

"You could," Inspector Harris said surprisingly. "But your cooperation in this would be helpful to our investigation. I understand it seems something of an invasion, but if you wish someone to accompany me...?"

"*I* shall accompany you," she said frigidly, and led the way from the hall where he had accosted her, upstairs to her bed-chamber. She sailed into Walter's dressing room and stood in the corner, glaring at Harris. It made her feel marginally better.

Until, she realized, watching him rake through drawers and cupboards, that he had actually *wanted* her presence. He did not appear to be finding much that interested him, but he asked her questions while he looked—increasingly personal ones.

"Was he an indulgent father?" he asked, pulling letters from a bedside drawer.

Deborah's gaze clung to them. Were they *her* letters? Should she have looked before the police got here? "Indulgent? No, he was a strict father. Kind but fair."

"Was it not indulgence to your son to let him waste his time and allowance in London?"

"He was looking about him," Deborah said with dignity, watching with difficulty as Harris skimmed his eyes over one epistle and flipped to the next. "Finding his feet in the world."

"That is not a privilege most of us are granted."

Deborah curled her lip. "Well, you are a policeman."

"Much to my father's regret. But at least I was earning. Did Mr. Winsom approve your daughters' suitors?"

"Peter, obviously. Of course he did."

"And Miss Ellen's suitors?"

"She is sixteen years old!"

"Yet I understand Mr. Davidson is quite assiduous in his at-tentions."

"Nonsense, he is just being friendly."

"Did your husband think so?"

"My husband entrusted such matters to me. He had many other things on his mind."

"Such as Mrs. Bolton?"

The blood left her face in such a rush that she felt dizzy and had to lean back against the wall. Even before a nobody like this, the humiliation was profound.

"I don't know what you mean."

"Yes you do, ma'am. If Mrs. Bolton had not already told us of her affair with your husband, these letters would have. According to her, you learned of it some weeks ago, and he ended the affair the night he died. Would you like to sit down?"

"What I would like—" She gasped and broke off, shuddering. "I find you impertinent. Our private affairs remain just that."

"Then you do not believe Mrs. Bolton took her rejection badly enough to kill him?"

Deborah stared at him. *What rejection?* "I cannot imagine what goes on in your life to make you imagine such a thing."

"It is other people's lives I am obliged to look into. Were you angry with your husband, Mrs. Winsom?"

What on earth did she reply to that? That she was? Would he then think her capable of murder? If she said he was not, did it make her an uncaring or complacent wife?

"Yes," she whispered, opting for truth.

"Did your children know?"

"Of course not! They thought the world of their father. It would have broken their hearts." She dropped her gaze again. "I might have hinted to Miriam. Mrs. Albright."

"And Mrs. Bolton? According to her and to all your family and guests, you bear her no ill will, nor she you. I find that hard to believe."

"I do not care what you believe," Deborah said. "Alice Bolton and I have been friends for years."

"And shared your husband for years?"

"How dare you?" she uttered.

"Then tell me the truth. When did it begin? When did you find out?"

She meant to stare him down, but he was clearly not going to crawl back under his stone. He held her gaze easily.

What did it matter anyway? Walter was dead.

"About a year ago, apparently. I found her earring in one of the spare beds last month, the day after they last visited us. And I could smell his soap on the sheets. I knew."

She still had his full attention. "Did you confront him?" he asked.

"I had his things moved to the dressing room. He knew what it meant."

"Did you know he had ended the affair the night he died?"

Dear God, was that kindness in his voice? Did he imagine knowing that made her feel better?

Did it?

She shook her head. *Poor Alice.* She had lost in the end. Though she still had her own husband.

As if he read her thoughts, the inspector said, "Did Mr. Bolton know?"

"I don't know. I hope not."

"Because he would be hurt? Or angry?"

"If you are implying Thomas Bolton killed my husband…"

"Did he?"

"Of course he did not!"

"How do you know?"

She stared at him. Was this a trap? What should she say? "I have known him for twenty years. He was my husband's friend and partner. I could never imagine his behaving in such a way."

"Nor Mrs. Bolton?"

"Don't be ridiculous."

"Did you go directly to bed the night of the murder, ma'am?"

"I already told you I did. It is still true."

"There was mud on the shoes you left in the passage for the

boot boy to clean that night."

"There frequently is," she said tartly. "I enjoy my garden."

"Were you in the garden after the rain that day? No one else saw you go further than the terrace, which is never muddy."

It had never entered her head that they would investigate anyone's movements so thoroughly. She had to swallow before she could speak. "Then they were not looking. Which is also entirely understandable."

CONSIDERING THE TRAGEDY that had occurred so recently in this house, Solomon was surprised to wake with a sense of eagerness and purpose that had been missing from his life for some time. It certainly had something to do with the mystery—was Constance right that he was prompted by guilt? He suspected novelty had more to do with it.

He had come to Greenforth because he was bored, and because it gave him one more chance, however faint, of discovering something more about David. He always hoped, but the strength of that hope faded with each passing year.

Now, even his business bored him. With the right people in place, it barely needed him. Finding the right people had been his biggest challenge. He could say the same for the charities he patronized. Apart from them, people had stopped interesting him in individual terms.

Until Constance Silver. The woman was a mass of contradictions, challenging his every prejudice. In fact, he hadn't realized he had any prejudices until he met her. She defied labeling, did what she pleased, went where she liked by any means available. He found he liked those things about her, even if they were not always strictly honest. She was young—younger than he had imagined on their first meeting, if she were really only twenty-five or six. She was also beautiful, vibrant, intelligent—charming when she wished to be. Or when one took her by surprise.

Why did she choose to waste such talents managing a brothel? Because she liked to defy the convention that madams were raddled old hags? Or because it was all she knew?

He did not want to think about that. And yet it plagued him as he walked briskly though the woods after breakfast. He meant to think about the mystery, not Constance, whom he had avoided after breakfast, even knowing she lurked nearby with the clear desire to speak to him. He did not want the distraction of her nearness right now.

Of course, she might have done it, he reminded himself. He had assumed she was looking for her father because family meant something to her, or because she meant to bleed him of a little coin. But what if she were seeking revenge on him? Perhaps for abandoning her mother, or some worse crime against her? He had never asked because it seemed intrusive. And because he couldn't believe her anyway.

But you are *believing her. You are trusting her.*

He had never frequented whores—at least not after one wild night in Port Royal when he was sixteen—but he had heard that the best of them could make you imagine you were different from their other clients, interesting and special to them.

Something clawed at his insides. She had nothing to gain from him, nor he from her. He had known purely mercenary people—still did—but she was not one of them. Life might have hardened her, but there was an odd vulnerability to her, a caring. Did that extend to a terrible vengeance?

Somewhere to his right, a twig cracked, as though stepped on by a heavy weight. The sudden sound dragged him out of his reverie. A few paces on, he heard something very similar and paused, listening. Apart from the fluttering of birds above, more distant singing, and the odd buzz of passing insects, the woods were silent.

He walked on, aware with every sense that someone or something was keeping pace with him, walking parallel to his course, maintaining the same distance between them. It could have been a dog, or a deer, maybe, but he suspected it was human.

It would not be the first time a human had objected to his presence. His very skin prickled with memory. Hiding among the tall sugar canes from a baying mob...

He walked with his hands loose by his sides, listening, watching, poised. For a time, his fellow walker shadowed him. But when he turned and headed back toward the house, he heard nothing more.

Imagination? Maybe.

In any case, why had it bothered him so much? He was living in the same house as a cold-blooded murderer.

He did not need to seek Constance out, for he saw her as soon as he entered the front door. Warm and bright as sunshine, she was placing a letter in the posting basket on the large hall table.

"It will be tomorrow now before it's posted," he said, "unless you take it to the village."

Her lip curved into a smile as soon as he started to speak, even though she didn't turn to face him at once. "I know. I have nothing urgent, just keeping in touch with home."

She didn't even say it to rile him. She really did regard her establishment as home.

"Then it wasn't you walking in the woods just now?" he asked.

At that, she faced him fully. "No, I haven't been out yet today." She indicated the letter. "I was busy. Why do you ask?"

"I had the curious fancy that someone was following me."

"And why would you imagine that someone was me?" she wondered, amused.

"Because you seemed to want to speak to me after breakfast."

"Actually, I do! Would you care to sit in the garden?"

Avoiding the swing area, they found a curved wrought iron bench by the ornamental pond. It was far enough away from the house for them not to be overheard, and between them, they could see anyone approaching from any direction.

"I wondered suddenly where Alice and Walter trysted," she said at once. "And I found what must be the place in the old wing. Unlike the larger room next to it, which is totally bare, this one has a made-up bed on the floor and a dressing table to make oneself alluring beforehand and tidy afterward. Also... I ran into someone there."

"Who?" he demanded, suddenly afraid of more than rotting floors.

"Richards."

He blinked. "Richards? What the devil was he doing there?"

"That's what I don't know. He said he looked over the wing every week to make sure there was nothing wrong. If that's true, then he definitely knew about the trysting room before, and he certainly knows now. But the thing is...he was different."

"In what way?"

"In a bully kind of a way. He didn't even pretend respect. He just wanted me out of there. Probably before I saw the trysting room. He wouldn't have known I'd seen it already. But this opens all sorts of different possibilities. We never even considered Richards or any of the servants before."

"Perhaps that was *his* trysting place," Solomon mused. "I wonder whom with? Did he take one of the maids there?"

"Or several?" Constance said with unexpected distaste. "Have I missed some fear and abuse in the servants' hall? He seemed so kind to young Owen."

"And yet he was there," Solomon said slowly. "Standing over him. He had no weapon that I felt when I struggled with him, but we have only his word that he was concerned for the boy, like us."

"He's in and out of the kitchen all the time," Constance said. "He could have taken the knife any time."

"He could," Solomon agreed, frowning. "Only, why would a respectable butler stab his master in the back? There has to be more to it than being caught tippling in the wine cellar."

"Maybe he's not respectable at all," Constance said. "Maybe—" She broke off with a sigh. "He's been here for a decade and more. Why should he turn on Walter now?"

"Perhaps Walter caught him making use of his—er...trysting place and tried to dismiss him."

"Risky," Constance said, "when Richards must have at least guessed it was Walter's. Aren't they more likely to have made an all-men-together agreement of silence? And yes, before you ask, I'm sure that is what goes on among the gentlemen who encounter each other in my salons."

"Whatever, I don't like this."

"Neither do I," Constance said with a shiver. "I will be very glad to leave here."

"Have you told Harris?"

"Not yet. He's been searching Walter's dressing room. Mrs. Winsom is outraged, though apparently they found nothing helpful. He was closeted with Alice Bolton when you came in."

He rose and, without thought, held out his hand to her. "Let's go back and try to catch him discreetly before he sees anyone else."

Though she took his proffered hand and stood, he had the feeling that his courtesies amused her, whether because she did not consider herself worthy of them, or because she thought he was mocking her. He wasn't, though neither was he sure what *did* compel him. One didn't hold doors for maids, after all—well, not unless their hands were so full they'd drop something.

By mutual, if tacit, agreement, they split up when they returned to the house. Solomon skulked in the hallway, waiting for the study door to open. Constance walked into the library and sat with a book open in her lap. He hoped it was the right way up.

Stupid. Of course she could read and write. He had seen her do so, and very neatly and stylishly, too. Where had she learned to do that? Someone had also taught her to speak like a lady. Unless she had been born a lady in the first place and the East End accent she had displayed to him the other day was the one she had learned.

So much of her life was a mystery to him... And would no doubt remain so.

The study door opened, and Alice Bolton sailed out, her cheeks flushed but her head held high. He thought she would walk right past him, but at the last moment, she seemed to notice him and a twisted smile tugged at her lips.

"I suppose it is a comfort that I am not the only suspect," she said brittlely, and walked on.

Since she hadn't troubled to close the door behind her, Solomon stuck his head around it. Inspector Harris sat at the desk, scowling at nothing, his hands dug deep into the pockets of his coat.

"May I have a word?" Solomon asked.

The inspector's scowl only intensified. "Another one?"

Constance had not joined him after all, so he closed the door and sat down. "What do you know of Richards the butler?"

"Nothing," Harris said shortly. "Barely spoken to the man. Flynn dealt with the servants, found nothing untoward."

"He might be worth another look."

Harris swore beneath his breath, though whether at Solomon or at the knock on the door that heralded Constance's arrival, it was impossible to say. Solomon rose, invited her to sit in his vacated chair, and brought over Sergeant Flynn's for himself. Harris watched these maneuvers with growing ire, until suddenly his face cleared and he sighed.

"I presume you haven't come to accuse each other. Tell me quickly."

Constance told him concisely of her encounter with Richards and their realization that the butler was, if not involved, then not quite what he seemed. Harris listened without comment until she finished.

Then he stood up. "Don't you think you're reading too much into what is probably just the man protecting his master's reputation? But I'll look into his background as well as yours. Now please go away. I'm busy."

At that moment, another knock sounded at the door, and before the inspector could respond, Sergeant Flynn entered with the force of a gale.

"Sir, I—" He stopped and inclined his head to Constance and Solomon.

"Well met, sergeant," Constance said winningly. "What have you learned?"

Flynn glanced at Harris, who, glowering at his visitors, merely pointed to the door.

Constance, accepting defeat, laughed, curtsied with some style, and glided out of the room.

Solomon, afraid she would seek out Richards herself, steered her across the empty hall to the door that led to the old wing. While she kept watch, he tried the door and found it locked.

"Surely it must usually be locked," Solomon murmured. "Too big a risk of discovery, otherwise."

"Then perhaps Alice has a key." She frowned. "But I got in easily upstairs this morning."

"Richards must have gone in that way, not meaning to be long." He met Constance's gaze. "So what was he doing downstairs? There must be something else there. How do we get hold of the key?"

As one, they moved apart, as Randolph prowled out of the morning room, a pile of letters in his hand. Constance walked directly toward him. Solomon wandered in the direction of the stairs, wondering if he could induce Mrs. Winsom to let him into the old wing. But something about Randolph's stance at the post table distracted him, so he paused, one hand on the newel post.

Randolph had picked up a letter from the posting tray and was gazing at it while he slowly lowered his own letters into the tray. His eyes lifted to Constance, who was walking up to him.

Before she could speak, he said clearly, "Why are you writing to the house of a notorious courtesan?"

CHAPTER THIRTEEN

U H-OH. SOLOMON'S CHIVALRIC urge to rescue her took him by surprise. Yet he waited, curious to see what she would do or say, and well aware she was used to looking after herself.

She had gone very still. "If I am writing to anyone, it must be because I have something to say. Though I fail to see that my correspondence is any business of yours."

Randolph waved the letter almost in her face. "This is your handwriting. You cannot deny it."

"I haven't." She held out her hand. "My letter, if you please. Since you are making such a fuss, I shall post it myself."

Randolph twitched it out of her reach. Solomon released the newel post and strolled toward them.

"Why?" Randolph asked tightly. "Who are you, Constance? *What* are you?"

"Aren't you making something of an assumption?" Solomon said quietly. "For instance, Mrs. Goldrich and I might wonder how it is you recognize the address of—er…a notorious courtesan. We would not mention such a thing, of course, since that would be rude." Casually, he removed the letter from Randolph's apparently nerveless fingers and presented it to Constance.

Randolph flushed hotly. "I have never—"

"Mrs. Goldrich does not question *your* charities," Solomon interrupted.

Constance cast him a glance of considerable respect, which for some reason meant more to him than the knowledge that he was not being strictly honest. Damn the woman, she was a bad influence on him.

The sound of the baize door to the servants' quarters seemed to remind Randolph the conversation could be overheard. He stepped back from Constance, and they all glanced down the hallway. Richards made his stately way toward the study and entered without knocking.

"Wretched policemen," Randolph muttered. "What do they want with Richards? They're disrupting the whole running of the house. This is too hard on my mother. Does she not have enough to bear?"

"I think you all do," Constance said with unexpected kindness. She even touched Randolph's arm in quick sympathy. "But you need to know, don't you?"

He met her gaze in silence. He looked suddenly very young, very lost. "I'm not sure I want to. Nothing will ever be the same."

The boy was having to grow up, not before time, perhaps, but before he was ready. Solomon could not imagine his doing this to himself, even in a fit of rage. And the stealing of the knife rather pointed away from rage to planning.

"Why the kitchen knife?" Solomon said aloud.

A spasm crossed Randolph's face, but he was listening. So was Constance.

"There must surely be better weapons in the house. Shotguns? Pistols? Hunting knives?"

Randolph nodded. "All these things. And antique swords. My father collected them at one time. Whoever did it was obviously trying to cast the blame upon the servants, though it didn't work."

"Actually," Constance said in an odd voice, "I think it did."

Solomon followed her gaze. Harris and Flynn had both emerged from the study, and between them, pale and shocked, walked Richards. Flynn took his arm as though to prevent his bolting.

"What the *hell*?" Randolph muttered beneath his breath. He

was already striding down the hall, Solomon and Constance at his heels. "Inspector! What are you doing?"

"I've arrested Richards on suspicion of the murder of your father," Harris said calmly. He did not even slow down in his march toward the green baize door.

"You can't!" Randolph exploded, following. "It's preposterous! Richards has been with us for a decade!"

"I am aware of that, sir. And it's possible further investigation will prove his innocence, but for now, everything points to him. My sergeant has suggested locking him in his pantry, meantime." The inspector pushed open the heavy door to the servants' quarters and held it for Flynn and the white-faced Richards to pass through.

In the kitchen, something like a copper pot fell to the floor, and the voice of Mrs. Corben the cook could be heard scolding. Flynn paused on the half landing beside a closed door Solomon had never noticed in his brief forays below stairs. The door was locked, which was interesting. Harris produced two rings of keys that he had presumably just taken from the butler.

Without a word, Richards pointed to the middle key of the smaller ring. The larger disappeared back into the inspector's pocket while he unlocked the door. The pantry was not large. It contained a few shelves of bottles, others of silver, an upholstered armchair, and a desk—on which were laid out an open book that appeared to be a diary, and several lists.

Randolph bundled in after Richards and the policemen. Sighing, Solomon stood aside to invite Constance to precede him. She did without hesitation, leaving Solomon to squash in after her.

Before he managed to close the door and create a modicum of space to stand in, he was pressed far too close to her. He could smell her skin, some soft, alluring perfume, and grew suddenly aware of just how lovely was her long, vulnerable nape.

He almost fell back against the door. Fortunately, no one was paying him any attention.

"What the devil...?" Harris began irascibly as he glared

around the suddenly full room. "Why are—"

"On what grounds have you charged my butler?" Randolph demanded.

Solomon thought better of him for his defense of the servant, but clearly Harris did not.

"On the grounds that he had access to the knife," he said impatiently, "clear opportunity, and the strongest of motives."

"Utter nonsense! What motive could he possibly have for murdering his master?"

"You really don't know, do you?" Harris said. "He didn't tell anyone. Sergeant Flynn here went to Winsom and Bolton's bank today, and among other things learned about the dismissal of one Harold Framley."

"Framley?" Randolph seemed to struggle for the memory.

"Indeed. Apparently this man swore at your father in the street one day when he was out with his family. He'd been dismissed for fraud."

"I remember," Randolph snapped. "But what has that to do with Richards?"

"They're half-brothers," Harris said with an air of understandable triumph. "Different fathers."

Constance cast a startled glance over her shoulder at Solomon.

"We know," Harris continued, "because Sergeant Flynn here had the gumption to call on the Framley family. After his dismissal, Framley's fall was spectacular. He could not get other work because everyone knew why he'd been dismissed, although he was never charged. He and his family were evicted from their home, and his wife took the children and went back to her mother. Framley took to drink, lived on the streets rather than seek help from the Richardses, and was finally killed when he fell drunk in front of a carriage in January."

It was a harrowing tale, and it silenced the room. Richards himself sat where Flynn had put him, in the hard chair at the desk, his face set, his mouth turned down.

"He was never charged," the butler said hoarsely at last. "It was never proved against him."

Randolph was staring at him as though truly seeing him for the first time. Then he blinked. "It still doesn't make sense. If Richards was so angry about it, why did he never speak before? Surely my father would have listened to so trusted a servant! And why wait so long to take his revenge?"

"Matters we would like explained," Harris said dismissively. "Our investigation is not completed, but…"

Solomon lost the thread at that point because Constance stepped back into him once more. At the same time, she glanced again over her shoulder and twitched her head toward the door in unmistakable command.

Somehow, Solomon reached behind him, opened the door a crack, and slid through with mingled relief and disappointment. Constance flitted past him and almost bounded up the stairs.

He followed quickly, hissing, "What's the rush?"

By way of answering, she lifted one hand and showed him a set of keys he had last seen in the inspector's possession. That silenced him until they were on the other side of the baize door. The parlor maid scurried past them.

"Worth a try, don't you think?" Constance murmured, a wicked gleam in her eye. She walked straight toward the locked door that led to the old wing.

Laughter caught in Solomon's throat. As he caught up with her, he glanced around the hall. Only the footman by the front door was visible, and he was gazing out of the little window beside his desk.

"Old habits dying hard?" he asked. The door was out of the footman's line of vision and, hopefully, of his hearing.

Constance was on to the second key, which didn't work either. "A girl's got to live, though I wouldn't like you to think I picked clients' pockets… Aha. Three was always my lucky number."

The key turned, she lifted the latch, and they both slipped

through the door. Solomon closed it behind him.

WHEN THE INSPECTOR went to explain Richards's arrest to Mrs. Winsom, Sergeant Flynn sat down in the study and took out the ledgers he had removed from the bank. The manager had been most unhappy and only agreed to it because they were copies and because Flynn had promised to tell Mr. Bolton he had them.

He hadn't seen Bolton yet. He wanted a head start, as it were. Flynn understood the basics of bookkeeping—it had helped in many cases of petty theft and fraud. But as he skimmed the many columns of the bank's huge ledger, he found himself literally scratching his head. He wondered if he would ever get his poor brain around this lot. The sheer size of the numbers was off-putting in itself.

He opened the other ledger, hoping this would somehow explain everything. It didn't seem to.

He was almost glad to hear the impetuous footsteps in the hall. He glanced up, and the door flew open to reveal Ellen Winsom.

She was furious, two angry spots of color flushing her cheeks, her eyes fiery. Her beauty took his breath away.

"Where is Inspector Harris?" she demanded as he stumbled to his feet.

"With your mother, I believe."

She seemed about to storm out again, but she hesitated, her fingers twisting the door handle. "Have you really arrested Richards?"

"Yes, miss."

"But why?"

Suddenly all the anger had left her and she resembled nothing so much as a bewildered child. It made her easier to deal with. He explained the butler's motive and his suspicious secrecy.

"Why is it so suspicious?" she asked at once. "Wouldn't you keep quiet if your brother was a thief and a drunk?"

"Perhaps. But you must admit, it requires further investigation."

"While poor Richards is locked in his own pantry? Can't you see what this will do to his authority with the servants?"

Flynn blinked. "If he's guilty, miss, that will be the least of his worries."

"And if he isn't?" she challenged.

He sighed. "Do you really think we can take that risk? What if he attacks other members of your family? Or Mr. Bolton, whom he must see as at least as responsible as your father."

She whitened, sinking slowly into the chair on the other side of his desk. "This is all a nightmare. I keep thinking—praying—I'll wake up. But I don't."

"I'm sorry, miss," he said gently. "I wish this hadn't happened, but I can't change it. I can only—*we* can only—try to catch whoever it was who took your father from you."

"Don't be *kind* to me," she spat, dashing her sleeve across her eyes. "It's so much easier to be angry with you than with—" She broke off, shuddering. She dropped her arm and looked straight at him. Her eyes were beautiful, sparkling with tears. "I'm sorry I was rude to you."

"You weren't, miss," he said gently.

Her eyes fell, clearly landing on the ledgers in front of him. "What are you doing?"

"Trying to make head or tail of the bank's finances."

"Ask Mr. Bolton."

"Limited use, miss," he said carefully.

"Because he is still a suspect, too? Even though you've arrested Richards?"

"We haven't charged Richards yet."

The boldness was back in her eyes. "Then you still suspect me, too?"

He could not prevent the flush rising to his face. He could

think of nothing to say.

Her smile was not childlike at all. "How can you do this work?" she wondered. Her voice contained mostly puzzlement, but it was not free of distaste.

"Because someone has to," he said, a shade more harshly than he meant to.

Without a word, she stood up and left the room.

DAYLIGHT SOMEHOW LEAKED in the boarded windows of the old wing, creating an odd, dappled effect on the walls and the floor. Between that and the two candles that Solomon lit with a match, Constance could see they were in a large, wood-paneled room, empty of all furniture except a bare old sideboard against one wall. A narrow staircase ran up the left-hand side. Flecks of dust danced in the sunshine.

Constance shivered. "I don't like this part of the house either. It should have ghosts, only they've all been scared off. I'll look around down here, if you want to see what's upstairs."

Grey moved away from her side, taking one of the candles, and she immediately wanted to grab his arm and drag him back.

Instead, she forced herself to walk across the room to the sideboard. The shelves were empty of everything except dust. She opened the drawers, felt inside them, then above and beneath them. There was nothing in the cupboard either, or on the floor underneath so far as she could see. She stood up again and wandered toward the fireplace. She wasn't quite sure what she was looking for, except some reason for Richards to come here.

She felt along the high mantelshelf, then peered rather warily up the chimney. She was reluctant to put her hand up in case it dislodged a deluge of old soot and rubble. *Last resort,* she decided, and turned toward the stairs.

It struck her that Richards might have crept in to watch Walter making love to his mistress—some men liked that sort of thing—but then, why had he come this morning? To cover up some peephole he had made? She could not quite imagine the dignified butler in such a situation, but she had been surprised before. Nor could she really see him plunging a knife into his master's back, even for his brother.

As she neared the top of the stairs, a shadow fell over her and she almost cried out. It was Grey, emerging from the door at the top of the stairs. Weak with relief, she looked beyond him and said, "You found the love nest, then? He didn't dismantle it. I wonder if he would hide it to preserve Winsom's reputation, even to spare Deborah some humiliation."

"He does not appear to be so selfless. Nothing downstairs?"

"Not as much as a scrap of paper. Did you look in the dressing table?"

"There's nothing there, apart from what's on the top. Nothing in the bedding or under the mattress, either."

At the end of the landing, another, even narrower stair led upward. Grey went first and she followed, her heart beating foolishly fast.

"The attic might be open to the main part of the house," he murmured.

It wasn't. They saw at once where the passage had been bricked off. Constance was secretly touched when he insisted on sticking his head into the first of the three rooms before standing aside for her to enter and then going to the second himself. She wasn't used to anyone looking out for her, taking care of her... Though perhaps that was exaggeration, more wishful thinking than anything else.

Oddly, this room was full of old furniture. Constance wondered if this were where the love nest furnishings had come from. It meant there were many drawers, cupboards, and shelves to look in. But there was so much dust that she didn't hold out much hope. Everything looked as if it hadn't been disturbed for years.

As they entered the final room together, Constance said, "I wonder Walter wasn't afraid of all this stuff falling through rotting floorboards on top him, especially in the throes of passion."

If she had hoped to embarrass Solomon, she was disappointed. His glance was merely sardonic. "The rot looks to have been just in that one patch where the repair was done. Shutting it off completely seems an overreaction. I would have thought the Winsoms would enjoy having a larger house."

"Perhaps they didn't have the money to renovate as they wished to," Constance mused, lifting the embroidered cover on a wooden cradle. "So they just concentrated on the more gracious part."

"Perhaps."

He brushed past her, large and lithe as a cat. She tried not to look. Not that she needed to—she was so aware of him that she could almost see him on the backs of her eyelids. He opened a wardrobe and reached up to the top shelf.

Constance, finding nothing in the cradle, moved past him to a chest of drawers. Her wide skirts brushed against his legs, but he did not appear to notice.

The top drawer was empty. She began to think there was nothing to find. Perhaps they should just be looking for a peephole after all. She opened the second drawer down, already preparing to close it again before she registered that it was not empty.

A bundle of cloth lay in the middle of it, scrunched up like a ball.

When she reached out and touched it, something pricked her finger.

"Solomon," she said huskily, unraveling the cloth with both hands. It wasn't scrunched at all, just carefully wrapped around several objects. A glittering diamond hairpin. One lady's silk stocking. Two perfume bottles, one square and masculine in style, the other curved and prettily decorated.

Solomon stood behind her, leaning over her shoulder.

Her mouth felt dry. "A bizarre little hoard," she managed. "Richardson's?"

She glanced over her shoulder and couldn't breathe. He wasn't looking at the "treasure" but at her face. His eyes were so profound that she felt she was drowning, and God, they were beautiful enough that you wanted to. She had never found a man's face to be beautiful before, but his was.

She licked her dry lips, and he looked deliberately downward at her find.

"Probably," he said. "Why else would he have come this morning?"

"True, but why didn't he take it away with him when he had the chance? He saw me on the floor below."

He shrugged, still so close that she felt even that slight movement reverberate through her whole body. "He thought he had frightened you off."

"I might have told Randolph or his sisters about his behavior."

"In the midst of all this...grief? I think he knew you would not. It doesn't seem to have entered his head that you would tell me, let alone come back."

With an effort, she forced herself to turn back to the "treasure." Her heart was beating like a captured bird's. He reached past her, his arm touching hers as he spread out the items on the cloth.

"Apart from the diamond pin, none of this can have much value," he observed. "Do you suppose Alice Bolton's handkerchief once resided here too?"

She moved slightly further away from him, just so she could think. "You mean he killed Walter and planted the handkerchief to cast the blame on her? What a...horrible thought. Why her? Why not Mrs. Winsom? I'm sure that must be her pin."

"A husband might easily carry something of his wife's. It wouldn't necessarily have the same meaning as clasping someone else's handkerchief."

Constance frowned. "He wanted everyone to know about the affair, as well as blaming her for the murder…"

"Maybe." He picked up the square bottle and pulled out the stopper. After a quick sniff and a grimace, he passed it to her.

"Walter's cologne," she said without doubt, taking the top from his slender fingers and re-stoppering the bottle.

He passed her the other. "Mrs. Winsom?"

"Alice," she said, frowning. Something bothered her about that, only she couldn't think what. "How did Deborah discover the affair? Alice said she knew, but how? She can't ever have come here, or the love nest would have been dismantled."

"Does it matter?" he asked.

"Probably not, but what is Richards doing with all this stuff? Was he deciding whom to murder and whom to blame, giving himself a few options?"

"Why don't we ask him?"

Constance met his gaze. "Inspector Harris wouldn't like it. And I stole the wrong set of keys."

"Can you give them back as easily?"

"Don't you think I should own up?"

"It depends how often you intend to do it."

"You are a surprising man, Mr. Grey."

"I thought I was Solomon."

Good God, was she blushing? "A slip of the tongue. I would hate to oblige you to call me Constance."

"Why?"

"You would not be comfortable."

"Would I not, Constance? How well do you imagine you know me?"

"How well do you imagine you know *me*?" she countered.

His rare smile dawned, weakening her knees all over again. "Not as well as I would like. But we seem to have gone beyond the formalities. Shall we get out of here with our treasure?"

She had almost forgotten she disliked the place.

CHAPTER FOURTEEN

T HERE WERE MANY areas of Miriam Albright's life that she did not like to think about. Her marriage was one of them. The murder of her father was most certainly another, which was why she kept herself almost feverishly busy.

She had taken on herself the running of the house, writing the death notifications—with occasional help from Ellen—and such other arrangements as could be made without her knowing when her father's body would be released to them. On top of that, she insisted on keeping up much of Peter's correspondence, which was what she was doing after tea when he found her yet again at the morning room desk.

He seemed slightly shocked by her activity, always tried to make her rest more, talk to her about God's will, and her own grief. Miriam bore these as patiently as she could and avoided them when at all possible.

"My dear, you will exhaust yourself," he said now, with the sort of anxious kindness that grated on her nerves. "There is nothing we can do about the arrest of Richards, except pray. Of course, the servants are upset, but I think you must let Mrs. Farrow deal with that. I myself will speak to them and lead them in prayer this evening."

She gave him a distracted smile. It was the best she could do, for she could feel the anger welling up in her again. She stood abruptly "I do not believe Richards did this."

"We must allow the police to know their own business."

"Must we? Would you say the same if they arrested me?"

For an instant, he looked startled, then his face smoothed. It seemed a long time since she had last wondered what he truly thought, which added to her guilt.

"Why would they be so foolish?" he said lightly.

She stood abruptly, striding to the window, then wishing she had gone to the door instead. The view from the window was too familiar to distract her for long, and her husband was still talking.

"I understand your distress. Richards has been with your family a number of years, but you cannot choose whoever you would prefer to be guilty."

"I am aware of that," she said stiffly. She heard him come closer and steeled herself. She knew he was trying and floundering in his attempts to ease her pain. He did not seem to understand that nothing could, and that annoyed her too.

"Such a terrible thing," he went on tritely, "but if it was truly one of the household who committed the crime, it is better it should be a servant than—"

"Than one of *us*?" she said harshly, spinning around to face him. "You think the scandal might be less this way, that we can somehow rise above it, and you will still be a bishop in five or six years?"

She knew she maligned him, and he looked so shocked by the accusation that it fed her guilt, and the guilt fed her fury.

"Does the truth not matter to us? Only what people perceive?"

For once, he did not trouble to hide his hurt. The mask of superiority and control slipped from his face, leaving it anguished. "Is that what you truly think of me, Miriam? That I am so consumed with ambition? Of course I would like to be a bishop, even an archbishop. I could do more good with such authority. I thought you understood that."

She closed her eyes against his pain. God, she had to deal with that too. Was there no end to this?

"Why don't you trust me?" he asked, his voice so sad, so

bewildered, that she opened her eyes again in sheer surprise.

Impulsively, she grasped his shoulder. "I do. I do. It's just..." Her fingers dug into his shoulder so hard it must have hurt. She gasped. "Oh, Peter, I have been so *angry!*"

He put his arms around her. She tried to pull away, but for once he was not tentative. He held her, hugged her. "Angry about your father's death?"

"About my father! I *saw* him, Peter. With her, in the garden, by the swing, embracing. How could he do that to Mama? To us? I hated him. Part of me still hates him, still rages! Even in death he hurts us, and God punishes us."

For once, he did not speak, did not lecture, only held her, stroking her hair, and for some reason a small stream of comfort began to trickle in. In truth, her anger had begun before her mother had told her about Papa's affair with Alice Bolton. She had been angry about marrying Peter to please him, angry with Peter for being her husband, with herself for allowing it.

Yet now she let herself feel the comfort of Peter's arms and recognized not just that he was a good man, but one who cared for her, loved her, as she did not deserve. She remembered she had liked him before their marriage. They had been friends.

Abruptly, she slid her arms around his neck, wondering if there were not after all many routes to love. And safety.

A knock sounded at the half-open door. She expected Peter to spring away from her to retain his dignity, but he merely raised his head from hers. "Yes?"

It was she who moved away, for it was Constance Goldrich who entered the room.

Miriam did not trust her. She was too beautiful, too self-assured, too confident in her handling of poor Randolph, who was so utterly besotted. Or had been. Why had she even come to Greenforth?

"Excuse me for interrupting," she said. "And please excuse me for what I am about to ask you."

"If it needs to be excused," Peter said, "perhaps it should not be spoken."

"Perhaps," Mrs. Goldrich said, "but the thing is, I think we all need to get to the truth of your father's death, particularly now they have arrested Richards."

Miriam frowned at her. "What is this to you, Mrs. Goldrich? Why do you keep interfering? It is the duty of the police to investigate, however unpleasant."

"Oh, I like to help," Mrs. Goldrich said vaguely. She twitched one side of her mouth into a self-deprecating smile. "And to own the truth, I would like to go home. The quicker we discover who killed your father, the quicker I am out of your hair. So please, help me reach the truth."

So she didn't believe Richards did it either. For her own reasons, Miriam needed to know why.

She waved her hand to one of the armchairs. "Please, sit."

Mrs. Goldrich sat with her perfect grace. Miriam wondered if she had studied to achieve it, and what Mr. Goldrich had thought of her.

"What is it you want to ask?"

"A delicate matter," said Mrs. Goldrich. "I think perhaps you were aware of your father's infidelity."

"One might ask how you think *you* are aware of it?" Peter said coldly.

"Because I have spoken to Mrs. Bolton," she said. "I am not here to cause trouble or gossip, let alone to judge. I just need to know how it was you knew, Mrs. Albright."

Miriam looked her in the eye. "My mother told me. Somewhat obliquely, but she told me nevertheless. She was too upset to keep it to herself, and she could hardly talk to Ellen about such things."

The woman nodded, then immediately asked, "And how and when did your mother find out?"

Interesting that Miriam could still feel something more than anger. Perhaps that had lessened slightly, thanks to Peter, and let in other emotions. The family had nothing more to lose, scandal-wise.

"Last month," Miriam said. "My mother was looking at the guest bedrooms after the Boltons had been visiting, thinking about the planning of this party. In one room, she found Mrs. Bolton's earring caught on a sheet. And she smelled my father's cologne on the pillow."

"A guest bedroom," Mrs. Goldrich repeated. "Which one?"

"The one now occupied by Mr. Davidson. Why? How is it important?"

"I'm not quite sure," Mrs. Goldrich admitted. "But I think it is." She rose. "Thank you, Mrs. Albright. Mr. Albright."

When she had left, Peter looked thoughtful. "I cannot quite make up my mind about that lady."

"Neither can I. Perhaps she will be good for Randolph after all."

CONSTANCE, MEANWHILE, WENT straight to her own room and seized the "treasure," which she had wrapped in a shawl of her own, and went in search of Mr. Grey. *Solomon.* She smiled for no reason as she moved from room to room and eventually found him playing billiards with Ivor Davidson.

Both gentlemen had their coats off. Solomon was walking around the table, cue in hand. He spared her only the briefest glance, but inclined his head as if he understood the presence of the shawl in her arms.

"Mrs. Goldrich," Davidson greeted her. "I challenge you to a game."

Constance had already made her own assessment of the game, which was almost over. "You can't expect me to play anyone but the winner. In any case, I suspect we shouldn't really be playing at all in a house of mourning."

Davidson kept his eyes on the table. "Special circumstances, I think you'll agree."

Solomon leaned across the table and struck his cue against the white ball, which cannoned across the table and knocked one of the two remaining red balls into the corner pocket. He straightened, walked past Davidson, and quite casually potted the final ball.

"Drat you, Grey—this speaks of a misspent youth," Davidson said. "Revenge, if you please."

"Only if Mrs. Goldrich does not defeat me, though I fear she will."

Davidson sighed and replaced his cue in the stand. "Then I shall seek some other amusement for half an hour." He picked up his coat, bowed, and sauntered out.

"I take it you don't want to play?" Solomon said, reaching for his own coat.

"No. It's time we took this"—she lifted the shawl bundle slightly—"to Harris. And to Richards. Deborah didn't find the love nest in the old wing. She was led to believe they used a spare bedroom—now Mr. Davidson's, in fact—by discovering an earring in the bed there. And a pillow smelling of her husband's cologne. Miriam told me."

Solomon paused, one arm in his coat, and looked at her. "They might have used both places to meet."

"Why risk it? Besides…I don't think Walter would have hurt Deborah in that particular way. The old wing is almost separate, as if he could think of it as not his wife's roof."

Solomon shrugged into his coat. "Could Miriam be lying?"

"I don't think so, though it's hard to tell. She is very…suppressed."

"What do you suppose she is suppressing?"

"Anger," Constance said. "She's angry about something."

"About her father's affair? Angry enough to give him away to her mother? You think she, not Richards, took and hid these things? And Alice's earring?"

"Maybe. Let's see what Richards says. He was still skulking

there." Constance walked toward the door, but Solomon stood where he was.

"Do you think she could have killed her father?"

"I'm beginning to think she could," Constance said.

Solomon moved forward at last, and they hurried to the study. Neither of the policemen were there. Constance went in and dropped the purloined keys on the floor behind the desk, ignoring Solomon's sardonic smile from the doorway.

"You don't suppose they've gone back to the inn for the night?" she said. "Or taken Richards off to jail?"

"Let's see." They went on to the green baize door, where they almost collided with a footman. He muttered a hasty apology and hurried on to the dining room. Whatever the upheavals, the business of feeding the family and their guests went on.

Voices came from the door on the landing, low and intense, and then Richards's, high with stress. "I don't care what you think! I know I didn't kill him!"

Solomon's eyebrows arched as he glanced at Constance. Then he pushed open the door to the pantry, and she sailed in, Solomon at her heels.

Richards, seated at his desk, stared at them without comprehension. He looked like a man in a nightmare from which he couldn't wake. The two policemen stood opposite him, Harris upright, Flynn leaning negligently back against the shelves.

The inspector glowered. "This is beyond a joke. You are both facing a charge of interference in police—"

"We found something, inspector," Solomon said, "which may be of interest to you. To all of you," he added, as Constance plonked her bundle on the desk in front of Richards. As she untied the shawl, she saw the precise moment when Richards's expression changed.

He recognized his own cloth wrapping, knew what was inside. His already pale, strained face whitened to his lips.

Not Miriam, then, Constance thought. *It was Richards after all.*

"We found these things in the old wing of the house that is shut off," Solomon told Harris. "Where Mrs. Goldrich encountered Richards this morning."

"You took these things, didn't you?" Constance said quietly to the butler, while Harris fingered the items, frowning direly.

"No!" Richards said desperately. "I've never seen them before in my—"

"Richards." Constance cut him off with one quiet word. "Your one chance now is to tell the truth. All of it."

"And be hanged?" he whispered.

"You'll be hanged if you don't," Harris growled. "That is a fact."

Without moving a muscle, Richards seemed to slump.

"Did you take these things?" Flynn asked him.

Richards nodded dully.

"Why?" Harris demanded.

"To sow discord among the Winsoms and the Boltons," Richards said.

"So you did blame them for your brother's fall?" Harris said.

"They *were* to blame for my brother's fall. At the very best, they let it happen when he had worked for them all his adult life. Turned their backs, without a word to him or even to me. My brother was not a thief—he was as honest as the day is long."

"And that made you angry," Flynn said.

Constance knew they had had this discussion before, probably many times. Richards nodded wearily. Perhaps admitting it for the first time.

"Very angry. After he died, I wanted—I *needed* to punish them. So I made it my business to pick up bits and pieces from both families."

"With the aim of discrediting them," Flynn said.

Again, Richards nodded. "And to show them how easy it was to lay a trail, false or otherwise, for other people to see. Mr. Winsom thought his son had stolen coins from him and lied. That was the true cause of their quarrel. Mr. Winsom was angry and disappointed, Mr. Randolph hurt and offended. They barely spoke, and that hurt Mrs. Winsom."

"But you took the coins," Harris guessed.

Richards nodded. "I didn't steal them," he added quickly. "I put them back in the petty cash for paying tradesmen."

A frown tugged Solomon's brow and vanished again. He was right. There was something oddly honest in the butler's insistence on his own honor.

"And Mrs. Bolton's earring," Constance said. "Did you take that too? Along with these perfume bottles?"

"I spilt perfume on the sheets of one of the spare beds, his cologne on the pillow. And I dropped the earring between the sheets."

"To make Mrs. Winsom believe the worst of her husband?" Harris said with distaste.

"Oh, that wasn't his worst," Richards said savagely. "He was *never* faithful to her. But I had no objection to ruining the outward happiness of his marriage, and I knew she'd never go into the old wing and discover him that way."

"Was that not unnecessarily unkind to Mrs. Winsom?" Solomon asked.

Constance blinked. He was full of surprises, was Solomon Grey.

"Unnecessarily? She stood by, did nothing when my brother was accused, even though she'd known him since her marriage."

"Did Mr. and Mrs. Winsom not know you were Framley's brother?" Solomon asked.

"Of course they did! It was why they took me on, because of my brother! Afterward, they seemed to think they were very magnanimous, doing me a special kindness by keeping me on when they had dismissed him without notice or character."

"So you punished them in your own way," Flynn said, understanding, even sympathy, creeping into his voice.

Richards grimaced. "In very small ways."

"So when did these small punishments progress to murder?"

Flynn asked.

Richards's gaze flew to his face. "They didn't!" he said.

"Of course they did," Harris said contemptuously. "You even tried to cast the blame for the murder on Mrs. Bolton. It was you who put her handkerchief in his hand, wasn't it?"

Richards closed his eyes. He nodded, his mouth curving down in misery. "I had it in my pocket. I'd been going to leave it in the mistress's bed that evening, only I never got the chance. So when my duties were done, I went outside instead to see who was creeping around—I knew someone was. I almost fell over his body. I couldn't quite believe it. I wasn't the only one who hated him."

"You're telling us he was already dead when you just happened to fall over him?" Harris said sarcastically. "It must have been like Piccadilly Circus in that part of the garden."

"Busier than you know," Richards retorted with a spurt of anger. "I heard someone else coming—two people, in fact, judging by the whispering. So I stuffed Mrs. Bolton's handkerchief into Mr. Winsom's hand and bolted. It was my last chance to discredit him in public, and had the added bonus of hurting both the Boltons at the same time."

"You wanted her to hang for a murder she hadn't committed?" Solomon said.

Richards smiled tiredly. "Frankly, yes. At best, I didn't care. My brother died in disgrace too, didn't he? And you needn't look so righteous either, Mr. Grey. It was you and her I saw creeping around when I ran off."

"Indeed?" Harris said with blatant disbelief. "And you imagine that is a more believable story than the denials you've given us before?"

"It's the truth," Richards said defiantly.

"You were at the scene by your own admission," Flynn pointed out.

"But he was already dead," Richards insisted. "And I had no reason to kill him when he was already suffering, had I? Can't you see that? Why would I bother with all this"—he waved his hand at the purloined items on the desk—"if I meant to stick a knife in his back?"

"Are you sorry he's dead?" Harris asked, switching tack.

Richards drew a shuddering breath. He glanced at Constance, then away again. "Truthfully, no, I'm not. I'd never have forgiven him for what he did. But neither would I stick a knife in his back and give them something to hang me for."

He had a point, Constance reflected. Why would he continue with the petty punishments if he simply meant to do away with the man?

"Did Winsom find you out?" Solomon asked.

"Him?" Richards scoffed. "He never looked further than himself."

Solomon glanced at Constance. He didn't think Richards was the killer. Constance didn't think so either. They both looked at Harris.

"I don't think it was Richards," Solomon said. "The body wasn't quite that newly dead."

"You an expert on the newly dead and those who've been dead five or ten minutes?" Harris growled.

"I've had cause to notice. But more than that, we'd surely have heard something, even the thud of his body falling. We didn't. And besides, he's right. The other punishment makes no sense if he planned to kill Walter anyway."

"You could have done both," Harris said to the butler. "I don't put it past you. But for the moment, I won't charge you. You can go back to your duties."

Richards laughed shakily. "Oh, I think I've just effectively resigned, don't you? Better than dismissal, of course."

Harris curled his lip. "You might even threaten a character out of them with what you know. And if I get even a whiff of that, you're clapped up again before you can turn round."

"Well," Constance said brightly, "back to the beginning. If it wasn't Richards, who *did* kill him? Who do you think it was,

Richards?"

"Mrs. Bolton," the butler said without the slightest hesitation. "Why do you think I left her handkerchief?"

"You've just told us it was to incriminate her," Solomon said. "Because her husband was equally responsible for your brother's dismissal."

Richards shifted impatiently. "More than that. I know she seems cold and haughty, but she isn't. She's clever and controlling and she's always been besotted with him, with Mr. Winsom. Believe me, she's too proud to take rejection well, and I know he ended their affair that evening. She killed him."

"WHAT DO YOU think?" Constance asked Solomon as they returned to the main part of the house. Without either of them suggesting it, they both turned toward the side door. "Is Richards right about Alice Bolton?"

"I don't know. He still has the best motive out of everyone, and he has a history of trying to blame others for things they didn't necessarily do."

Constance pounced. "Does he, though?"

Solomon opened the door, and she sailed through, impatient to talk without being overheard. Randolph was striding down the path from the stables, so she turned toward the garden instead. No one else was around at this time, since the gardener had finished for the day and the household would be changing for dinner. Even in a crisis like this, formalities were rigidly observed. They seemed to be all that held these people together.

"Does he blame others falsely?" Solomon said. "He admitted it."

"No, his proof might have been false, but his accusations weren't. Alice and Walter *were* having an affair. And he believes she killed him."

"Randolph didn't steal the coins."

"No, but it could be argued he is living off his father and contributing nothing. Not uncommon among the upper classes, where work is a dirty word, but among normal people, it is not admired."

Solomon cast her a curious glance. "And Walter worked for the money they all lived off. You see Richards as some kind of moral arbiter?"

"Hardly. But he has his own code. You saw that, too. I don't think he's a murderer, just an angry, grieving, misguided man."

"A generous interpretation. So you believe his accusation against Alice Bolton?"

"Emotions run high when people are intimate. What may begin as casual, transactional, need not remain that way for either party. And I think she loved Walter for years before their affair began."

"Servants do see a different side of people," he allowed. "They can bear the brunt of bad moods and ill nature and see private moments because their masters get so used to their presence that they are not noticed."

"Exactly. I could imagine Alice hurt and humiliated, angry to have her excitement, her joy in life taken away. Beside Walter, her husband is a somewhat…colorless man."

"Do you find him so?" Solomon sounded surprised.

"Don't you?"

"No, but then, I prefer subtle people."

Her insides twisted. *I have to stop taking his every remark as personal.*

"We're no nearer a solution, are we?" she said lightly. "It could still be any of them. They all have a motive of some kind, and the garden seems to have been so full of people around the time of his death that I'm surprised we didn't fall over each other."

CHAPTER FIFTEEN

C OMING BACK FROM the kennels, Randolph saw Constance emerge from the side door. His heart lifted because she looked so lovely in the late afternoon sunshine, hatless and carefree. The troubles weighing him down began to lift at the very sight of her, even though he had twice now offended her by saying the wrong thing or asking the wrong questions.

He had recognized her handwriting on the letter earlier that day. He should never have looked, let alone admitted it, but the address had shocked him.

Not that he had ever been to Constance Silver's discreet establishment in Mayfair. It was as difficult to get into as the most exclusive London club. But a friend had once promised to get him a card, and described the wonders of her salons and her girls. Randolph had been undeniably shocked that his Mrs. Goldrich should be writing to someone there. And then came the stunning realization of the same Christian name. Constance Silver. Constance Goldrich. It had felt like a connection, and he had blurted something stupid and offensive that allowed Grey to tell him off in front of her.

Now, at least, he had the opportunity to apologize and make everything right again... Only Grey was behind her again. Irritation threatened to surge into anger, especially when he was sure she saw him and yet turned away toward the formal garden, apparently deep in conversation with Grey.

What is he to her? She is my *guest, in* my *house.* There was an insidious, guilty pleasure in those words. *My house. My bank.*

He strode into his house, seething.

Mrs. Goldrich had once seemed so immeasurably out of his reach that he had been amazed she actually accepted his invitation to Greenforth. Now at least he was a man of substance. And yet she had hardly paid him any attention since she had arrived, preferring the company of his father, his sister, even Davidson, and now Solomon Grey.

Wealth-wise, of course, Grey was in a different class. But was he even a gentleman? Randolph had never met him during the Season, nor at any of his clubs. He only knew the man's name through overheard business conversations. Surely Constance would not be influenced by mere wealth?

Perhaps they shared charitable interests in reforming prostitutes and drinkers. His mother had met him on some charitable board and invited him because of that and his connection to Jamaica. No doubt they also shared membership of the anti-slavery societies that still existed after abolition in British territories in order to end the practice in the rest of the world.

Constance's interests were clearly wide, and yet they did not appear to include Randolph. She treated him like a boy. In fact, he realized now she always had. Resentment and outrage boiled up inside him, not least because he suspected she might be right.

What had he ever done in his twenty years?

He was only wealthy now because his father was dead.

My father is dead. The knowledge swept over him in great waves of guilt and grief and exultation.

In the hall, he met Richards coming the other way and almost passed him without acknowledgment. Before he recalled the man had been locked up in his pantry by the police.

He halted abruptly. "Richards. They let you go, then?"

The butler inclined his head, almost his old, haughty self. "Indeed, sir."

"Good thing," Randolph said gruffly. "Bloody idiots. Don't know what they were thinking of to arrest you in the first place.

Where are they?"

"The policemen, sir? I believe they have returned to the inn for the night."

Randolph nodded and carried on his way to the staircase to change for dinner. Constance was still at the forefront of his mind, though, preventing him from calling in on his mother, as he had intended. He changed quickly, admired his dramatic good looks in the glass, and twitched his necktie to make it perfect. Then he hurried down to the drawing room early, in the hope that Constance would do the same, or at least that he could corner her as soon as she arrived.

He poured himself a large brandy and sat down on the sofa, brooding. In a certain light, he could imagine Constance had been avoiding him since she got here. He had put it down to winning his parents' approval, but other possibilities reared their ugly heads.

He was actually startled when she walked into the room in her burgundy evening gown, a necklace of jet around her throat emphasizing both its slenderness and the creaminess of her skin. If she were surprised to see him down so early, she didn't show it. Nor did she bolt under some pretense, as he almost expected.

"Randolph," she greeted him as he sprang to his feet. "How are you?"

"Apologetic," he said ruefully. "Again. May I fetch you a glass of sherry?"

"Thank you."

However, since Richards came in just then, Randolph left him to do the fetching, while he gestured for Constance to sit beside him. Unexpectedly, she did. It struck him that she did not seem surprised to see Richards back about his duties. Word spread quickly. There had been a certain air of relief among the guests after Richards's arrest. Randolph supposed the tension would be back in full once more.

He took the glass from Richards's tray and presented it to Constance himself before sitting down beside her. Richards bowed and departed, no doubt to inspect the dining table.

"What are you apologetic about?" she asked lightly.

"My rudeness over your letter. I offended against your privacy and your good name. I didn't truly mean to do either. The words just came blurting out."

"You are under a lot of strain," she said, patting his sleeve. "Think nothing of it."

"I am ashamed that I gave Grey cause to defend you when that honor should be mine."

"Nonsense," she said. Her eyes betrayed amusement that began to rile him all over again. "If my honor ever needs defending, I shall do it myself."

"You are very independent."

"I have had to be."

"Being a widow," he said, slightly ashamed of himself. "Are we friends, Constance?"

"Of course we are." Her voice was friendly, though entirely lacking the special warmth he longed for. "Although I feel you should call me Mrs. Goldrich."

It felt like a red rag to a bull. "Why did you come here, *Mrs. Goldrich?*" he demanded. "Why did you accept my invitation to my parents' house on such a short acquaintance? It was not because you liked me, was it?"

She met his gaze, her own as alluringly mysterious as ever. He doubted she could help that, but there was also a pride in her eyes that told him she would not answer.

"Did you use me in order to meet someone else?" he asked. "Grey? My father?"

Her lips quirked. "The latter." She twisted the stem of her glass in her fingers, then said abruptly, "There are enough secrets in this house, so I shall tell you the truth and let you do what you will with it. I accepted your invitation because I thought you might be my brother."

His mouth fell open. "Your *brother?*" he said with horror.

"My mother was abandoned by a gentleman. I thought I

might have discovered his identity."

Randolph felt numb. "Had you?"

"I don't know. He died before I could ask him."

Other people came into the room then. Constance rose and moved away, and very soon he was walking into dinner with his mother on his arm, patting her hand in a soothing, inattentive kind of way.

Hurt and furious, he could not bear to look at Constance. Though it did strike him, savagely, that revenge for her abandoned mother made an excellent motive for murder. A word to the police inspector and…

He who laughed last laughed longest. He could have the perfect revenge *and* get rid of the police and their insolent, upsetting questions, thus killing two birds rather neatly with one stone.

DINNER WAS EATEN that evening largely in silence, as though since Richards's arrest and release they were now afraid to say anything at all about the murder or the police, and yet those things were clearly at the front of everyone's minds.

From time to time, Solomon observed each of his fellow diners. Posture tense, faces bleak or falsely smiling, they made brief remarks about the weather or the food and ate quickly in order to get away as soon as possible.

Miriam and Ellen tried to persuade their mother to eat, but she mostly shuffled her knife and fork around her plate and left the contents. Solomon watched her, her drooping shoulders and almost blank expression. He found it interesting that no one was seriously considering the widow as a suspect, although arguably she had been hurt more than Alice Bolton by Walter's infidelity. Exactly how hurt, how humiliated, he still could not tell. She had not shunned Alice, but then, this was probably not the first time her husband had strayed. Could she have finally had enough with this double betrayal and lashed out?

In her own way, she had been fighting back. She had decided to flirt with Solomon to make her husband jealous, which had made her feel guilty when Walter died. But her sense of guilt could be over something else. She could even be planning to punish Alice in some similar fashion, although her listlessness argued against it. She would have to be a very clever actress.

Alice was more obviously strong, physically and mentally. And then there was Miriam, devoted to her mother, who had known about her father's infidelity and perhaps resented being pushed into her own loveless marriage. Ellen, restless and distracted, probably had the strength but not the character to plan so dispassionately as to take the knife in advance.

Had a woman really planned and carried out so violent an attack? Solomon did not look at Constance, but he had never seriously considered her as the murderer. And yet if one put a madam beside these respectable and respected women, which was the likeliest culprit in the eyes of the world?

Randolph glanced in her direction. Solomon did not quite like his expression, which looked more speculative than besotted. Was he beginning to suspect Constance was not who she claimed to be? Would they all demand her arrest? Not that Harris seemed a man to be bullied...

He realized the women were leaving, and hastily stood up. Richards placed the decanters and fresh glasses on the table. Solomon had given up hoping to learn anything in such gatherings, and indeed, no one had anything to say. The post-prandial drink was quick and perfunctory, the trip to the drawing room merely to say goodnight. No one wanted to talk to anyone else. No one trusted anyone else.

Did the Boltons trust each other? Did the Albrights? If not, it was a long time to be shut up in a room alone together...

Constance walked past him, her skirts brushing against his leg.

"Goodnight, Mrs. Goldrich," he said civilly.

She inclined her head in return, and he knew from that brief meeting of eyes that she wanted to talk to him.

Accordingly, when his goodnights were said, he walked across to the library, openly in search of a book to read. He left the door open, assuming she would join him when she could do so discreetly. However, while he wandered around the shelves, footsteps and voices faded to quiet. Davidson glanced in, said goodnight, and moved away.

The hall lights were dimmed to almost nothing. Giving up, Solomon seized a book at random and walked out. A light shone from under the billiard room door.

Drat the woman—how was he expected to guess she would go there? He moved silently across the hall and along the short passage. Voices drifted from the billiard room, but neither of them belonged to Constance.

Suddenly much more alert, Solomon stepped nearer.

"You see my problem?"

At first, Solomon could not recognize this rather stiff voice, though at once he knew the man who replied.

"I do, Peter, I do," Thomas Bolton said sympathetically. "You spent the money before you had it in your hand, and a vicar in debt is not a reputation you want."

Peter Albright, then. In debt? That was something Solomon had never considered.

"The vicarage is charming, of course," Albright said, some of the stiffness fading from his manner, "but it was not great for entertaining on any scale. Mr. Winsom saw that at once and gladly lent me the money to make improvements. We went a little too far, and he was glad to lend the rest to cover the expense, only he died before he could."

"If the work is only just completed, then you have a little time," Bolton said. "At least—"

"That is the problem," Albright interrupted, all the stiffness back. "It was completed months ago, and he kept forgetting to

MARY LANCASTER

give me the bank draught."

"Forgetting?" Bolton said with undisguised disbelief. "Walter?"

"I cannot otherwise account for it," Albright said coldly.

"Sadly, I can," Bolton said. "He never intended to give you the extra money. I think you know that."

"How dare you, sir? I am not in the habit of lying! Nor was my father-in-law."

"And yet you have said yourself there is no record of this arrangement. I cannot act without it, and nor can Randolph. You must reapply for the extra money in the usual way."

"Sir, I am family! Randolph would never wish his sister to be in such a position!"

"Then you should not have put her there."

A cue bumped against the door, and Solomon quietly retreated before he was discovered. But the odd conversation gave him considerable food for thought.

He lit a candle from the lamp at the foot of the stairs and went up to his room. Apart from the billiard room, the house appeared to be silent. In order to get to his own room, he had to pass the door he knew was Constance's. A light shone beneath it.

The temptation was too great.

He paused, looked back and forth along the passage, then scratched softly at the door. It opened at once, taking him by surprise. The sight of him clearly surprised her too, for he could have sworn even in the flickering candlelight that color suffused her face. Even fully dressed as she was, she could not afford to linger with him in this position, so he stepped forward into the room, causing her to back away.

He closed the door softly behind him, and by the time he turned to face her, she had recovered fully enough to mock him.

"Why, Solomon. You are indeed a man of many surprises."

"No, I'm not," he said. Her room was surprisingly neat and tidy, the bed still made, no clothes left lying about. Even her cloak and bonnet hung on a hook on the door, next to the rather delicious robe he had seen her wearing in the kitchen. He brought his attention back to her face. "You wanted to talk to me."

"I had thought the garden when everyone was asleep."

He blinked. "Because that turned out so well the first time?"

"Someone had to find the body. And now I'm already on thin ice. If you're found here—"

"On thin ice how?" he interrupted.

"I had to tell Randolph why I came to Greenforth."

"Does he know?"

"My name? I expect it won't take him long to work it out. You might find me gone at any time." She frowned, which somehow never marred her looks. "It is inevitable, of course, but I am loath not to finish this."

"Whatever their outrage, I can't see Harris letting you go until it *is* finished."

"There is that." She lifted her chin. "Will you still speak to me, Solomon Grey, once I am exposed as the notorious Constance Silver?"

"Yes. I'll go to the garden and wait for you."

She reached to stop him, then dropped her hand without touching him. He found himself curiously disappointed. He liked her to take his arm, pat his hand, even in jest. "You're here now. Any fresh information, or insights to offer? What should be our next move?"

She sat down sideways at her desk, casual and graceful, leaving the nearby armchair for him.

He sat, trying not to see the bed at the corner of his vision and to concentrate on the ideas that had been spinning around his head.

"Peter Albright borrowed money from Walter to extend his vicarage. Apparently he was promised more and did not receive it. As a result, he is now in debt. From what I overheard, Walter kept putting Albright off. Either that or Albright is trying to pull the wool over Bolton's eyes—which is what Bolton clearly thinks, because he's refusing to do anything about it or treat him any differently to any other customer of the bank. He is a harder man than he looks."

Constance nodded, accepting that. "And you think that is a motive for Albright to kill his father-in-law? Shouldn't he have got the money out of him first?"

"Not if Miriam inherits a good enough sum. But there's more to it than that. What if the bank isn't really doing as well as everyone thinks?"

"You said you had looked into it," she reminded him.

"I asked around. It's not exactly the same as auditing their books."

"Do you think they need it?"

"Think about it. Wouldn't a proud and doting papa simply *give* the money to his daughter? Why make it a loan? And why not bail her out when she needs it? Then this business of the bank fraud—they didn't charge Framley. Maybe that *was* in considera-tion of his family and his previous loyal service, but it *could* have been to save their books from coming under scrutiny. A bank thrives or dies according to its reputation. Then again, Ivor Davidson made them money not so long ago, and yet Walter refused to invest in his new scheme. What if he couldn't?"

Constance rubbed her forehead, thinking about it. "If it's true, does it change anything? Does it give anyone a stronger motive?"

"Not that I can see," Solomon admitted. "I just can't help thinking it's important somehow."

"If it's true," she said. "Can you find out if it is?"

"Probably. In time. Do we have time? We can't all remain trapped in this house indefinitely. We must already know all we're likely to find out. Any of them could have committed this murder, for any reason we know of, or one we don't. Either we have to think our way to the correct solution—and prove it— or..."

"Or what?" Constance prompted when he trailed off.

He looked up and met her eyes. "Or set a trap that will force the culprit to reveal himself. Or herself."

Her eyes sparkled. "Oh, I like the sound of that. What do we do?" Without warning, her face changed and she stood up, creeping rapidly across the floor in her stocking soles while she flapped her hand at him, clearly encouraging him to keep talking. She must have heard something he had not.

"That's the problem," he said, pulling words out of the air as he stood up. "I really have no idea. I'll think about it."

Her fingers closed around the door handle and yanked it open. Solomon threw himself forward to her side. But no one threatened her. No one could be seen in the passage in either direction, even when Solomon picked up his sputtering candle from the table and lifted it high. No open doors, no light, no person.

They slipped back inside, and Constance closed the door, her eyes wide as they stared into his.

"Someone was there in the passage," she said. "I heard them. They brushed against the door."

"I believe you. The question is, did *they* hear *us*?"

"Perhaps we sounded so threatening, they'll bolt and give themselves away."

It bothered Solomon more that it might make the killer stand and fight. "Well, it can't be much surprise to anyone in the house that we discuss the matter. We've been asking questions since he died. It is possibly of more concern to our eavesdropper that I was in your room."

"It will be interesting to see if that story spreads. Who will regard me now as the scarlet woman?"

"The prospect does not appear to trouble you," he said, searching her face.

She shrugged. "My masquerade is almost over. It is time to go back to reality."

There was a hint of defiance in the eyes that met his, and yet she accepted it. Solomon did not.

"There are ways out, Constance. You can change your reality."

"As you did?"

He acknowledged the attack with a small nod. "Yes, I suppose so."

"But did it make you happy, Solomon Grey?"

For a moment, the words stuck in his throat. Memory rushed on him so fast, so vividly, he could *feel* the fun, the sheer joy of playing in the sunshine, the laughter, the companionship that he took for granted until it was gone. And the coldness of being alone, of being just one. That was a reality he could not change, only how he dealt with it. He had made a good, successful life, and he grasped that knowledge with both hands.

"I am not unhappy," he said evenly.

She took hold of his arms, gave him a little shake. "That is not the same thing. And you know it. I saw it in your eyes. You know the kind of happiness I mean—a comfort, a contentedness, and moments of pure joy. I have that, Solomon." *You don't.*

The last words were not said, but he heard them anyway. And she was right, but he was not thinking of himself. He was thinking of her, and this new pain was unfamiliar.

"The men make you happy?" he said, trying to understand.

She smiled. "Not the men, Solomon. The women. Friendship. Fun. Creating happiness for others."

He believed her. There was a vitality, a warmth in her that could not be faked. It fascinated him, perhaps because somewhere he envied it. He tugged his lips into a one-sided smile. "And you're still not talking about the men, are you?"

"There, you *do* understand."

"Only in part," he said honestly.

Her hands slid down his arms until they found his fingers. "You are my first male friend."

Startled, he gazed into her face. Her eyes were warm, serious, completely free of teasing, of mockery. He found himself absurdly touched by her declaration. Proud. He curled his fingers around hers and held them.

"Perhaps you are *my* first friend." Why had he admitted that? Why did he even feel it?

Her long eyelashes, alluringly darker than her hair, swept down. He would have thought she was hiding except that she suddenly lifted his hand to her cheek. So soft and smooth and warm. Like all of her.

Then she released both his hands, and he was sorry. With an effort, he forced his mind back to practical matters, in particular to their eavesdropper.

"Take care, Constance," he said urgently. "Go nowhere alone, or even with just one companion. And let's think of a trap for our murderer before he comes up with one for us."

CHAPTER SIXTEEN

THE REVEREND PETER Albright woke with a sense of wellbeing he had not experienced for a long time. It took him only an instant to remember why. For the first time ever, Miriam had initiated their physical love last night, and clung to him with a tenderness and a need she had never shown him before.

They had always been friends, of course, a partnership, but it had taken him several weeks after their marriage to realize she did not love him, longer yet to recognize that it hurt him. How ironic that it was her father's death that had finally brought them closer and given him hope of something more.

He turned his head on the pillow and found her eyes already open and on him with a slightly embarrassed affection. It seemed a shame to risk that, but he could no longer put it off.

"I borrowed money from your father to pay for the building work."

"I know."

He blinked. "You do? Did he tell you?"

"Of course not. But I manage the household, Peter. I know what you earn and where it all goes."

"It seemed a good idea at the time."

"It *was* a good idea. I am very happy with the changes, and it made entertaining the bishop and his family much easier."

"It cost too much," he confessed. "I rather assumed your father would cover that too, but he didn't. I'm sure he thought I should stand on my own feet, and he was right."

She gazed at him expectantly.

He swallowed. "I am in debt, Miriam. I cannot pay the tradesmen who are in greater need than I. I asked Mr. Bolton to cover it, as your father had once implied he would. He told me to apply through the bank."

Miriam's eyebrows flew up. "I call that shabby."

He smiled ruefully. "I call it disastrous."

"Of course it is not," she said in surprise. "We can pay it now with my dowry."

He sat abruptly. "That is for you, for our children…"

"Peter. There is no *me* and *you* in this. Only *us*. So we will pay our debts, and when my inheritance is released we can pay back the dowry money."

Peter closed his gaping mouth. She was so matter-of-fact, stating the simplest solution. Weeks of worry—months, even—slid off his shoulders.

Miriam was frowning. "I'm surprised at my father, though."

"I thought he was angry with me."

"Why would he be angry with you?" she asked, clearly surprised.

"I thought he knew, that you had told him…you were not happy with me." It was difficult to say, but he met her gaze as he did so.

A hint of color, perhaps shame, tinged her cheeks. "I am not unhappy. Perhaps I needed time to adjust, to work out why I was…angry."

"And have you?" he asked gently. "Have you worked it out?"

She nodded slowly. "I was angry with him. With Papa, for deciding who and what would make me happy. Because he wasn't even concerned with that. He wanted a gentleman in the family to counter his own fall into trade. You are a nobleman's grandson in a respectable profession. And I am an obedient daughter."

His hurt must have shown in his face, for she cast herself into his arms. "I let it sour me. I thought it wouldn't matter if I was just a good wife to you. Actually, I like being your wife. It was my father I could not forgive for his utter selfishness, not just to me but to my mother and Mrs. Bolton, and all the previous women." Her fingers dug hard into his shoulders. "I am glad he is dead," she whispered, chilling his blood with terrible suspicion. "I shall go to hell, but not yet. Not yet."

HE CALLED ME *his friend.* Constance rose with the pleasure of that thought in her mind. If felt like an achievement, even though the realist in her knew that they were barely acquainted, and that his feeling was inspired largely by their cooperation on the mystery of this murder.

More importantly, her awareness of his loneliness had been intensified since last night into something very like a mission. There was danger in that, for her. She was not used to physical attraction, and she hadn't expected it to deepen as she grew to like him, with his subtle humor and his unexpected insights.

But she did like him, and she could not bear him not to know happiness, even those odd moments of reasonless joy that could come so unexpectedly, whether from laughter at a shared joke, some moment of beauty, or a friend's well-earned success. It was almost as if he had cut himself off from such feelings, because he was so alone. He had no one to share with. He had lost more than a brother. He had lost a part of himself and found nothing— or allowed nothing—to grow in its place.

Except his work. He had turned himself from a struggling plantation owner into a shipping magnate, a wealthy importer with such a wide variety of business interests that even the abject failure of one could not touch his overall success. She knew this from Lord James Andover, who had once suspected Solomon of stealing his own diamonds and setting James up to take the blame. It hadn't been true. Everyone said he was an honest man, if a hard one to cross or to get the better of. Solomon Grey was one of the benevolent rich who gave their time and money to worthy causes.

But he brushed off questions about his work. She suspected it no longer interested him, but he had nothing else to replace it in his life. No wife or family, no great cause he valued above all others. No true friends, only acquaintances with whom to enjoy the fruits of his success.

Except me. I will be your friend. I will make you happy again if it's the last thing I do.

A grand ambition, she mocked herself, and doomed to failure if she didn't accomplish it in the next few days. After this murder was solved, she was very unlikely to see him again. She was a friend of the moment, not of his life.

But she would not let that sadden her. She had to stop thinking about him and think of the killer and how to trap him. Or her.

Having washed and dressed, she sallied forth to breakfast.

On impulse, she detoured to the study to see if the policemen were there. They were, poring over two large ledgers and looking baffled.

Surely these must be the bank's ledgers? In which case, they would reveal whether or not Solomon was right in his belief that the bank was struggling.

"Good morning," she said brightly. "Can I help?"

They both straightened and frowned at her. "Good morning," Inspector Harris said, "and unless you understand bookkeeping, I'm afraid not."

"Of course I understand bookkeeping," Constance said. "I keep accounts for my household and my business."

Flynn blushed, bless him. Harris frowned at her, then, after a quick exchange of glances with the sergeant, waved his hand at them. "Please do. We can't make head nor tail of it."

Constance tried not to preen as she took the sergeant's chair. It was as well she didn't crow, for it did not take her long to realize this was beyond her.

"Are these from the bank?" she asked. "They are rather more complicated than a small business or household. I know someone who could do it for you, but she's in London."

"She?" Harris uttered in disbelief.

"Oh, you'd be surprised by some of the skills my girls have acquired." She spoke with her usual humor, which she rather expected to go over the policemen's heads, but fortunately, Solomon Grey strolled in and acknowledged the sally with a crooked smile.

"Don't be deceived, inspector. Some of the young women who leave her establishment emerge as cooks, secretaries, shop assistants, maids, and housekeepers. An accountant would not surprise me. However, if you will allow me a glance…"

Constance rose, and was about to leave them to it when a thought struck her. "Does Mr. Bolton know you have these?"

"Yes," Flynn said at once. "If I hadn't told him, the manager at the bank certainly would. He was very reluctant to let me take anything at all. Mr. Bolton never batted an eyelid. He seemed quite happy for us to look."

Not the behavior of a guilty man. But perhaps that of a man who had other things on his mind—like the guilt of his wife? Did he really not know about her affair with his partner? Would he even care? Most men regarded women, particularly wives, as their possessions…

As she wandered along the hall toward the breakfast parlor, she thought that Solomon, who had after all been born into a society that kept slaves, did not appear to think that way. As far as she knew. But how interesting that he was aware of her girls going into other work… Had he asked Elizabeth? Or come across one of them in his own employment? Was that why he was so surprised she did not abandon her profession herself?

And why did every line of speculation come back to Solomon? Her mind should be on the mystery and finding the murderer. She needed to get back to her own life soon. Even though she still didn't know if the Winsoms were her family. Even if she wanted them to be. She did not care for what she knew of Walter, however warm and charming he had been. His children were a different matter. They seemed to need looking after, somehow. That was Constance's forte.

Her other forte, of course, was that she understood people. She had seen the good and bad in most. Moreover, the livelihoods and the very lives of herself and her employees depended very largely on her judgment. These people were not so very different from the men who spilled through her establishment doors every night, or the women they came for.

She had been too diffident, too wary in her judgments at Greenforth. Because somewhere she wanted to be one of them. Because she knew she wasn't. She had imagined she didn't understand them, but she did. They had the same weaknesses, the same emotions and ambitions as anyone else. It was she who had hampered herself from looking, from relying on all the instincts and experience that had kept her alive and made her rich.

The tension in the breakfast parlor was palpable. The longer the uncertainty dragged on, with its inevitable suspicions and fears and doubts, the more powerful the strain on nerves, relationships, even sanity. Was the murderer just hoping it would all die down with no culprit ever found? After all, it was Richards who had sought to blame Alice Bolton, not whoever had actually done the killing.

It was possible Richards would still be charged with the crime, but Constance didn't believe he'd done it. The first pain and rage at his brother's death hadn't made him start killing Winsoms and Boltons. Instead, he had begun a much subtler revenge. He was no killer.

Harris's best guest was Alice Bolton, who stood beside her now at the sideboard, helping herself to kedgeree. Constance didn't believe that either. But then, she had some sympathy for a strong, passionate woman tied to a weak, cold man whose entire focus was his work.

"The scrambled egg is cold," Alice told her with distaste as she was about to take some. "If you want it, ring for more."

"I'll just have toast," Constance said. "I'm not really hungry."

The table was unusually crowded this morning, with everyone present at once, except for Solomon and Mrs. Winsom. Perhaps no one had slept well. Strain and tiredness showed in everyone's face—except Peter Albright, who looked even more tranquil than normal, despite what Solomon had overheard last night. Perhaps, in the end, he had talked Bolton into a favorable loan. Or perhaps Randolph had helped.

With her revived confidence in her own instincts, Constance chose to take the vacant chair next to Ivor Davidson. Had it been him skulking outside her door last night, listening? Certainly, his eyes were veiled as he wished her a pleasant good morning. And there might have been significance in his amiable question, "Did you sleep well?"

"As well as could be expected in these difficult circumstances," she replied. Across the table, Randolph was watching her. It could so easily have been him at her door, as he had been the night of the murder. Only he knew now her suspicions about their relationship... She turned back to Davidson. "Did you?"

"Like a baby," he said lightly.

He was lying. There were deep shadows under his eyes. The man was exhausted. And scared.

"Excellent," she said, "then you will be ready for that long-threatened game of billiards this morning."

"Is that quite appropriate?" Alice said, sounding genuinely shocked.

"I doubt my father would object to his guests playing billiards," Miriam said with unexpected shortness.

"I was thinking more of your mother," Alice said.

Miriam stared at her. "Were you?"

It was the first sign of hostility to Alice that Constance had seen from any of the family. Ellen dropped her fork in surprise. Thomas Bolton stared studiously into his teacup.

"I was," Alice managed. Her face had paled, her lips stiff as she spoke. "But you are right to point out that this is not my house or my concern. I beg your pardon." She rose and left the room.

Randolph frowned at his sister. "Was that necessary? Do we have to be at each other's throats?"

Miriam met his gaze. "You decide, Randolph. You are head of the family."

Everyone else finished breakfast in an uncomfortable silence. Constance, considering everyone with new dispassion, found it interesting that Mr. Albright did not censure his wife by as much as a look. In fact, when she was finished, he held her chair for her to rise, and left with her.

Constance left shortly afterward and found Davidson at her heels.

"Now?" he suggested.

She glanced at the rain drizzling down the front hall window. "Why not?"

"Do you play often, Mrs. Goldrich?"

"When I have the opportunity."

He bowed her into the billiard room. "I imagine there are not so many of those for a widow."

"Do you find it sad that I play against myself?" she asked.

"At least you will always win."

She laughed, and he smiled as he took two cues from the stand and offered her one. She took it, then rummaged among the others, choosing another that she swapped for the one Davidson had given her. He watched the process with tolerant amusement.

"You have a suspicious nature, Mrs. Goldrich."

"I have a careful nature and have grown used to making independent decisions."

"So who made the decision about you and Randolph?" he asked. The table was already set up, so he gestured toward it to signify she should begin.

"What decision was that?" She chalked the tip of her cue.

"Well, he no longer lives in your pocket. Does he imagine he can do better now he is the head of Winsom and Bolton? Or have you jilted the poor fellow for Grey's riches?"

She eyed him thoughtfully. "I can't make up my mind whether you are deliberately offensive for theatrical affect, or whether you really don't have any manners."

His smile only broadened. "And what—er…independent conclusion have you come to?"

"I'm still debating the issue. I don't believe you are an idiot, so I rather incline toward theatrical effect. Though of course you may be so in love with your own cleverness that you believe you can make such remarks without anyone understanding the offense. You can carry the act of 'blunt new man' too far."

"It's not an act. I *am* a blunt new man."

"And you feel that, as such," she said, bending over the table and smoothly hitting the white ball with her cue, "you are free of the obligations of a gentleman?"

"I see no reason to flatter just because someone calls herself a lady."

"Why, Mr. Davidson, you have taken me in such dislike, I am surprised you wish to play with me."

"I don't dislike you in the slightest." He took his shot. Constance barely looked at it. "In fact, you intrigue me greatly. What do you believe makes a gentleman? The mere luck of his birth?"

"Of course not. It is a matter of behavior. Take our murderer, for example."

Davidson, about to take his next shot, mishit the ball and scowled at Constance.

She smiled seraphically and stepped forward to the table.

"You think murder is only committed by those not regarded as gentlemen?" he mocked.

"Oh, no, I am not so naïve. By its very act, murder is hardly gentlemanly conduct. And yet there is a belief that a gentleman kills face to face—like a soldier, or a duelist. Mr. Winsom was killed by a stab in the back."

"Therefore, not by a gentleman?" Davidson said in disbelief.

She glanced back at him from the table, and her stomach gave a sickening jolt, for his expression had turned ugly.

"Are you and Grey trying to push the blame for this murder onto me? Because I am a self-made man and not a gentleman born?"

He lunged at her so quickly she would have been pinned to the table had she not whisked herself aside, almost falling back against the wall. He followed her, swinging up his cue as though to strike her.

It was a long time since she had been in such a situation, since she had allowed such a situation. But old instinct refused to let her show fear. She gazed into his eyes, her brows slightly raised, even as the cue descended toward her face. At the last moment, he shifted the angle and held it horizontal across her throat.

"I could kill you now," he sneered. "Face to face. Would that make me a gentleman?"

Somehow, she held on to his gaze and her own sense of worth. "It would certainly make you the prime suspect in two murders."

IT DIDN'T TAKE Solomon long to understand the difficulty with the books. Bolton's system merely borrowed from the usual, and it had been so heavily modified that it was almost impossible to follow the money from one column to the next, one book to the next. Eventually, by following one particular amount, he began to see daylight.

Still, the system was unnecessarily complicated. Why?

He had focused on another figure, to try to prove his theory, when a footman knocked at the door. Habit made him call, "Enter," before he recalled that this was not his own office.

Fortunately, neither of the policemen were present.

A footman entered carrying two letters on a silver tray. "For you, sir."

"Thank you," Grey said, taking the letters. Dragging his brain away from the numbers, he said, "How did you know I was here?"

"You were not at breakfast, sir. Miss Ellen told me I would find you here."

Miss Ellen did not miss much. Solomon nodded dismissal to the footman and laid the letters on the desk. He turned back to the ledger, then paused and looked again at the letters. Picking up the first, from his warehouse manager at St. Catherine's Dock, he saw that the one beneath was from his traveling secretary, whom he had asked to look into the business of Mr. Ivor Davidson of Norwich.

Opening it first, he swiftly read the contents until he came to the line, *He has overextended and is in dire need of investment. If he doesn't get it within the next month, maybe two, he is going under. With such rumors, no one will touch him.*

In which case, no wonder Davidson was so eager for Winsom's partnership, and furious when he didn't get it. Making a play for Ellen had been a desperate alternative... A desperate man committed desperate deeds. A desperate, angry, worried man. Had he taken the knife from the kitchen in a moment of fury? Then perhaps calmed himself, and then—perhaps even on his way to returning the knife—he could have spied Winsom in the garden with Alice Bolton. Would he not then have become enraged all over again by the self-righteous nature of Winsom's refusal?

Though it was hardly proof of murder, Solomon could almost see these scenes playing behind his eyes and they brought a chill to his bones. Davidson hurtled to the top of Solomon's list of suspects. Or perhaps joint top.

But Constance, who had always suspected Davidson, did not have this information. He didn't put it past her to chase the man down, ask him questions that were too bold. If he was volatile enough to turn on his host...

Solomon was already out of his chair and striding for the door, stuffing his scrunched-up letter into his pocket as he went. In the hallway, he encountered the stately Richards, looking a trifle haggard yet as haughty as ever.

"Do you know where Mrs. Goldrich is?" he asked. *Don't be out walking alone with Davidson...* He had warned her not to, even knowing she obeyed no one and trusted too much in her own ability to control any scene.

"I believe she is in the billiard room." A gleam of malice shone in Richards's eyes. "With Mr. Davidson."

CHAPTER SEVENTEEN

T HE UGLY TEMPER in Davidson's eyes flared brighter. Constance held herself very still, pretending she barely noticed the cool, hard wood against her windpipe—not pressing or hurting, just touching firmly enough to show her how vulnerable she was to his strength.

She met his gaze without flinching, hoped he could not feel the hammering of her pulse. To her unspeakable relief, the anger began to die back.

The cue left her skin. Davidson turned it and stepped away. "You are quite right. I'm sure I'm already the chief suspect. As if I don't have enough to worry about. You smell delightful, by the way. Are you wealthy, Mrs. Goldrich?"

"Wealthy enough that I need never marry a fortune hunter, though I appreciate your honesty. And your desperation." She barely knew what she was saying. The cue was still in his hand, and he still stood too close for comfort. "What are you worrying about? Apart from the murder."

He gave a lopsided smile, but before he could speak, the door burst open and Solomon stood there. Relief flooded her, turning her knees to jelly as the fear had not.

Davidson swung around to face him, and Constance slipped out of his reach, strolling around the billiard table on her trembling legs.

"Care for a game, Mr. Grey? I believe I am almost beaten." Amazingly, her voice was very nearly steady.

And Solomon understood. She saw it in the flicker of his hard eyes. He didn't move as Davidson walked steadily toward him.

"Take my place, Grey. I find I don't care much for billiards anymore."

Constance forced her legs to move faster, to prevent the inevitable confrontation. The eyes of the two men locked.

"Oh, Mr. Grey!" a female voice hailed him from the foot of the stairs.

Mrs. Winsom.

Grey did not move, let alone turn.

"Your pardon, sir," Davidson drawled. "Mrs. Winsom wants you, and I want past."

To Constance's relief, Solomon stood aside and Davidson sauntered past. She heard him greet Mrs. Winsom on his way.

The lady appeared just outside the door in dark outdoor clothes, black crepe on her bonnet. "Mr. Grey, might I have your escort? I find myself eager to walk now the rain has gone off."

Indeed, a beam of watery sunshine had brightened the room. Solomon greeted his hostess with a bow, though his frowning gaze quickly returned to Constance.

She did not want him to see her weakness. She did not want to be weak. "I shall leave you to it," she said lightly. "Enjoy your walk."

His brow twitched. For a moment he seemed about to dig in his heels, however much it offended his hostess, the recent widow, and that warmed her heart, though she needed him to go.

She willed him to see it. *Go with her. You might learn something important.* They would need to very soon, for she had this sick feeling in the pit of her stomach that the tension at Greenforth was about to snap into fresh catastrophe.

He turned away from her and politely offered his arm to Mrs. Winsom.

Constance waited, listening to their footsteps recede across the hall and the murmur of their polite voices. But only when the front door had closed behind them did she draw in a shuddering breath and leave the billiard room.

Despite what her head knew, she did not feel safe. She longed for the stout, loyal footmen of her own establishment, whose very presence protected her and her girls. Had she become too dependent on them? Too fearful?

No, she was just a realist who had faced much worse than one angry, selfish man with a billiard cue. And yet she was undeniably shaken. She looked about the empty hall as she crossed to the stairs, felt the hair on the back of her neck prickle as she climbed. She was ridiculously glad to see the chambermaids in the passage as she made her way to her own room, where she closed and locked the door behind her.

Only then did she sink into the armchair and wait for the trembling to stop. It had been too long since anyone had threatened her. She had grown too soft.

But she had survived. Even before Solomon had come—why *had* he come?—she was back in control. Still, he would have stayed with her had she shown the slightest need, the slightest desire for his company. And that was sweet.

"I HAVE NOT left the house for days," Mrs. Winsom said as they walked through the gardens toward the woods. "I began to feel trapped there."

Solomon nodded. "A little fresh air and exercise are necessary to all of us." Although he could have done without it at this moment. He was more worried about Constance. She had smiled and looked as self-assured and unconcerned as always, and yet he knew she was not. More, he knew Davidson was the cause.

"Mr. Davidson has almost beaten me." She meant he had not touched her, but he had come close. He had threatened, and that, Solomon would never forgive. But she was his first concern. He did not want to be with the grieving widow right now, though he

pitied her. He had to make the effort to concentrate on her, for apart from anything else, she could well hold the key to this whole mystery.

"I had almost forgotten it is summer," Mrs. Winsom said. She sounded bewildered. "It feels as if months have passed instead of a mere couple of days. Or perhaps as if time has stopped in one terrible moment."

Solomon nodded. "It will be hard to adjust. But you are not alone. You have your children."

"I am blessed," she said, with a slight crack in her voice. "Shall we walk through the woods?"

"If you wish, though the ground will be wet."

After recent events, the wet clearly did not even register with her. She walked in silence for a while. Solomon assumed he was there merely for companionship, perhaps for the familiarity of a male escort.

"He was having an affair, you know," she said abruptly. "My husband. With my friend."

"It must be very painful."

"She was not the first. I doubt she would have been the last. Nor am I the last wife who will suffer in such a way." She swallowed. "It's odd how much I miss him."

"He was a very likeable man."

She nodded. "Too likeable. He assumed he would always be forgiven. Like a beloved, overindulged child."

He looked down at her, aware that no one had ever seriously considered her as a suspect for more than a moment. "Do you forgive him?"

She looked away, her smile faint and rueful. "Not for dying."

"Someone else is to blame for that," he said gently. "All of us, particularly you, need to know who that was."

"You are right, of course. But somehow it seems less important than the fact he is dead."

She was burying her head in the sand, and she knew it.

"You will live more easily, and keep yourself and your family safer, when you know."

She did not answer or look at him, and with a sudden jolt he wondered if she did know. Or merely thought she did.

He must tread carefully here. One hint of interrogation and he would lose her.

"You know everyone at Greenforth better than anyone else," he said carefully. "You could help Inspector Harris to find the truth, to end this awful uncertainty for you and your family."

Unless it *was* one of her family. Who else would she cover for?

She nodded slowly. "I will think," she promised. "Seriously." She walked on, taking a narrower, less-trodden path into a thicker part of the wood. There was no cornflower or meadowsweet here to distract her. She just seemed to be going as far away from the house as possible. He felt a stab of sympathy for that.

"The police inspector wants me to say it is Alice," she confided. "But I know it is not. She is as grieved as I." A mirthless smile dawned and vanished. "In her own way. It must be a stranger, and yet one he has annoyed." She glanced up suddenly, catching his eye. "It must be either Mr. Davidson, because Walter refused to invest with him, or Mrs. Goldrich. I still don't know why she is here, but it is clearly not for Randolph. I think she came for Walter."

"Then why would she stay?" Solomon was only half listening. As before in these woods, he had picked up the sounds of another presence, unseen but close enough to be alarming.

"I suppose she could have fled before the police arrived," Mrs. Winsom allowed. "But surely the police would have suspected her more and found her anyway?"

Not if they hadn't known her real name. Would Solomon have told them? "How well do you know Ivor Davidson?" he asked instead. "Did you know he is in financial difficulties?"

"No. But then, I would not normally hear such things."

Solomon, his skin prickling all over with unease, turned her back the way they had come. "I think we should return to the house. This is far enough for your first outing in days."

She accepted his dictate, clearly used to obeying the superior wisdom of men. Though after only one step, she halted, frowning. "Do you hear that?"

He did indeed hear the rustling in the undergrowth, and it was drawing nearer. Then he heard something else, an animal's growl, and instinctively stepped in front of Mrs. Winsom, putting himself between her and whatever animal this was. Yet surely it could only be a dog...

"Keep walking," he said quietly. "Don't run."

But she seemed rooted to the spot, resisting his urging, staring into the undergrowth. A huge bull mastiff loped out, its tread purposeful, its lips curled back in a snarl that showed his slavering fangs. Randolph's pet, Monster.

"Oh, no, he's got out!" Mrs. Winsom wailed in fright. She flapped her arms wildly at the dog. "Go home, Monster!" she all but squealed.

The animal tossed its head, not slowing in the slightest. Then it leaned back to spring, and Mrs. Winsom gave a squeal of terror. "He goes for the throat!" she shrieked, her voice still high with fear. "Stay still! Don't move a muscle! I'll fetch Randolph—he's the only one who can handle Monster!"

Before he could stop her, she snatched her hand from his arm and dashed along the path. The dog immediately swerved toward her, so Solomon, almost resigned to his fate, lunged into the beast's path. Distracted again, it halted and stared at him from its muddy, malevolent eyes.

How long would it take Deborah Winsom to return to the house and bring Randolph back with her? Too long. It was up to Solomon to save himself. Or not.

"What are you doing out here?" he asked it conversationally. "Are you not supposed to be eating your head off in your kennel? Or did you bring Randolph with you?"

The dog cocked one ear. Its lip uncurled.

"Ah, you recognize your master's name. That's good." *I think.*

"What's the matter? Are you hungry?" He'd never met a dog that wasn't, but this one, by all accounts, including the gamekeeper's, was seriously disturbed.

Solomon moved very slowly, lifting his hand to his pocket. The dog took a step nearer, growling deep in its throat. Just a warning. It wasn't a snarl. So Solomon took the chance, curling his fingers around the horse treats in his pocket. He brought his hand out very slowly, hoping the food smell would appease Monster. Though how well slightly fluffy pieces of carrot and lumps of sugar went down with dogs, he had no idea.

Monster was still looking him in the eye.

"Sit," Solomon said, firm but friendly, and with very low expectations he hoped the dog could not read.

Monster did not obey. But he dropped his eyes to Solomon's open hand.

"Monster, sit," he said more severely.

To his astonishment, the dog sat back on its huge haunches. Solomon threw it a piece of carrot, which the dog caught in its massive jaws with a lightning-quick snap that was still somehow terrifying, even though his tail actually twitched.

Monster barked, and Solomon threw another piece of carrot. It seemed they would be fine until the vegetables ran out.

DEBORAH WINSOM WAS panting as she almost fell in the front door of Greenforth House. She had not run—she couldn't—but she had walked very fast, as though all the fiends of hell were after her. At any moment, she expected to hear the screaming as Monster attacked. Perhaps the dog would get bored and leave him alone...

"Randolph!" she cried as soon as she was over the threshold. James the footman gaped at her. "Where is my son?" she demanded.

"In the library, ma'am, with Mr. Bolton."

"Fetch him!" she commanded, collapsing, wheezing onto the ornate but uncomfortable chair that was kept in the hall for visitors one didn't want even in the reception room.

James started across the hall immediately, but the commotion of her arrival must have already alerted most of the household, who had begun to gather for luncheon. Miriam and Ellen rushed out of the morning room. Peter leaned over the banister. Constance Goldrich seemed to be flying down the stairs. Randolph stuck his head out of the library door.

"Mama? What the…" Seeing her all but collapsed, he strode toward her, Thomas following more sedately, a concerned frown upon his face.

With a massive effort, Deborah heaved herself to her feet and staggered to meet her son. "Randolph, Monster is loose! He has poor Mr. Grey cornered in the woods! Near the cave where you used to play as a boy. You have to stop him before he kills someone! Shoot him or lock him up or—just *go*, Randolph! You're the only one who can do this!"

White-faced, Randolph stumbled past her toward the door.

"Wait," Thomas said urgently. "You'd better take a gun. I'll fetch the key to the gun room."

"How did he get out?" Miriam demanded as Randolph brushed past her in Thomas's wake. "You should have shot him when he attacked the kennelman."

"Easy to be wise after the event," Deborah said. She was recovering her breath now, though she still trembled with fear. "It's not so easy to kill a creature who loves you. Oh, hurry, Randolph!"

Ellen, the dear child, put her arm around her mother. Randolph, his set face determined, hiding his fear of what he would find and what he would have to do, marched past, armed with his shotgun. However this ended, it was going to be so awful for him. Deborah could not bear it.

"Don't worry, Deborah," Thomas said in passing. "I'll go

with him, and we'll deal with it. All will be well."

When he touched her shoulder in a comforting sort of way, she wanted to shake him off. Instead, she stumbled after them out the front door. Ellen hung on to her as if afraid her mother would try to go with them.

Which seemed to be what Mrs. Goldrich was doing. With neither bonnet nor cloak, her face white to the lips, her eyes dark with some turbulent emotion, she stormed past Deborah. The others emerged from the house too, all talking and whispering at once so that she wanted to cover her ears.

And then came a bark, so deep and powerful that it could only belong to one animal. Deborah froze. So did everyone around her.

Monster loped around from the side of the house, with Solomon Grey at his side. Tall and elegant as ever, there was a casual rakishness about him that she couldn't quite fathom until she saw that he wore no necktie. That indispensable item of a gentlemen's attire was looped through the dog's collar as a short, makeshift leash that he held in one alarmingly strong hand.

Deborah's legs gave way. She would have fallen if her daughters had not been holding her up. A collective gasp sounded from all the watchers.

After an instant of stunned paralysis, Randolph started forward. So did Monster, who had been walking quite sedately at Grey's side. Everyone else fell back toward the house.

"I brought your dog back," Grey said mildly.

It was, in its way, rather magnificent.

WHEN THE COMMOTION arose, Constance had been in her bedchamber, writing down every fact and every suspect she knew of, and connecting them up with lines. By the time she heard Mrs. Winsom crash into the house, calling for Randolph, she had paper spread all over the floor. But at the panic in the widow's voice, she sprang up and ran from the room, bolting for the stairs.

Even now, her terrible vision of Solomon being dragged to the ground by the snarling mastiff, its teeth tearing at his beautiful golden throat, faded slowly. It took a moment to adjust to the unlikely reality of Solomon strolling so carelessly beside the beast, connected by his necktie.

"I brought your dog back."

Solomon and Monster might have been the best of friends, although Monster clearly reserved that honor for Randolph. With another earth-shaking bark, he jumped, placing his huge paws on his master's shoulders to lick his face.

Solomon released the end of the necktie and looked at Constance. She wanted to slap him for scaring her so horribly, for the unwelcome glimpse into the depths of her own emotions, her own loneliness. She wanted to fling her arms around him and hold him and never let him go, to sing and laugh, just because he was safe.

She did none of these things. She dragged her gaze free and watched Randolph lead the docile Monster on toward the kennels. Everyone else was laughing with nervous relief, especially Mrs. Winsom, who appeared to be on the edge of hysteria as they went back into the house for luncheon.

Constance seemed unable to move.

"What happened to you?" Solomon said quietly.

She blinked and turned at last to stare back at him. "To *me*? You're the one who was having his throat ripped out by that ravening beast! Why didn't it happen?"

"Carrots," Solomon said.

The terrifying experience must have turned his mind. "Carrots," she repeated.

"I keep them in my pockets, for my horses. Turns out Monster likes them too. Or, at least, he likes catching them. I don't think anyone plays with him, and Randolph doesn't pay him enough attention."

She regarded him with fascination. "You are saying the dog tears people's throats because he is lonely and misunderstood?"

"And scared," he added.

"Solomon, you... I... Damn you, Solomon!" Striding the few paces between them, she grasped him by the upper arms as she had done last night, squeezing hard, just for an instant before she pushed herself away.

"Constance." He caught her hand, drawing her back to face him. "What did Davidson do?"

Davidson. It seemed a lifetime ago. "Displayed his temper. He is a very worried man, wound tight as a drum and ready to take offense at anything and anyone. We are all fair game."

"Including Winsom?"

They discussed the theory of Davidson's taking the knife in a fit of rage one night, calming down, and then using it during a subsequent fit. "It suits his character," she finished. "Sort of."

"Just *sort of?*"

She frowned, trying to put her instincts into words he would understand. "I think he's a bit like Monster. Volatile, worried, living on his nerves, taking offense, and lashing out first. But he can be quelled."

"Meaning a man of Winsom's strong character could have quelled him if he tried?"

"I would imagine so. If he got the chance. I doubt he did, because he was stabbed in the back. I don't think Davidson would have done that. Violence flares in him, he needs to frighten, to *see* you're frightened, but he doesn't...*hurt.*"

He held her gaze. "You looked hurt to me."

Heat surged into her face. She didn't know why. A strange kind of shame, perhaps. "He didn't hurt me. He took me by surprise. I have grown...unused to that kind of threat."

His eyes searched hers, a frown tugging his brows. Disgust, perhaps. "The worst thing is that you were ever used to it. I'm sorry."

Surprise held her speechless. He gave her no time to recover, merely placed her hand on his arm, pulling her toward the house.

"The dog," she said, managing to drag her thoughts back to Solomon's escape from harm. "How did he get out?" Her stomach twisted as her original suspicions flooded back. "Do you think it could have been deliberate? Because the killer was listening last night and was afraid of our traps?"

"I don't know yet. We should talk after luncheon. We need to finish this, Constance."

On that, she was in complete agreement.

CHAPTER EIGHTEEN

I N CONTRAST TO the long, tense silences of breakfast, luncheon was almost hysterically lively. Bizarrely, no one asked how Monster had escaped, as though he had simply barged out or eaten his way through the bars of his kennel. For Constance, now that she knew Solomon was neither dead nor injured, that was the whole point.

He was asked to tell his story, which he did as humorously as possible, and Mrs. Winsom, more animated than she had been since the murder, told of her terror and her mad dash to get Randolph to recue Solomon from his pet.

Someone had let Monster out. Constance had every intention of examining his kennel, though she imagined Randolph had already made certain it was secure.

Randolph. From what she had heard, only Randolph had the courage to open the kennel door, and why would he? Why would anyone? Just in the vague hope of causing mischief? Or had it really been an attack against Solomon? Or against Mrs. Winsom?

She thought about who had been in the hall when Mrs. Winsom had been shouting for her son.

Where had Davidson been? Where had Alice Bolton been? And did it matter? The dog must have been released long before that. Only, who was brave enough to open the kennel door?

Both the chief suspects seemed on edge. Davidson, who cast her several covert glances, might have been waiting for her to denounce his unacceptable behavior. Certainly, he didn't seem terribly interested in the tale of Monster and Grey, though he kept a pleasant smile on his face. Alice seemed distracted, merely pronouncing herself glad no harm had been done and that all was well in the end.

"I do trust you'll lock him up more securely, Randolph," she said. "He is not really a *safe* dog, is he?"

Randolph scowled at his plate full of chicken in an excellent wine sauce but agreed that Monster was a little unpredictable.

As soon as she decently could, Constance excused herself and walked around to the kennels. Monster was lying down in his own vast kennel. He opened one sleepy eye as Constance approached but didn't otherwise stir. He also ignored the calls of the hunting dogs who were running and playing around their own separate paddock in the sunshine.

Keeping a sensible distance, Constance eyed the apparently undamaged kennel door, which was bolted. The far end of the kennel was open to the paddock beyond, so she walked around the fence, looking for holes or even recent repairs. The repairs she did find looked weathered and old.

As she returned to the front of the kennel, Randolph was approaching along the path.

"He's exhausted, poor old fellow," he said, when the dog thumped his tail but didn't otherwise move.

"How did he get out, Randolph?" Constance asked.

He sighed. "No idea." He cast her a glance. "A lot of weird things have been happening at Greenforth since I came home."

That was an understatement. But she was distracted from asking him what precisely he meant by Solomon's strolling along the path to join them.

Randolph's expression changed. It wasn't unfriendly. "Mr. Grey, come to visit your newest friend?"

"I thought I might look in on him."

Monster swished his tail against the straw again.

"I owe you an apology," Randolph said awkwardly. "You and my mother both, though it was you who was left to face down the beast. I know he's scary, but you seem to have handled him just right."

"Oh, I think he probably handled me. Certainly he had me playing 'catch' with him."

Randolph grinned, and Constance remembered why she had liked him in the first place, why she had hoped he was family. She'd set about finding out all wrong, of course. She had lied from the beginning, because it had seemed the only way, but she saw now that even if he were her brother, her deceit was unforgivable. It hurt, but she had only herself to blame.

"I should have warned everyone," Randolph said, his smile fading. "I just didn't want to upset my mother. I never even thought of her walking in the woods, for she never does so, even at the best of times. I assumed he would come back when he was hungry, and so asked Hudson the gamekeeper to keep an eye out and bolt him in as soon as he was home."

Constance's eyes widened. "When? When did he get out?"

Randolph shifted from one foot to the other. "Yesterday evening, I think. I went to feed him before our dinner, as I usually do, and he was gone. I thought Hudson, who helps me look after him, must have left the door unbolted by accident. He said *I* must have."

She remembered seeing him yesterday coming from the direction of the kennels. She had been with Solomon and deliberately avoided him. And when they met later, he had been on edge. He must have been worried about the dog, and then she flummoxed him further with their possible relationship.

Guilt twinged. "So he was out in the woods all night?"

Randolph nodded miserably. "That's what bothers me. Why didn't he come home? He likes me—he *trusts* me."

Solomon stirred. "Has he done this before?"

"He bolts sometimes. Usually takes his chance when the kennel door is open to feed him or something. He nearly always heads into the woods. I often take him there myself because he likes all the scents. But when he gets out on his own, he *always*

comes back for his dinner. Even the time he leapt at the kennelman and trampled him to escape, he came back."

"Do you think someone frightened him?" Solomon asked.

"I think it's more likely he did the frightening."

"Who else feeds him?" Constance asked. "Apart from you and
your gamekeeper?"

"No one," Randolph said in surprise. "Even the kennelman
gives him a wide berth now, and I honestly can't blame him for
that."

"So no one else goes into his kennel or his paddock?" Solomon asked.

"Only when I take him for a walk, if the kennel needs
cleaned."

Solomon turned back to the dog, clearly exhausted after his
night's adventure. He didn't look very fierce. "I don't suppose
anyone's *not* scared of him?"

"Not apart from you."

"Oh, I was scared too," Solomon said. "We didn't become
friends until I was resigned to being eaten."

"He smells fear, and that frightens *him* so that he attacks.
Stupid, great beast." Randolph frowned. "He'd be better if I could
take him into the house, where he'd get used to people and see
they're no threat, but my parents would never let me."

Solomon regarded him in silence until the younger man
flushed with sudden understanding. "It's my house now, isn't it? I
can take him inside if I wish. Only I don't wish to frighten my
mother."

"Of course you don't," Solomon agreed.

Still, Randolph looked thoughtful as he ambled away toward
the house.

"I don't *think*," Constance said, "that that is the reaction of a
man who killed his father for freedom and financial gain. And I
believe he was genuinely worried about the dog—to say nothing
of his mother and you. I definitely don't think he let it out."

"I believe we're narrowing our list. But are we right to include the dog's escape in our thinking? It's hardly a sure means of attack. Whether aimed at me or at Mrs. Winsom, it was always likely to fail."

"A sign of our murderer's desperation?" Constance suggested. "After overhearing us last night?"

"Possibly. Though it could be someone trying to protect the murderer."

"By committing murder themselves?" she said doubtfully.

"A murder made to look like an accident. The entire household and no doubt several neighbors could swear to the dog's viciousness."

She frowned. "It bothers me."

"It bothers me," Solomon said with an odd fervency that refocused her attention.

"You know something!"

He shook his head. "Only that you were in last night's conversation too. We both need to be careful."

The intensity of his gaze unnerved her, even while she basked in his concern. She resorted to mockery. "Why, Solomon, you *do* care."

"Is that so hard to believe?"

"No, I am everyone's favorite."

He caught her arm as she swung back toward the house. "I am serious, Constance," he said urgently. "No more billiard games with just one, no *tête-a-têtes* or solitary walks."

"I do understand, Solomon. I am not an imbecile."

He let her go at once. "I beg your pardon."

"If we are to be so careful of ourselves, how do we bait this trap we were discussing?"

"By being prepared," he said, surprising her yet again. "And by pretending more knowledge than we have."

A wave of excitement swept over her. "You have a plan," she breathed.

SOLOMON HAD NOT been strictly honest with Constance. Though he did not know with any certainty who had murdered Walter Winsom, a new theory that seemed to fit everything was bouncing around his mind, looking for proof or refutation.

It all stemmed from one of the chaotic thoughts swirling around his brain as he made tentative friends with Monster. Had Deborah Winsom brought him here deliberately and then abandoned him to his fate? He remembered her flapping her arms in the dog as though shooing him away, and yet she knew movement excited him.

The suspicion didn't really hold up to much scrutiny, especially now he knew the dog had escaped last night. There was no way she could have known the dog would still be free, let alone that he would come to that precise place at that precise time. Unless she had a partner who had brought the dog to the vicinity.

Although he had absolutely no proof of that, it did get him thinking along different lines.

What if there were not one murderer but two? Ready to provide each other with information and alibis in order to make the crime easier to commit and to divert investigation?

The most obvious pairings were married couples, already dependent on each other. Which meant the Boltons or the Albrights. And yet neither marriage was close and loving. Would Alice really ally with her husband to kill her lover? The other way around would have made more sense. And would Miriam really kill her father, whatever he had done? Somehow, he couldn't really imagine the vicar committing so heinous a crime either.

No, the theory was foolish, which was why he didn't mention it to Constance. He refused to analyze his reluctance to look foolish in her eyes. He rather liked her current friendship and the way she trusted him.

Since everyone had dispersed and the house was quiet, he

accepted her invitation to look at her lists and connections.

Paper was spread all over her bedchamber floor, some of it closely written, with inked arrows pointing to other pieces of paper that she had numbered, presumably to keep track of when she picked it all off the floor.

He crouched down, examining it with her, while she sat on the other side, her legs drawn up beneath her billowing skirts. How on earth did she control them?

Concentrate, Sol, concentrate.

She pointed at one piece of paper with the word BANK in large letters. "What do you make of the books? Anything?"

"They seem deliberately impenetrable, which tells me something in itself. But banks are secretive by nature and necessity, so it may mean nothing. Still, I'll work on them some more this afternoon. And Harris and Flynn have gone to speak to the bank staff and the solicitors, so they may well find out more. At least whether or not the bank is in trouble."

"What difference would that actually make?" she mused. "Removing Winsom will not aid its recovery, although I suppose it limits the number of people who share the profits. In which case, Bolton and Randolph are the main beneficiaries."

And Randolph would have known Bolton all his life. Were they the allies he was looking for? If the bank was failing, would it even matter how many people it needed to keep?

He read every piece of paper again, followed every arrow. She was thorough, remembered every detail, even quoted a few things people had said that seemed significant.

"This is helpful," he said at last. "Clarifies... Though everyone here is connected somehow to everyone else as well as to the victim. And if we discount married alibis, anyone could have committed the murder. *And* let Monster out."

"Meaning we are no further forward," she said, sighing.

"No, we are. I can't help feeling we have all the information we need to solve this, and I think we know everyone involved much better than we did." He passed his hand over the paper diagram. "The answer is here, somewhere."

"So let us bait our trap," she said. "And see who falls in."

SHE DIDN'T LIKE his plan, of course, largely because it kept her out of the thick of things. Although she did eventually see the need of another witness, and possibly of rousing the household if necessary to save his life.

"Not that I am anticipating difficulty, you understand. But one never knows."

He left her after that, to go and pore over the bank ledgers once more. A thankless task, he thought gloomily after an hour. The trouble was, one needed all the books, not just these two, to follow the complete trail of particular amounts.

He hoped the police could obtain access to them—and preferably to someone who understood them better than he.

And then he saw it. One single discrepancy from one book to the next, based on a hard-to-read figure that could have been a 1 or a 7, transcribed downward after the first of the far too many column entries. Which made no sense if the bank was covering up the fact that it was failing. And he could see no sign of that. Certainly the profits were down in the last couple of years, judging by the figures in the final books, but they were not yet in trouble. They were just being careful.

On the other hand, if six thousand pounds were unaccounted for… And these were not the day-to-day accounts, but the monthly figures… If such mistakes had been scattered throughout the weeks, then the fraud could be massive.

His heart was thudding. Framley, who had been with the bank for years, had been the only employee who had access to these books. Walter had discovered the fraud and blamed him.

What if he had then discovered the same fraud continued after Framley's dismissal? And now the only person who had access to those books, apart from him, was Thomas Bolton.

"Got you," he whispered, throwing himself back in his chair.

Only he hadn't, not yet. One mistake did not mean massive fraud. But it was a significant one, and any replication would surely prove it.

Bolton, the cold, insignificant man with the beautiful wife, constantly overshadowed by his larger-than-life partner, even in the eyes of said beautiful wife. Had he stolen to give her things? Status and more wealth? Or just because he could, because he reveled in deceiving his arrogant friend?

And Alice had covered for him. In the end, perhaps because Walter had ended their affair, she had sided with her husband. He knew the house and grounds better than any other guest. He could easily have let Monster out last night, perhaps knowing only that the dog would stalk threats in the woods and crossing his fingers.

Because he had overheard Constance and him talking of trapping the murderer? That conversation had happened *after* the dog had been freed, though Bolton might have somehow frightened it into bolting again after it came home as usual. That would explain its odd behavior in staying out all night and the next day. Monster really was more fearful and less terrifying than everyone thought. Bolton, the frequent visitor, could have known that...

Of course, so could other people. It was no proof of Bolton's guilt. He had not been worried by the police looking over his books. He thought they were impenetrable, and he was mostly right. But if *Solomon* was right—and this, finally, *felt* right—then Bolton had the best motive of anyone to murder Winsom.

He sprang to his feet, closed the ledgers, and shoved them into the desk drawer. He locked it with the keys Harris had given him, then blinked in surprise at his watch. It was almost dinner-time and he was desperate to talk to Constance, not because he thought they should change their plan, just because he wanted to share with her.

He locked the study door behind him again, then had a quick look in the library, the drawing room, and the garden room. Finding them all empty, he ran upstairs, taking two at a time. But as he raced along the passage to her bedroom, the Albrights emerged from theirs, and he had to greet them pleasantly and keep on walking to his own.

He changed quickly into evening garb, then stared at himself in the mirror, striving to lose the gleam of triumph in his eyes. To bait the trap effectively, he would need to strike just the right balance. Gloating would not help. He needed to look knowledge-able and just a little naïve, conscious of his own power, but not overstating it. Nor did he want to look too gullible, or assume that his audience was.

Constance would help there, of course. If she kept to the script they agreed. He realized that he was not sure she would. She went her own way, did Constance Silver, confident in her own judgment and courage.

His reflection smiled, not the faint amusement or cursory amiability of his social smiles, but one that took him by surprise. He realized he was excited by this chase, filled with anticipation and determination. How long since he had felt this way? Years. Since he had expanded his shipping empire and found success to be easy.

Right now, he was no longer bored.

Beyond that, he would not think. He had enough on his mind.

He twitched his necktie to perfection, as Constance had once done for him, and flexed his fingers. Then he strode confidently down to dinner to bait his trap.

CONSTANCE, UNEASY ABOUT her own meager part in Solomon's plan, followed her own instincts that afternoon by sending for

Owen the boot boy. She waited for him in the hall, just beyond the baize door. The other servants must have been teasing him that he was in trouble for poorly polished shoes, for he emerged very warily, an inch of him at a time.

"It's only me, Owen," Constance said. "I need your help."

As she had intended, the lad was flattered, squaring his shoulders and marching rather than slithering the rest of the way over to her.

"And you need to keep it secret," she added. She kept her voice very quiet, made sure they were not overheard from behind any door or staircase.

Owen's eyes gleamed as he nodded.

"Can you stay awake into the night? Or, better, wake yourself up at a certain time?"

"Depends," he said dubiously. "*What* time?"

"Midnight?"

"I can listen for the clock chiming. You can hear it in the kitchen. I don't usually notice now, except when I need to get up, but I can tell myself to listen for the twelve chimes. I can count to twelve."

"Good for you. You won't be punished if you don't wake up, but it would be a big help to Mr. Grey and me if you could come up at midnight and wait for me here, or at the library, which is behind that large door. Mr. Grey will be in there. You might need to wait a long time, but don't let anyone except us see you."

"Course not. What d'you want me to do?"

"Be an extra set of eyes. You might be the only one who can help us."

"Really?" he said in the disbelieving tone of one who knew when his leg was being pulled.

"I'm serious. I think you see more than you know, even when you're asleep in your cozy corner. Don't you half wake sometimes when the other servants are still up and talking? Or when someone sneaks into the kitchen for a midnight snack?"

"I dream it sometimes. I'm not afraid," he assured her quickly, "'cause I like to hear the others. I know I'm not alone."

Her heart went out to the boy, though she knew he wouldn't thank her for the sympathy. The other servants were probably the only family he'd ever known, the only people who'd ever been kind to him.

"But you remember those dreams," she guessed. "And I'll bet Mr. Randolph is one who sneaks into the kitchen in the middle of the night."

Owen grinned. "Middle of the day, too. I know him."

"Then I expect it's not really a dream when you see him at night, helping himself from Cook's larder."

"Well, it's a bit hazy-like. Misty. So I don't know. In any case, he don't do it so much now."

"Who does?"

"Don't know. I don't see the family, except the mistress, or the guests much, so I don't know 'em."

Her pulse quickened. "Then you have seen—or dreamed— someone else in the kitchen, someone who's not Mr. Randolph, taking food, perhaps?"

"Don't know. I think it's just a dream."

"Would you know them again? This person from your dream?"

"Maybe."

She gave him a little nudge with her elbow because he was looking worried. "It doesn't matter if you can't. Anyway, do your best to meet me here again at midnight and wait, will you?"

"Course I will," Owen said. "Can I go now? Cook wants me to wash them pots…"

"Until later, then," she said conspiratorially, and he grinned as he swaggered back off to the kitchen.

Constance, feeling one step closer to success, returned to her room to change for dinner.

She went downstairs early, in the hope of a last-minute dis-cussion with Solomon. But she found the Albrights already in the drawing room, and, in fact, Solomon was the last to enter, just before dinner was announced.

He looked so splendid that her breath vanished. It felt almost like the first time she had seen him, when he saved her life. Only this time, he had everyone's attention. The hum of somewhat strained conversation dropped suddenly as he drew all eyes.

That was when she realized it was deliberate. He could blend in or dazzle as he chose. And tonight, he meant to make his presence felt. Judging by his reception, he had begun well. She could almost see everyone watching him with fresh appreciation. He was not the kind of man who needed a billiard cue to inspire awe. He was every subtle inch a powerful man.

"Forgive me," he said, bowing to Mrs. Winsom. "I appear to be late."

"Not at all," said the widow, slightly flustered as she went forward and took his arm. "In any case, after your heroism of this morning, we are all inclined to be lenient." She seemed oddly energized after her earlier adventure, perhaps because she regarded Solomon as having saved her life. She certainly seemed inclined to cling to him, which was annoying when Constance wanted a private word.

"Policemen are not gentlemen, are they?" Ellen said to Constance, who turned to her in some surprise.

"I expect they are commanded by gentlemen," she replied cautiously. "Why?"

"Oh, I was just wondering about ours. They don't seem common to me."

"Nor to me," Constance said. If the policemen were "common," what would they call her? Criminal?

But it was a curious subject for discussion, and Ellen's color had heightened. "They are different, though."

"Does that bother you?" Constance asked. "Do you mind them being in the house so much?"

Ellen shook her head. "Actually, no. I thought I would mind, but I don't. I think he—they—are good men."

Over Ellen's shoulder, Constance met Solomon's gaze for the

briefest instant. He wanted to speak to her, too. But Richards announced dinner, and Mrs. Winsom, still on Solomon's arm, led the way to the dining room. Constance sat between Randolph and Thomas Bolton, so there was no opportunity to speak during dinner either. She would just have to comply with their agreement, follow his lead, and observe.

Strict table formality had fallen by the wayside since Winsom's murder, so conversation tended to be general.

Ivor Davidson said, "Where have our gallant police detectives gone today? Dare we hope they are leaving us in peace?"

"I doubt it," Bolton said with distaste. "They were at the bank today, poking around and asking questions. Or so Blackford, our manager, informed me."

"Couldn't they just have asked *you* whatever they wanted to know?" Mrs. Winsom said.

"They would not believe anything I said. I am a suspect, after all. We all are."

"Don't," his wife said shortly. "The situation is distressing enough."

Solomon lifted his napkin to his mouth and let it fall. Constance knew it would be now. Of the servants, only Richards remained in the room, and the subject had been raised perfectly.

Solomon said, "At least it should be quickly over now. I believe they are closing in on the culprit."

Everyone stared at him. He certainly had their attention, and they all looked anxious.

"What makes you say that?" Randolph asked uneasily.

"I've been talking to them, and their line of reason and evidence is very similar to my own. If I know who killed Mr. Winsom, so do they."

Constance played her part, speaking into the uneasy silence with a deliberate trace of mockery. "Yes, but *do* you know, Mr. Grey? Or are you just speculating, as I'm sure we all do privately?"

Solomon gazed from her to Davidson and onward around the

table. Constance looked too, observing the stunned and uneasy faces, until she came to Solomon's own. There was no doubt that he dominated the room.

"I have proof, of course. The only question I have in my mind is what I should do with it." He fixed his gaze on Mrs. Winsom. "We all know this was a vile and heinous crime. Whatever the circumstances, murder cannot be tolerated. And yet the punishment of the perpetrator affects everyone concerned, almost as much as the original crime. The scandal may be great. Perhaps you, as the victim's widow, should decide what must be done in order to keep your family safe."

"I?" Deborah squeaked. "What am I against the power of the law? Which I am *not* against, in any case!"

"Of course you are not. Nor am I."

"You owe it to us to tell us what you know," Davidson said, shoving his plate aside.

"That isn't necessarily the case," Solomon argued. "I know who committed this wicked act, but I don't know why. I'm not sure the why matters, although the law prefers it, so perhaps we should too. So here is what I propose..."

Here it comes, Constance thought uneasily. *Will they believe in his arrogance? Allow him to take control in this way?* Davidson and Bolton were frowning. Alice looked unexpectedly dazed. Randolph seemed impatient, as he often was. Mrs. Winsom was clearly frightened. But only Ellen looked angry.

"I shall keep the name of the culprit to myself for tonight, giving him—or her—the chance to explain to me why they did this thing. Once I have this last fact, I shall lay the whole before Mrs. Winsom. Or before the police, whichever she prefers."

"You cannot lay such a burden on my mother!" Miriam burst out. "Has she not suffered enough?"

"Too much," Solomon said gently. "Which is why she needs to choose the best way to spare herself and her children yet more. Obviously, if Mrs. Winsom refuses to hear, then I shall go straight to the inspector. I know I should in any case."

"Do you expect us to confess over the dinner table?" Ellen demanded fiercely.

"Of course not. Immediately after dinner, I shall retire to the library and remain there all night. If the murderer comes to me and explains, then I will have a complete picture to present to Mrs. Winsom."

"To all of us," Miriam said tensely. "We should all decide. Except the person who killed my father."

"Perhaps. Either way, we will have to agree to abide by whatever decision is made."

"But you said the police have solved it, too," Constance argued.

"*Suspect*, not yet solved. I have the proof."

"Which you would really destroy if my mother asked it of you?" Randolph said in a voice of disbelief, overlaid with contempt.

"Sometimes justice needs to be flexible."

"Not in this country!" Albright said angrily. "The law is absolute and with reason. There is no justification for murder!"

A look of weariness crossed Solomon's face. "When you have knocked about the world as much as I have, you learn there are circumstances which might justify almost anything. My proposal is not to create anarchy but to protect friends."

"One law for this household and another for the rest of the country?" Ellen exclaimed.

"If that is what it takes," Solomon said steadily. He glanced around the table. "Look, you don't need to agree with me. If you don't, speak to the inspector, who, I'm sure, will be here first thing in the morning. But I shall be in the library all night."

"Aren't you afraid?" Constance taunted him. "To invite a murderer there in the dead of night? A man—or woman—who has killed before and who has nothing to lose? I'm sure they would rather murder you too than depend on the mercy of Mrs. Winsom."

"No," Solomon said, with a blind, naïve sort of arrogance that almost had her convinced, and she knew what he was about. "I have come to know you all during these last few difficult days, and I know that one of us is eaten with remorse and shame, even if they don't yet know it. They will not hurt me, for if they do, they have lost their last chance of redemption. The rest of you will not remain silent, and the police will know to arrest their suspect. Then the matter is out of all our hands."

"I for one will have nothing to do with this," Bolton announced.

"Nor will I," said Peter.

"You don't need to decide now," Solomon said. "You might change your mind overnight. Either way, I shall be in the library. No one has anything to lose by this proposal."

"Except you," Mrs. Winsom said hoarsely. "Mrs. Goldrich is right about the danger."

Solomon smiled. "I can look after myself. But I won't have to."

It was supreme arrogance. Constance saw the contempt and the pity in the faces around the table. No one betrayed fear or determination. But then, she already knew their murderer was skilled in hiding.

In the early days, she had once had to winkle a thief out of her establishment. It had been one of the girls who was loudest in her praise of Constance. Constance had caught her by guile. She tried to tell herself that this was no more serious, but her stomach was clenching.

"Good luck, my friend," Davidson murmured.

He will need it.

CHAPTER NINETEEN

A s FAR AS Solomon could tell, they all believed he meant it, even Richards, who stood by the door, his lip curled at this proof of how the gentry regarded themselves as above the law. And Constance had played her part well, voicing derision and letting him brush it off to be all the more convincing.

No one lingered over the port. Solomon only entered the drawing room to bid everyone goodnight and announce that he would be in the library in five minutes. He then went upstairs to splash water on his face and fetch a blanket—and a small, accurate pistol—which he took with him to the library.

He hoped to meet Constance on the way, just to be sure she would take especial care around Bolton—in fact, around both Boltons if he was right about Alice being in league with Thomas, at least after the event in covering up the crime.

Deliberately, he turned up the lamps, left the curtains open, and chose a book to read before he settled in one of the armchairs and prepared for a long night.

The drawing room clock chimed the eleventh hour.

Solomon fully expected Bolton to come, although not until much later. It was, he reflected, a nice touch to have announced he would have nothing to do with the proposed scheme. It fitted the character Bolton portrayed, of slightly prissy, inflexible accountant who thought all of life was as disciplined as numbers. But the worm had turned.

He had probably known he could not kill Winsom face to

face. He could only do it in the dark, from behind. And whatever nonsense had been spouted during dinner, Solomon had no intention of allowing the murderer to escape the law.

He tried to concentrate on his book, but thoughts of Constance distracted him. Worse, he didn't mind. He liked thinking of her, liked the visions of her that danced behind his eyes. She had really feared the dog would harm him.

He was not used to people caring.

The clock struck midnight.

Solomon rose and turned down the lamps, leaving only the one beside him shining brightly. Moonlight streamed palely through the windows, not as strong as the night of the murder, but enough to make out any figure approaching the window or entering by the door.

He loosened his necktie, then sat back down and spread the blanket across his knees. Taking the pistol from his pocket, he laid it in his lap and placed his book over it to hide it. All he had to do now was stay awake. Which, normally, was easy.

Normally.

AS THEY HAD agreed, Constance retired to her bedchamber when everyone else went to theirs. Mrs. Winsom tottered off first, accompanied by Miriam, who did not return to the drawing room. No one discussed Solomon's proposal, but everyone seemed to be thinking about it, for they were mostly silent, gazing at their hands or into the empty fireplace.

Everyone else went upstairs together, perhaps to prove they were not sloping off to the library to confess. As they said polite goodnights, Constance wondered if in just a couple of hours, they would really know the identity of Walter Winsom's killer.

On reaching her own room, she did not undress, but stood gazing out at the moonlight for several minutes.

Somewhere, it still grieved her that she would never know now if that flawed, vital, charismatic man was her father. Whatever he had done, taking his life was not the answer. She swallowed foolish tears and turned back to face the room. As planned, she placed the upright chair as close to the door as she could without impeding its opening. Then she wrapped a shawl about her shoulders and made herself comfortable enough in the chair not to wriggle, yet poised enough to act immediately when she heard the first sound.

Beside her, on the candle table, the lamp was turned down low and shaded on one side with a towel to prevent the light showing under the door. It was the best she could do to pretend to be asleep and yet still move quickly when she needed to.

Below, the drawing room clock chimed midnight. She knew that Solomon, alert at his post in the library, heard it too. This was the hour in which the murder had taken place, but she doubted this evening's action would happen so early. Surely the murderer would give everyone time to fall asleep, however reluctantly.

She kept herself awake by thinking of Solomon, of the danger he was putting himself in for the sake of people he barely knew. This whole mystery, harrowing as it was, seemed to engross him. As if he had grasped it with both hands because it was new and different.

The clock below chimed one. Poor Owen was having a long wait, if he had managed to wake himself. Constance smothered a yawn and waited. And waited.

And then she heard it.

The faintest click of a door opening. She could not even tell from which direction it came, though after a few moments she made out the hushing sound of soft footsteps. She rose, her heart thundering, ready to follow when she could not be seen. It wasn't as if she didn't know where the murderer was going.

Oh God, please look after Solomon Grey, who is a good man...

The faint footsteps didn't fade. They stopped right outside

her door. Now her heart twisted in fear. She was afraid to breathe.

Then came a scratch at the door. The same sound Solomon had made when he came here. Her stomach turned over, though whether in relief or a different kind of fear, she could not tell. What was he doing? Had the murderer confessed already, and she wasn't even there to witness it?

She reached for the door, softly opened it a crack, and then wider.

No one was there.

Feeling behind her, she picked up the lamp, looking warily to each side. Then, hearing and seeing nothing, she stepped out into the passage. By the lamp's glow, she saw at once that the door to the old wing of the house stood open.

SOLOMON WOKE WITH a start. Disoriented, he knew only that a noise, a threat, had roused him. What on earth had he been thinking of to fall asleep at such a time?

The plan rushed into his brain at the same time as he realized the library door was being pushed slowly open. A quick glance at the window on his other side showed him no one had entered that way or stood on the other side of the glass to shoot him. Hastily, he shoved one hand beneath the book and curled his fingers around the handle of the pistol. He had time to be grateful he hadn't dropped the weapon to the floor, and then his visitor was inside.

The visitor carried a lamp held low, and at first all he could make out was skirts.

Constance? Fear for her clutched at his chest. But no, this woman did not move like Constance. Of course it was Alice Bolton—oddly enough, the weak link in the chain of her husband's crime. She closed the door behind her and stood as though frozen, or perhaps just assessing him.

He didn't stand up. He wanted to offer no threat. And he certainly didn't want to scare her off with the sight of the pistol.

"Welcome," he said quietly. "I knew one of you would come, but I confess I expected your husband."

"My husband?" she said in a peculiar, startled voice. "Mr. Grey, are you quite well?"

She walked into the light of his lamp, and he saw his mistake. Not Alice Bolton—Deborah Winsom.

⇢⇢⇢⟨⟨⟨

IN THE PASSAGE, Constance hesitated. Why had Solomon deviated from the plan? He was obviously so eager to get to whatever he had learned about that he could not wait for her, merely showed her the way. Beyond the doorway, she could just make out a bobbing light within the old wing.

Eager to know what he had discovered, she snatched up her own lamp from inside her room and crept as quickly as she could along the passage and through the old door. Was she supposed to close it to prevent anyone following them? Or did it no longer matter?

She pulled it closed anyway.

She could no longer see Solomon's light, only the bare walls and the badly repaired floor of the large chamber. She moved through it, shining the light on the floor to be sure where she stepped, and into the makeshift bedroom where Alice had met Walter. Nothing had changed, so far as she could see.

The door to the passage was open. Walking toward it, she glimpsed the moving light once more, near the staircase.

"Solomon!" she hissed. "Wait!"

He didn't answer, but the light vanished. What was he playing at?

Her heart lurched. Had someone attacked him? Were they

not alone here after all? Had they been tricked in turn?

She paused, listening intently. Nothing moved. If anyone else breathed, she didn't hear them. Her lamp trembled as she held it higher and made out the open door of the small room at the head of the stairs.

She had barely noticed it the last time, beyond the fact that it was entirely empty. She went closer. Her lamp's light flickered over the bare walls—and a pile of rags at the far corner that had certainly not been there before. It was terrifyingly body shaped.

Oh no… She sped toward it. *Don't be dead, don't be dead…*

She stopped hard once more, for she could see now that her imagination had been playing tricks. There was no body inside those rags.

A blow to her back sent her staggering forward. The floor beneath her feet gave way and she fell through the darkness. There was the shock of landing, staggering pain, and then only blackness.

➵➵➵⋘⋘

"MRS. WINSOM," SOLOMON said. Had he got everything horribly wrong? Everything, *everything* pointed to Bolton.

He rose to his feet, dexterously lifting book and blanket with him to hide the pistol.

"You seem surprised," she said, moving toward him. She had changed from last night's black evening gown into a simpler, less fashionable affair. She looked small and brave and entirely unthreatening. "I suppose I should be flattered."

"What have you come to say to me?" he asked, feeling his way.

She set down her lamp on the nearest desk and took the chair opposite his. Oddly, she looked more serene than at any point since his arrival at Greenforth. And yet the lines of grief and worry remained, along with the puffiness and bruising around the eyes that spoke of too little sleep.

"I am responsible for my husband's death."

Even through the shock of his error, he acknowledged the odd phrasing.

She shuddered. "No, I did not stab him. But I know who did, and why. I am why."

She lapsed into silence, her eyes distant, her expression one of misery.

"What happened?" Solomon asked.

His quiet voice seemed to drag her back to the present. She even smiled, without mirth or pleasure. "I fell in love."

"With whom?" he asked. He was adjusting his theory, but not by much. He thought he knew.

"With my husband, a long time ago. Everyone did, of course. I was one of many, even then, but he chose me. I was so devoted that I accepted his infidelity as part of a wife's lot in life. One does, you know. But one doesn't always appreciate the hurt that builds and builds over the years, the weariness... And then came the ultimate betrayal."

"Alice Bolton."

"Alice, my friend. The wife of *his* friend, his partner." She stopped talking again. Her fingers pleated and pinched at the fabric of her gown. "I suppose it was my fault. By all my tolerance and turning of blind eyes, he thought he could do anything he liked, and I would neither notice nor complain."

"Did you?"

"Complain? No. I went to Thomas. I've known him almost as long as I've known my husband. He was a friend."

"You told him?"

"Yes, I told him. The thing was, he already knew. People underestimate Thomas. They think he sees nothing but numbers. They're wrong. And he was devoted to Alice. He would do anything for her. I went to their house one day, when I knew Walter was with her in town." She smiled, this time with unexpected warmth. "I had never been drunk before."

"You went when you were intoxicated?"

"Oh, no. I arrived stone-cold sober. We drank together, Thomas and me, and talked and talked. I wept, and he comforted me, and still we talked. I had always known Thomas's was the brain behind their partnership, though a business needs the kind of charisma and confidence that Walter brought. On that day, I saw that Thomas was the quiet hero, responsible for all our prosperity, and yet he allowed Walter to take not only the credit but a higher proportion of the bank's profits. He said that was because Walter put up the first money that founded the bank, but I think it was just his way. The money didn't interest him. He wanted to see if he could *do* it, build their own successful bank."

Her distant eyes came back into focus on Solomon. "He is strong, you know, much stronger than Walter, who always stole the limelight without trying. And yet I was so comfortable with Thomas… As I say, I fell in love. Again."

"So while your husband was with Alice, you began an affair with her husband?"

"I didn't mean to," Deborah said, as though she had merely dropped something. "It just happened, and afterward, I was not remotely sorry."

"It felt good to have your revenge on both of them."

Annoyance flared in her eyes and then died. "Yes, probably it did. I don't know how much was true emotion, and how much was vengeance. It doesn't really matter."

"So why am I at Greenforth?" he asked.

She blinked, then smiled. "I liked you. I wanted someone at this party who was genuinely interesting and attractive, unknown to any of the others. I wanted to show you off. You were my coup. A distraction, if you like, from the rampant adultery of the rest of us."

"Someone to entertain the children?" he said sardonically.

"Perhaps. But then I found the earring in the spare bedroom, and I knew he was making love to her under our own roof. I don't know why that should seem the ultimate betrayal. After all, he had made free with our parlor maids in the past. I would not risk the bank by flaunting my affair with Thomas in front of him. But I had no objection to flirting with you under his nose. It felt dangerous and exciting, and it took him by surprise."

"It took me by surprise, too. Was I also to take the blame for your husband's murder?"

Her eyes widened in shock. "Of course not! Walter's murder was not part of the plan."

"I beg to differ. The knife was taken from the kitchen one night and used the next. You and I both know who by."

Tears sprang to her eyes and began to course down her cheeks. She didn't seem to notice.

"He did it for me," she whispered.

Abruptly, Solomon had had enough of the lies and deceit of this house, the excuses for every bad behavior and every crime.

"Rubbish," he said flatly. "He did it because Walter found out he'd been doctoring the books and stealing from the bank to keep Alice in jewels." The blank shock in her face was genuine, but he pressed his advantage ruthlessly. "You knew Bolton had murdered your husband, your children's father, and you remained silent. Did you know he had freed the dog? Is that why you took me to the woods this afternoon?"

"No!" she gasped in outrage. Then she wriggled in her chair like a schoolgirl caught out in some misdemeanor. "Well, he told me we needed to scare you off because you and Mrs. Goldrich were poking your noses in everywhere and might lead the police to him. I was to take you to the center of the wood, the place the children used to play, but I didn't know what he had intended, and I certainly didn't know then he had freed Monster! The dog terrifies me."

"But the dog didn't find us by accident. And Bolton was with Randolph, not guiding Monster to us."

"Thomas couldn't guide the dog if his life depended on it," she said. "But he'd been talking to Randolph. He knew where the dog went when it bolted, and he knew about the cave." She licked her dry lips, and her voice dropped further. "He told me after you came home. He hid a sheep's carcass in that cave. So he knew Monster would lurk there and guard it from us."

"He wasn't very careful of you, was he?"

She shook her head, closing her eyes.

"Is that why you're confessing?"

She nodded. "Partly. I don't want anyone else to die."

Partly.

His breath caught. "Deborah, did he send you here?"

Her eyes flew open, stark and fearful. She was in a nightmare she didn't seem able to wake herself from.

Constance.

He sprang to his feet, just as a soft knock sounded at the door and Owen the boot boy slunk in. His eyes were huge, his face white and scared and determined.

"Sir, she ain't come down," he blurted, totally ignoring his mistress. "And what's more, there's smoke in the house. I can smell it."

CONSTANCE STRUGGLED INTO consciousness with a weird crackling in her ears and pain in her head. When she managed to open her eyes, everything was fuzzy like fog, with lights flickering wildly. It reminded her of the night she had first seen Solomon, when police lanterns pierced the misty darkness. But the face above her was not his.

Thomas Bolton stared down at her, his eyes glinting red in the flaring light. He stood quite still, something dangling from one hand—a club of some kind. Why did he need such a thing in—

"I fell," she said stupidly. "I fell through the floor."

"I pushed you."

Of course he had. With the club. That was what he had

jabbed into her back, casting her forward into darkness.

"Having previously taken the trouble to remove the floor-boards," he added. "You're just too nosy, Mrs. Goldrich. You and your wealthy lover. I've done you a favor. You may die together, like Romeo and Juliet."

Alarm jolted her brain back to work. *Where is he?*

She threw herself into a sitting position to see better, but immediately she choked and a searing pain sliced through her head. She let out a groan. Her whole body hurt and she couldn't breathe for…smoke.

There was no mist, no fog, no flaring lanterns—only smoke and the crackle of flames leaping up the moth-eaten curtains and the bare, dry walls. He had set fire to the old wing.

"You'll kill everyone!"

"No, no," Bolton said. "I'm off to raise the alarm."

"Wait!" she cried, grasping the fabric of his trouser leg. She had to make him stay a moment longer, come nearer, for she knew he would never take her with him. "You—not Alice—*you* killed Walter."

He laughed, high and terrifying in the hell surrounding them. "You didn't know! He doesn't know either, does he? I suppose yours was a better trap than I thought." He crouched down to look into her eyes. "But mine is better. I killed Walter, and though you don't seem to quite know it yet, I've killed you and Grey too." He leaned nearer, and even through the smoke she could smell his breath—beef and brandy, fear and excitement.

She clutched his arm, his shoulder. "You can't leave me here to burn! You can't!"

Her right hand found his coat pocket and delved, somehow still as lightly and easily as breathing. Old habits did indeed die hard. She was looking for a weapon. He had to have a weapon or he could not make her stay… But it was a key her fingers closed around.

He meant to lock her in.

She moaned, letting her right hand dangle by her side as if it was too injured in her fall.

"I *can*," he said almost euphorically. "I really can do anything. I took Walter's money. I took Walter's wife, and I took Walter's life. Deborah will still lie for me, while Alice and I live in wealth and happiness."

"Deborah?" she repeated, stunned.

"Who do you think will bring Grey here to save you? In just a few—"

Abruptly, the door to the main house flew open and the light flamed over Solomon. Bolton jumped to his feet and flew across the room so fast it was frightening. The club came down hard before Solomon would even have seen him for the smoke.

By then, Constance was crawling along the floor toward them, mostly because she wasn't sure she could stand. Only then it came to her there was less smoke nearer the floor. She could actually see Solomon's dark head quite still in front of her. Then she saw the lantern flying through the smoke above. For an instant, she thought it was Bolton fleeing up the staircase to leave by the upper door, but glass shattered on the wooden steps and they burst into flames. He had thrown an oil lamp.

Then the door slammed shut and Bolton was gone. Constance crawled on, gasping out, "Solomon! Sol—"

She found his hair, grasping it between her fingers. She must have tugged it hard, for he groaned.

"Oh thank God," she muttered. "Solomon, we have to get out of here!"

"He's locked us in." Solomon reached up, grasping her hand. The heat was unbearable, the flames burning ever closer. "Help me up so I can break in the door or the window boards if I can. I'm sorry. I came to save you, but we might have run out of time."

Constance thrust her hand in front of his face and opened her fingers.

Solomon stared at the key in her hand and laughed. The sound changed immediately to a choking gasp. She threw her arm around his shoulder and they staggered to the door.

CHAPTER TWENTY

THOMAS BOLTON ONLY realized he didn't have the key after he'd slammed the door to the old wing and reached in his pocket. He must have dropped it inside!

Panic surged, for footsteps scurried across the hall toward him. He peered into the light, knowing his face must be blackened by smoke.

Deborah was hurtling toward him from the foot of the stairs. The stupid cow had sent Grey five minutes early, before he was ready, before he was certain enough of the fire... On the staircase, a line of frightened people in nightclothes were rushing down. She had roused them early too, but at least Alice was among them, thank God. He didn't care about anyone else.

"Outside, outside!" he ordered them. "Send for help before the whole house goes up!" He kicked at the door. "Grey is in there! I think Mrs. Goldrich is also."

"Why would they be in there?" Randolph demanded, striding across the floor looking too damnably like his father. "Grey should be in the library!"

"Oh, those two are playing some deep game of their own! They use the place for assignations. Get everyone outside, Randolph, and I'll see if I get in upstairs."

"Thomas, no!" Alice exclaimed as he shooed them all toward the open front door. Her cry warmed his heart as he ran up the stairs.

"I'll only be a moment. You must take everyone out, Alice.

Make sure they're all safe, including the servants…"

He almost laughed. You could make people do anything with a little conviction, a little courage.

He was grateful to Walter, in a way, for finally inspiring that courage. It hadn't taken very much bravery to steal from the bank, for he'd known no one would ever find out. The same when he'd taken Deborah. No one would ever believe it of him, and Walter himself was too occupied with Alice to notice his own wife was unfaithful. It had been rather delicious.

Until, inconceivably, Walter had noticed the discrepancies were still going on, and known only Thomas could be responsible. Nothing else mattered but to be rid of him. *That* had taken courage.

Until, the kitchen knife hidden in his coat, he had followed Walter outside on his walk. He had seen Alice with him by the swing. They were locked in a passionate embrace.

He had never seen them together before, although he had known for months what was going on. And so, cold fury in his heart, he had lurked in the shadows until Alice fled back to the house.

Then he had run across the flowerbed behind Walter and spoken his name.

"I don't want to talk to you," Walter had growled without even turning.

So Thomas didn't talk. He plunged the knife into Walter's back and watched him fall forward. His old friend's face, turned to one side, hadn't even looked surprised as the life faded from his eyes. Thomas was glad his was the last face Walter had seen. They had been friends, and he had almost been sorry.

Almost.

He had turned and walked back to the house, the same way as Alice. She was already in bed when he arrived there. But just as he'd known she would, she had lied that he had been there all night. He hadn't even needed to ask her.

Smoke was oozing under the upper door to the old wing.

Bolton amused himself for a little, kicking at the door and calling out to Grey. It shouldn't be too long before the pair were overcome by smoke. His own lungs felt sore and burned. After that, it wouldn't really matter if they put out the fire. Grey and the Goldrich woman would already be dead, or as good as. And he would be safe. He would sell the bank to Randolph, at a vastly inflated price, and take Alice abroad, away from the scandal and Deborah and all the other Winsoms.

It really was perfect.

The door was hot to the touch now. Downstairs would be an inferno. He gave one final kick to the door, splintering the lock, and risked a quick foray into the smoke to blacken his face and clothes a little more. Then he left, closed the door, burning his fingers on the metal latch in the process—it would look good to the police that he had tried to save even Walter's evil killers.

Thinking himself into the role—he had been acting for most of his life, after all—he staggered downstairs and out into the blessedly chilly night. Smoke had dulled the silver gleam of the moon, but there were so many lanterns scattered ahead that didn't seem to matter. He was slightly surprised not to see the sky orange and bright with flame.

"Thomas!" It was Alice's panicked voice, calling to him because she needed him. How long had he waited for that particular tone? Euphoric, he wanted to swagger up to her. Instead, he staggered a little, coughing without having to act.

His throat rasped when he tried to speak. "I couldn't find them. I got no answer when I called. I'm afraid they're dead already…"

All the same, he felt slightly uneasy about the fire, which was no longer burning out of control. No flames leapt from the roof or through the shattered windows, though through the billowing smoke, he could still see patches of orange glow.

An organized line of servants and tenants and villagers were heaving buckets of water into the building. Some were up ladders, trying to keep the main house wet and safe and to quench the fire in the upper floor. Among the helpers, he picked out Randolph, Peter Albright, and Davidson. And surely that was Sergeant Flynn?

But the night had been his so far. He had done enough. Alice clung very tightly to his arm. Deborah was with her daughters, shivering uncontrollably. Inspector Harris seemed to have materialized in front of him.

"Who is dead already?" he asked sharply.

"Grey and Mrs. Goldrich. They were in the old wing—they must have knocked a candle or something and not noticed. But I couldn't find them, and they didn't answer when I called..." *Careful.* He mustn't repeat himself. "I was driven back by the smoke and the heat. I couldn't save them. Perhaps we can get in now... The housekeeper will have a key!"

He started toward the house again, pulling free of Alice, but it was the inspector who stayed him.

"No one is to go back inside the house until it's safe."

"But we can save them now from the worst of the fire—"

"There's no need, sir. What makes you think they were in the old wing?"

"I saw them go in."

"When was that, sir?"

"Just after midnight. I daresay you know Grey had this ridiculous idea that one of us would go to the library and confess to killing poor Walter, after which *he* would decide what to do about it! I confess I was curious to see if anyone would go. So I went downstairs, and that was when I saw him with Mrs. Goldrich, slipping through the door to the old wing. He must have given up on confession. Perhaps she convinced him of his stupidity."

"Not many people call Solomon Grey stupid," Davidson remarked.

"And yet we are all here," Bolton snapped. "And he is in *there!*" He gestured toward the smoking building. Which was when he realized what he should have observed from the beginning.

No one was concerned for the pair trapped in the fire. No one was trying to save them.

Because…

A foot crunched in the gravel behind him. His neck prickled and he turned very slowly to face Solomon Grey. In his black-streaked white shirt, his short hair awry, he should not have been able to look elegant or superior. He managed both. And beside him, her hair tumbling around her shoulders, looking like a decadent angel, even with a bandage around her head and Grey's coat around her shoulders, was Mrs. Goldrich.

He had told her everything. The urge had been irresistible.

He swung back to the inspector. Deborah stood just a little way from him, flanked by Miriam and Ellen. Alice had let go of him. Her face showed he had never won her, only a last trickle of dying loyalty. It had never been enough.

And Deborah…

"You told them," he said in disbelief. Despite the danger to herself and her family, the damage of such scandal, she had blabbed.

"You wouldn't stop," she whispered. "I had to do the right thing. Finally."

Miriam put her arm around her mother's shoulder. Ellen stared at him. Walter's children.

"Thomas Bolton," Inspector Harris said, "I am arresting you for the murder of Walter Winsom, for the attempted murder of Solomon Grey and Constance…er, this lady."

THE RESIDENTS OF Greenforth all slept elsewhere that night. The Winsoms were taken in by neighbors, the servants scattered.

Ellen barely slept. She felt stunned by the revelations of the night, wondering if she should despise her mother for her moral lapse. But a new kind of adult understanding was seeping into her, a sympathy with making mistakes in impossible, tragic situations. Was there really nothing in the world to look forward to except heartache and an unfaithful husband?

Not all husbands were like that, of course. Peter was not. But then, she could never imagine being married to Peter. He and Miriam seemed to have grown closer over these last difficult days. She hoped that would last. Miriam deserved to be happy.

If any of them could be now.

Outside the window of her guest bedroom, the sun shone. *Incongruous.* Over the fields and hedgerows, she could still see the gray cloud over Greenforth House. *In more ways than one.*

Dressed in the ill-fitting gown loaned by the squire's daughter Amelia, she left her room and prowled the quiet house where her hosts still slept. She hoped her mother and her siblings did, too.

She was crossing the entrance hall toward the front door when someone sprang up from the old-fashioned wooden settle that lived there to discourage unfavored visitors.

"Sergeant Flynn," she said in surprise.

She ought to be annoyed to see him here, bothering them even now, and yet she wasn't. He had helped extinguish the fire last night. He had taken her father's murderer away to prison. She still couldn't think of the murderer as the same man she had known all her life.

"I'm sorry to come so early," Flynn said. "After the night you've all had, I didn't really expect to find anyone up. I really just wanted to pass on the message that the sooner your mother writes and signs her statement, the better it will be. Also for Mrs. Bolton."

Ellen frowned. "Where *is* Mrs. Bolton?"

"With the vicar and his wife."

Ellen rubbed her forehead. "This must be as awful for her... I don't really know what to do."

She didn't like the helplessness in her words or her voice, but they were at least truthful.

"Were you going for a walk?" Flynn asked. "I can walk with you for a little, if you like. Or not," he added hastily.

It brought a smile flickering to her lips. She liked the sergeant. He had no pretensions, no axe to grind or role to play. He had honest eyes, a touch of sardonic humor, and a really rather wonderful smile.

"I *would* like," she said.

They walked into the sunshine together, quiet and companionable.

"It will take time," he said at last, "to adjust to everything."

She nodded. "Will we able to go back to Greenforth? If my mother wishes to."

"I believe so. The only damage is to the old wing. It will have to be rebuilt. It will be an interest, perhaps. A distraction."

Her lips twisted. "From the unpleasant reality that our neighbors won't speak to us once the whole scandal comes out?"

"It needn't *all* come out, except in court. The inspector will see what he can do to limit how much is reported in the newspapers."

"That is kind of him."

"We're all human."

"And all afraid of scandal, how it will affect our standing in the world, our career—poor Peter!—our marriage chances…"

"Poor you?" he asked sympathetically.

She sighed, gazing out over the fields to the horizon, imagining the vast world beyond. "I don't think I want to be married. Ever, if I have to live like my mother. Certainly not yet. I flirted with Mr. Davidson, you know. I thought it might be fun, but it's just dishonest because neither of us means it." She cast him a quick smile. "I think I might have just grown up. At least enough to know that I don't want to sit sewing samplers until some man I don't hate deigns to take me off my mother's hands for my fortune."

"No, that does sound a dreary life," he agreed.

"I shall be bored," she said. "I think I was bored already. Perhaps I should become more involved in causes. Like the anti-slavery society."

"A cause worthy of your time," he said. "Like many others."

"I know nothing of the world," she said, almost surprised by the discovery.

"Young ladies are sheltered to protect them."

"And if we don't want to be protected?"

"You should." He sounded stern, but there was no criticism in his eyes, only concern. She saw with some surprise that he liked her. And she liked that much more than Ivor Davidson's fulsome compliments and secret touches.

"Maybe it's the *kind* of protection you need to question," he suggested. "You must be safe, but everyone should have that right. If you want to see the world, you really just need to look beyond sending a pot of jam to your poorest tenants or cast-off clothes to the deserving poor in London. There is a whole world of poverty and sickness out there. Much of it leads to crime, so I see an awful lot of it. The poor need work, decent housing, warmth, and water. They need education and self-respect and hope."

Ellen took his arm, happy to have found a friend of her own, and suddenly much more interested, even excited, about the future. "Tell me more."

CONSTANCE FOUND THAT the Greenforth servants had packed all her bags and brought them to the inn, where she had spent a few uncomfortable hours dozing through pain. She was very glad to wash from head to toe—again—and dress in her own clothes. She didn't think her hair smelled of smoke anymore, but she could not be sure. It seemed to linger in her nostrils and her throat.

Wincing, she put a clean dressing on her head and kept it in place with a dashing scarf rather than a bandage.

Disappointingly, there was no sign of Solomon when she went downstairs for breakfast, though the maid assured her he was fine and had eaten before he went out early with the police inspector.

Constance could not really do justice to the inn's generous breakfast. Her throat was too sore. But she ate some soft, crustless new bread with a little egg, and drank lukewarm coffee.

She was even contemplating a second cup from the pot when Randolph entered the inn.

"How are you?" he asked anxiously. "May I join you?"

"Only a little the worse for wear," she said lightly, "and of course you may. How are you? And your family?"

He grimaced. "In shock, I think. My father was an old goat, of course, always had been, but my mother and Bolton?" He glanced hastily in the direction of the kitchen. "You won't speak of this, will you?"

"Of course I won't. And the inspector will try to keep newspaper reports to a minimum."

"My mother might still be charged," he said, staring at his hands.

Constance poured him some coffee into the cup provided by the smiling maid. Randolph waited until she had gone.

"She didn't know what to do after he killed my father," he said urgently. "She hadn't even guessed what he intended, though she knew immediately who was responsible. I think that's why she fell so utterly to pieces. If she denounced Bolton, she would have to say why, and that would ruin us all. It was only after the dog incident that she realized he would kill again to save himself and knew she would have to tell everything. A pity the policemen chose that day to stay away, though I was very glad to see them last night... It's a devilish mess, isn't it?"

She knew he didn't mean the house. "It will be difficult. But it's not insurmountable, Randolph. Not for you, if you put your mind to it."

He glanced at her with a hint of the old warmth, but a new

ruefulness too. "I don't suppose you'd care to help me with that? We're not related, you know."

She looked up at him quickly, and he took a folded paper from his pocket, pushing it across the table to her. She gazed at it. He had sounded very certain.

She said, "My name is not Goldrich. It's Silver."

"I had already guessed. In a way, it makes you even more wonderful."

"You are very kind to say so, but I was never for you, Randolph."

"Perhaps. But I'm sorry you're not my sister." He touched the paper on the table. "My father did have an illegitimate daughter of around your age. Her mother was a girl in Norwich who died a year after the birth. My father paid her an allowance, which I will continue. I believe she has a very nice milliner's shop, should you ever be in Norwich."

Would I have made a good milliner? Would Solomon look on me differently then? Beyond the silly surface thoughts, the old, familiar ache came back, because she was still no one. She still had no family to look out for, even if she never saw them or spoke to them. Except her mother, of course, which was more than the milliner in Norwich had.

And she had a friend. Randolph had not needed to come to her with this. He had enough on his mind and his shoulders. And yet he had thought of it and done it.

"Thank you," she said warmly. "You are becoming a very fine man, Randolph."

He looked away. "My father was fine, in some ways."

"He was. But you will be better."

"I will try to be."

She smiled, pushing the unread document back to him. "What will you do? Hope the bank will ride out the scandal?"

"I'm not sure yet. I need to think and consult with wiser heads than mine."

"You could do worse than talk to Mr. Grey."

"I intend to. I'm going to see him in London next month."

"Good. I wish you well."

He smiled back, then rose from the table and said goodbye.

She doubted she would see him again.

She finished what was left of the coffee and went back to her room. Perhaps a walk would be in order. She did not want to return to London until her bruises had faded and her head healed.

Feeling suddenly tired, she sat down on the windowsill and rested her forehead on the glass. Now that she knew, she found she didn't actually mind that she had not found any family. She had accomplished what she had without them, and any bizarre urge toward respectability was surely nipped in the bud by the very fact she'd had to lie her way into Greenforth. Even if Walter had been her father, she would have achieved nothing by this escapade.

And yet she was glad she came. She had done a good thing in helping to solve the mystery. And Solomon Grey was her friend.

The noises of a coach-and-four pulling into the inn yard below dragged her out of her thoughts. Baggage was packed on the roof and the coachman looked vaguely familiar. No wonder. It was Solomon who alighted.

She smiled, her tiredness dissipating like a summer cloud. But the coachman did not dismount as Solomon strode inside. No one unloaded the bags.

He was going back to London.

Of course he was. He had a business to run, and...and she had been fooling herself to think he was truly her friend. They had never been more than temporary allies. Although he was unmarried—she knew that much about him—he was bound to have a special lady awaiting his return, a lady he could never introduce her to. Solomon Grey did not want or need a woman like Constance in any part of his life.

Reality was a slap in the face. She knew that, and yet she always dreamed beyond it. He had come to pay his shot at the inn.

She would spare them both the farewell and absorb the pain alone, in private, as she always did.

She stayed where she was, not looking below but across the gently rolling hills in the distance. The countryside was pretty. She should spend more time outside the city. Perhaps she should close the house for a few days next month, take everyone on holiday to the seaside. Clacton, perhaps. Southend. Even Brighton...

A knock interrupted her.

Hastily, she dashed her sleeve across her face, so as not to appall the maid. "Come in."

Not the maid, but Solomon. He entered and took off his hat, inclining his head with his usual courtesy. "I'm glad to see you up and about. How are you?"

"Sore but proud," she said lightly. "How are you?"

"Likewise," he said with a quick smile. "I thought you would like to know you were right about the muddy shoes. Flynn found a pair of Bolton's uncleaned, with traces of the flowerbed in question on the soles."

She grimaced. "It didn't help catch him, though, did it?"

"It is useful evidence to help convict him."

"Maybe."

He said, "It's reprehensible in the face of such tragedy, I know, but I enjoyed it."

"A guilty pleasure. I understand the Tizsas better now."

"I think we have earned their approval."

She rose from the window seat. "You are going back to London."

"I need to. There are things I have been neglecting. I would offer to take you, but I don't think you are fit to travel."

I could be. With you.

Foolish. Foolish.

She walked toward him, her hand held out, her friendliest smile on her lips. "I shall be more comfortable in a day or two. Goodbye, Solomon Grey. You're right. It has been fun."

He took her hand in his firm grip, his dark, perceptive eyes searching hers. "Perhaps we shall do it again some time."

"Perhaps," she said, still smiling, because she knew they would not, and the hurt intensified. *Please just go. And be happy...*

He leaned closer and dipped his head. In astonishment, she felt his mouth cover hers, soft and infinitely gentle, and gone in an instant. But the world stood still.

She found herself staring at his back, at the door closing behind him.

Wonderingly, she touched her lips and smiled.

"*Au revoir,*" she whispered to the door. Because she knew now that she would see him again.

ABOUT THE AUTHOR

Mary Lancaster lives in Scotland with her husband, three mostly grown-up kids and a small, crazy dog.

Her first literary love was historical fiction, a genre which she relishes mixing up with romance and adventure in her own writing. Her most recent books are light, fun Regency romances written for Dragonblade Publishing: *The Imperial Season* series set at the Congress of Vienna; and the popular *Blackhaven Brides* series, which is set in a fashionable English spa town frequented by the great and the bad of Regency society.

Connect with Mary on-line – she loves to hear from readers:

Email Mary:
Mary@MaryLancaster.com

Website:
www.MaryLancaster.com

Newsletter sign-up:
http://eepurl.com/b4Xoif

Facebook:
facebook.com/mary.lancaster.1656

Facebook Author Page:
facebook.com/MaryLancasterNovelist

Twitter:
@MaryLancNovels

Amazon Author Page:
amazon.com/Mary-Lancaster/e/B00DJ5IACI

Bookbub:
bookbub.com/profile/mary-lancaster